WHEN ZOMBIES ATTACK

Sara led the way, bounding up the stairs two at a time. I couldn't really blame her for wanting to rush out. Yet she stopped at the door, blocking the way out.

I started to ask her what was wrong, but the words trailed off as a foul stench wafted into the room. All the anger faded away like smoke on the wind as the combination of death and rot invaded my nostrils like a physical assault.

The vampires behind me started complaining—some of them blaming Brendan for the stink—but then Sara was stumbling back into me, and I didn't have time to worry about where it was coming from.

Bloated, discolored fingers with long, jagged nails were grabbing at Sara's shoulder and arm, dragging her out through the door. By the time I got over my shock enough to reach for her, she was gone. . . .

Books by Jess Haines

HUNTED BY THE OTHERS

TAKEN BY THE OTHERS

DECEIVED BY THE OTHERS

STALKING THE OTHERS

FORSAKEN BY THE OTHERS

Collections

NOCTURNAL
(with Jacquelyn Frank,
Kate Douglas, and Clare Willis)

THE REAL WEREWIVES OF VAMPIRE COUNTY
(with Alexandra Ivy, Angie Fox, and Tami Dane)

Published by Kensington Publishing Corporation

FORSAKEN
BY THE
OTHERS

AN H&W INVESTIGATIONS NOVEL

JESS
HAINES

ZEBRA BOOKS
KENSINGTON PUBLISHING CORP.

http://www.kensingtonbooks.com

ZEBRA BOOKS are published by

Kensington Publishing Corp.
119 West 40th Street
New York, NY 10018

All Kensington titles, imprints and distributed lines are
available at special quantity discounts for bulk purchases
for sales promotion, premiums, fund-raising, educational
or institutional use.

Special book excerpts or customized printings can also be created to fit specific needs. For details, write or phone the office
of the Kensington Special Sales Manager: Kensington Publishing Corp., 119 West 40th Street, New York, NY 10018.
Attn. Special Sales Department. Phone: 1-800-221-2647.

Zebra and the Z logo Reg. U.S. Pat. & TM Off.

ISBN-13: 978-1-4201-2403-3
ISBN-10: 1-4201-2403-X

First Mass-Market Paperback Printing: July 2013

eISBN-13: 978-1-4201-3205-2
eISBN-10: 1-4201-3205-9

First Electronic Edition: July 2013

10 9 8 7 6 5 4 3 2 1

Printed in the United States of America

Chapter 1

Every part of me ached. Though I was wrapped up in blankets, curled up on my side in bed, I was cold, too. Maybe it was my own shivering that stirred me out of sleep. Whatever it was, I didn't want to move right away.

Then something cool and spidery shifted under the covers, brushing over my stomach.

Startled, I screamed and twisted away, flailing at the sheets to bat it off. It only tightened against me, yanking me back against a hard, male body.

A clearly naked—*quite* hard—male body.

"Shush, now. You'll wake the whole building."

Oh, hell.

My voice was a lot more gravelly and perhaps a touch more peeved than it needed to be. "Let go."

"Hmm. Someone is not a morning person."

Annoyed for no reason I could readily put my finger on, I shoved at Royce's arm, trying to get him off me.

It was like trying to move a boulder. The rumble of his laughter vibrated through my body, my hot skin pressed to his cold. It was only when he took hold of the wrist of the hand I'd locked on his arm and rolled so he was on top that it struck me how easily he overpowered me.

Which served as another reminder. The belt was gone. I wasn't turning Other.

I should have been happy, I suppose. Maybe the twinge of disappointment I was feeling came from trading one version of my own personal idea of hell for the uncertain future of being a legally bound and contracted vampire's toy.

Bitter? Me? Perish the thought.

Wriggling, I pushed at Royce's arm with my free hand again, wincing as the pressure of his body rubbing against mine revealed a whole slew of hurts from my battle with Wesley—and more than likely from the far more pleasurable activities that had come after.

He didn't let go, one hand coming up to tweak one of my nipples. "Much as I enjoy that delightful squirming you're doing, I wish you would relax. I know you're feeling regrets—don't bother trying to deny it; I can feel it as well as you can—though I'll be damned if I understand it."

That did it. Snarling, I slammed a fist against his arm. Most likely it was surprise rather than pain that made him move, but he finally let me go and pulled back, putting enough distance between us for me to whirl on him. I twisted around onto my knees, leveling a shaking finger at him.

"Don't even pretend like you don't know. You feel what I'm feeling, don't you? Don't you know just how damned *creepy* that is? How invasive?"

The thought alone made me ill. I was his property now, and not just on paper.

He owned me, body and soul. Not only had I abandoned my morals and common sense last night, I'd *liked* it. Liked the feel of his lips and tongue and fingers and other parts so intimately pressed against mine, all over, inside me, all while he drank my blood. What the hell was wrong with me that I'd *liked* being wrapped in Death's arms and pounded into the mattress while my life was siphoned away a sip at a time?

Images of all of the ways he could take advantage of me while I was unable to defend myself whirled through my head like a maelstrom of horror-show terrors, a painful reminder that now I was just a blood whore, a plaything, and that I'd willingly put my life in his hands. Something very close to terror warred with the anger, but I wasn't about to give in to the desire to run screaming from his bed. The things he could do to hurt me ran far deeper and were many times more intimate than the threat of what he could do with his fangs or physical strength, and running from them—from him—wasn't an option.

"Shiarra, I'm hardly—"

"Oh, fuck *'hardly.'* You know exactly what you've

done. Instead of being Other, I'm just Other property now. A toy, right? One you can use or discard or bleed dry—"

"*Shiarra.*"

The sharp tone of his voice cut right through the head of rant-fueled steam I was working up. He could have stopped a charging bull with that tone.

I shut my mouth and glared at him. He met my gaze squarely, his dark eyes narrowed and unflinching.

"You know better by now. You know you're not just a meal on legs. You know you're more to me than entertainment."

That was . . . not what I had been expecting him to say.

"You," he continued, and this time I didn't withdraw as he leaned forward to gather my shaking hands in his, "have continued to frustrate and fascinate me since we first met. Do you realize that not one of my people noticed anything was wrong with me when I was under the influence of the *Dominari* Focus? Not one of them, Shiarra. Yet you, someone I could have hurt or destroyed in so many ways, chose to save me rather than leave me to my fate. Why would I ever hurt someone who did something so selfless on my behalf?"

A growing lump made it too hard to squeeze any words out in answer. I turned my eyes down, unable to meet his stare, focusing on our entwined fingers instead. He might have had a point, but it didn't mean I was ready to put my trust in him.

His grip tightened, just a bit, before he pulled one hand free and shifted on the bed. He brushed the back of his hand against my cheek before sliding his fingers under my jaw to tilt my head up so I would look at him. Stubborn to the end, I closed my eyes.

"I've been over this with you before. You still have doubts. Why?"

After taking a few moments to swallow the emotions clogging my throat and to collect my thoughts, I attempted to answer him. He was being candid with me. Even if the only way I could get the words out was slow and halting, I'd try to do the same for him.

"Doubting is one of the things I do best, I guess. It's just that being with you like this—like last night—it means my dad was right. I'm not a Waynest anymore. Not myself anymore. Just another vampire's puppet."

I peered up at him through my lashes, trying to figure out if that damning little tidbit had upset him. Royce's expression was unreadable, his gaze burning into mine. I wasn't sure if he was angry with me for being honest with him, but it was far too late to take the words back, and I'd never been good at hiding my thoughts from him. Especially when he was staring at me so intently, like he could see right past my eyes to the darkest thoughts buried in the back of my mind. Like he knew all the horrible things I didn't want anybody to know. He might not judge me for them—but that didn't mean I wanted him to know every thought inside my head as intimately as he'd come to learn the secrets of my body last night.

Practically vibrating with tension, I buried my face against his chest so I wouldn't have to think about how he was already in my head. Maybe I could pretend when I wasn't looking into his eyes that it made some kind of difference. It was as dumb as wishing for some way of taking back all the stupid things I'd done in the last month or so, but that didn't mean I wouldn't make a valiant effort at denial.

I think he got the picture that talking about the situation was only making things worse. His voice, when he finally spoke, was strangely gentle, and made me feel like an even bigger fool for finding comfort in it.

"Even after last night—you still think that I was only using you, or would abandon you once I got what I wanted?"

I nodded, not trusting my voice. He ran his fingers through my hair and down my back, not saying anything for a time. It took awhile, but after the worst of my trembling tapered off, he slid a hand between us and nudged my chin up again so he could peer into my eyes.

"What is it you fear has changed about you? What do you feel I have taken from you?"

Biting my lip, I looked away again before answering him. Though it was hard to speak without breaking into tears, making the words soft and breathy, I'm pretty sure he still heard me just fine. "My soul. My free will."

Shaking from a mix of stress and fatigue and a sickness more of mind than body, I jerked out of his grip and put some distance between us, turning my back on him as I swung my legs over the side of the futon—not that there was far for my feet to go to reach the floor—and put my head in my hands. He might own me now, but that didn't mean I had to like it.

What hurt worst of all was knowing that my dad was right. I wasn't fit to be a Waynest. I wasn't even my own person anymore. Without the belt, I was just another helpless, hapless human, at the mercy of a monster who could feed off of or kill me at any time with no cost to himself. No safety nets. No taking it back. I'd put myself here, and now I would have to suffer the consequences of my own choices.

The vampire's hand settled on my shoulder. The irony of that possessive gesture coinciding with my thoughts wasn't lost on me. If anything, it made it harder to get the tears under control. When I didn't turn around, he gripped my upper arm, not tight enough to hurt, but definitely enough to keep me from pulling away from him again.

"Shiarra, please look at me."

I wouldn't—couldn't do it. He made a soft, frustrated sound in his throat before speaking.

"I wish I had some way of expressing to you how much you mean to me in a way that you would accept. You saved my life, Shiarra, back when I meant nothing to you. You're brave when you have every reason to run scared, you've shown a remarkable ability to think on your feet, and you're resourceful. You've faced many of your fears, which is more than could be said for some of the most loyal of my number—but you hold to this idea that belonging to me makes you less than a person, and it's simply not true. You are no less the woman you were before you let me touch you last night, and I have no intentions of discarding you like some broken toy."

"This isn't something you can fix, Royce," I said. My voice might have been thick with tears, but I was proud of myself for being able to say what I was thinking for once instead of choking on my own angst like a brooding teenager. "You were just . . . you. It was my choice. I let it happen."

His voice was deadly cold and quiet. "Are you telling me you consider last night a mistake?"

I twisted to look at him, shocked.

He leaned in, using his grip on my arm to push me to my back. Before I knew it, his fingers, icy and implacable, tightened around my wrists. The growl rumbling in his throat made my knees quiver, and I gasped as my hands were abruptly pinned above my head, his lips brushing over my throat with a teasing rake of fangs as he leaned into me. His usually smooth voice came out rough, ragged, and I could very nearly taste the anger and frustration radiating from him around the bitter flavor of fear on my tongue.

"Why is it you can't accept that I don't intend you any harm? I have fought everything that I am to be what I thought you would desire of me. I have left you to live your life as you wished it, rather than as I willed it. Do you know how difficult it was to wait idly by while you hemmed and hawed about whether you could trust me? Don't you know that the temptation to interfere with your choices was nearly unbearable?"

"Don't you know that's what scares me about you?" I shot back.

That seemed to startle him out of his sudden surge of anger. Though he drew back, peering down at me, his eyes still glittered with a hint of red deep in the pupils, pinpoint sparks gleaming like the reflection of light on his fangs.

His voice, though it had deepened with his anger, was steady. "I have been as kind and generous and understanding as I know how to be, Shiarra. I waited for you to come to me of your own will—and now that you have, you think that what we did was a mistake? After all that I have done? Still you spurn me, fear me. Am I not generous enough? Have I not been merciful? What must I say or do to make you understand that I have leashed *everything* that I am so that you would choose me of your own will?"

"I don't know," I cried, voice breaking even though I was doing my best not to let him see how much the truth of his words stung. "Don't you think I know it's stupid? For God's sake, look at you! You're a walking wet dream, you're great in bed, you've got money and power and you have this fascination with me I can't even begin to fathom. I *know* you haven't done anything to hurt me, but I keep waiting for the other shoe to drop— I just don't know, Royce! I wish I had a neat answer wrapped up in ribbons and bows to give you, but I don't know what else to tell you. I'm so scared of what I've done and what I'm becoming that I can't even think straight anymore. For crap's sake, I barely trust myself, let alone someone I hardly know who holds the power of life and death over me. I'm not even close to coming to terms with what I did this month, so to ask me to come to grips with how I feel about you, too—please, just give me time. Please."

An aggravated hiss escaped from behind his clenched teeth before he leaned in. He closed his eyes, his hair becoming an inky curtain as he rested his brow lightly against my own. It took him a bit to speak again. Probably trying to collect himself so he wouldn't throttle me out of sheer frustration.

"If you think I'm about to let your inaccurate, specious beliefs about me continue to stand, you are very sorely mistaken. You are every bit as human now as you were when you first entered my home last night. I have done nothing—*nothing*—to change that. Don't hate yourself for letting me make you feel good. Giving in to me isn't a crime.

Liking the things I make you feel isn't a sin against your family or your God. There is no shame in it. I won't tolerate these misconceptions any longer, or see you destroy yourself, physically or emotionally, now that you're finally mine—do you understand? You mean too much to me for me to allow that to happen."

I shuddered at his pronouncement. Though a part of me was absurdly pleased with his words, the rest of me was screaming in horror at that *finally mine* part. It only validated the terror of losing my own identity, only to be overshadowed by a new "master" I couldn't live without.

"Damn it, Shiarra, look at me!"

I did. His normally black eyes were blazing red with anger, shining like bright beads of precious stones set in a lake of tar. His grip shifted, and he twined his fingers with mine before lifting one of my hands to press it to his cheek, much like we had done last night.

"Why do you not believe me when I say you will remain your own person? You know I still taste you, crave you, want to be inside of you again. Can you honestly tell me you don't want that too? That you don't want me?"

I wanted it. I wanted it so badly I could taste the remembered mint and copper of his mouth on my tongue.

But I wanted to stay *me*, too.

"Please," I croaked between shallow pants, my

fingers against his cheek lightly stroking his skin, pressing the length of my body against his to ease the growing heat and need, even though I knew I should have drawn away. "Please, Royce, I can't take this anymore. I can't even figure out who or what I am, let alone what you are to me. Please."

"No more tears. Not because of me." His hands cupped my cheeks as he tilted my head up so he could briefly press a kiss against each eyelid, his cool lips following the path of my tears as he whispered against my skin. "You don't need to be frightened anymore, my little hunter. You'll always be safe— and yourself—with me."

When he loosened his grip and coaxed me to embrace him, I wrapped my arms around his neck and clutched at him. The hurting, lonely, emotional side of me that wanted to believe it all—heart and soul— was winning out over the dark part whispering what a terrifically awful idea it was to trust him.

"You aren't a pet or some mindless puppet, Shiarra. I'll only take what you'll freely give me, never force anything from you. I might tease you now and again, but it will remain no more than the occasional attempt to fluster you or coax you into trying something beyond your comfort zone." The fanged smile that curved his lips spoke of wicked things he already had in mind to talk me into. Even my dark, rational side admitted that might be some fun to go along with. "You have my word."

It might have been more stupidity on my part, but I believed him. He hadn't hurt me, hadn't driven me away, hadn't done anything other than reassure and comfort me. True, his methods were sometimes abhorrent, but his intentions, though not always clear, were good. I was the one with the hang-ups here, and I felt no small measure of shame for constantly treating him as the bad guy or thinking him responsible for every evil that had befallen me since I'd been drawn into the doings of the Others in this city.

I pressed a kiss to his chest before ducking my head, mumbling a few words that might or might not have been coherent. Spitting out the truth hurt, but I meant everything I said. "Sorry . . . I'm sorry, too. Shouldn't have said—shouldn't think so little of you. I'm sorry, Royce."

He rested his cheek on the top of my head as his fingertips ran soothingly along my back, just holding me. It took awhile, but eventually my tears tapered off.

I'd done some terrible things during that time I had thought I might be turning into a werewolf, but maybe, with Royce's help, picking up the shattered pieces of my life wouldn't be as hard as I feared. Tackling everything alone had been incredibly foolish—as had my decision to go to the White Hats for help—so why not accept that the vampire could assist me? Aside from when he hadn't really known me, or when he had been forced to by someone else, he had never done anything to hurt me. Doing things alone and ignoring his offers before had only gotten me into more trouble.

When I tilted my head back to give him a speculative look, considering the possibilities, he leaned forward just enough to brush a kiss over my brow.

"It's been an intensely stressful month for you. If you can't bring yourself to trust me now, at the very least, give me the opportunity to earn it. I imagine there may be other times in the days ahead when you will need reassurance. There is no need to suffer in silence. You will come to me and allow me to help you instead of rushing off on your own now, yes?"

That hit a little too close to home. I gave him a sharp poke in the side, followed by a disgruntled snort. "Can we talk about anything other than that right now?"

"After you promise you will come to me if you need assistance."

I squirmed under his weight, frowning up at him. His pointed look as he rolled to the side, curling his arm under his head as he stared back, gave me the courage to say exactly what I was thinking.

"Fine. I promise"—Royce's triumphant smirk faded when he realized I was tagging my own stipulation onto the deal—"*if* you promise you'll stop trying to blackmail or manipulate me every time you want something."

His smile became more genuine. "Is that all?"

I thought about it. "You're also going to answer some questions. I'm tired of being scared and left in the dark. I hardly know anything about you. I want that to change."

"A reasonable request. Agreed."

"Good. Then I have something to ask right now." He nodded for me to continue. "What the hell is with the futon?"

He blinked. Then another slow smile spread, followed by a chuckle. "I suppose you were expecting some vast acreage of satin sheets and mounds of pillows, hmm?"

I knew I was turning red, could feel the heat blossoming in my cheeks, but I folded my arms and gave him a raised eyebrow while waiting for him to answer. "Maybe I was. You're not some college frat boy who can't afford better, and every other piece of personal property of yours I've seen, from your clothes to your office—offices—whatever—practically screams 'look at me, I have more money than God!' So, explain it to me. Make me understand this piece of you."

He'd lived up to a number of vampire stereotypes in our previous encounters, being broody and dark and mysterious—but I knew there was more to him than that. The odd choice of furniture was one piece of the puzzle that didn't fit, and I thought it might be a safe place to start learning more about the man hiding behind the mask of a monster. From the looks of things, he didn't mind my prying, either. He rolled onto his back and folded both hands under his head, giving me a boyish grin and an excellent view of the scars ranging across the toned muscles of his chest.

"Yes, I lived up to the cliché. Up until recently, I

had the huge bed and all the necessary accessories to make this place a suitable haven to live out every imaginable debauched and depraved sexual fantasy that I desired." As hard as it was, I kept my gaze steady on his, even though I was pretty sure I was about to ignite from my own embarrassment. "Do you know, less than a year ago, a woman—a human woman—reminded me how very important it was to value my freedom and humanity?"

I was getting an inkling that he was referring to me, but I still didn't see what that had to do with his futon or the sexcapades he was referring to. I'm sure he gathered I was confused. As he continued speaking, he rolled onto his hands and knees and crept toward me. I lay back as he approached, a teensy bit apprehensive about the predatory nature of his movements; he didn't stop until he was positioned above me.

"A very brave and foolish girl saved me from the very fate I had subjected countless others to. She freed me from what could have been lifetimes of slavery to someone who cared nothing for who or what I was. And while she could have taken that artifact and used me for her own ends, she did not. Though I wished that she would let me do something to show her how thankful I was to her for showing me such mercy, she would not have me."

I bit my lip and pressed my palm to his cheek, not sure what to say to this strange confession of his. He was still smiling, so I knew he wasn't angry with me, but it was surreal to hear him talk about me like I was some brilliant savior. Considering how little I knew about his world, that could be taken as very flattering, or very alarming.

"When I saw how humbly she lived, it served as a reminder of who I really was and where I came from. A futon is not quite the same as the bedding from my home on the farm when I was human, but it serves as an adequate reminder. Every night—from the moment I wake, and again, before I take my day's rest—I am reminded that despite all of the luxuries available to me, they are not to come at the expense of another's freedom. That there is no shame in taking the weak and making them strong." He leaned in to kiss and nip at a spot that nearly had me come off the bed. ". . . And, perhaps now I can get that great big bed back and keep you close instead. What do you think? Will you remind me when I should show mercy?"

"If you keep doing that thing with your tongue." I tangled my fingers in his hair, gasping when he repeated the motion. "I'll . . . I'll . . ."

He paused, glancing up at me with a fangy grin and raised brows. "You'll what?"

I laughed and pushed him back. "I'll think of something. Don't stop!"

And after that, he didn't.

Chapter 2

Christ, it was weird to be a vampire's toy.

I had about a million and one questions for Royce, but we kept being interrupted by phone calls. He'd forbidden anyone to enter his room, so it seemed just about everyone in New York had to call him *right then* to talk about something more urgent than my burning desire to know stuff about him. Like why, since he was technically dead, he could still get it up. Plus I needed to know if he had any way to find out if Jack and the other White Hats had survived the fight last night against the Raven-wood werewolves.

Maybe a teensy part of me wondered—very guiltily—if Chaz had survived, too.

While some of my senses still seemed abnormally heightened, for the most part I could only make out Royce's side of the conversations. It was at turns fascinating listening to how he ran his empire—and picking up some juicy tidbits about a missing case of some expensive-sounding wine from one of his restaurants, making the private investigator in me itch to know more—and boring as hell. The parts about quotas, headcounts, and company stock nearly put me back to sleep.

"I'm sorry," he said to me at one point, covering the mouthpiece of his phone so the lawyer on the other end wouldn't overhear. "Things have gotten a bit out of hand without John here to field the mundane issues. Angus and Jessica have stepped in to a degree, but there is only so much they can deal with on their own."

I eyed the screen of the laptop he'd popped open a few minutes before, curious about the mountain of e-mails he hadn't yet tackled. From where I was sitting, it looked like he got more legitimate e-mails in a day than I did in a month. "Maybe I should grab a shower and get dressed."

"Hmm? Oh, just give me a moment to wrap this up. I'll join you." Then, into the phone, more forcefully, "Glen, I'm done. Save the paperwork for when I visit the firm next week."

The lawyer was obviously peeved. This time I could hear the speaker loud and clear. "Those interrogatories you put off are due in less than a week. I need to prep you for the depositions scheduled—"

"Yes, and we'll discuss this later," Royce said, with far more patience than I would have been able to muster in his position. "I'll call you later tonight. Give me an hour or two to get things settled and get ready."

"An hour, Alec. I know you hate the legal bullshit and red tape, but we're running out of extensions, and there's only so much I can do to cover your ass when you don't work with me."

I couldn't believe Royce was letting someone talk to him like that. The vampire made some sounds of contrition before he snapped his cell phone shut and then turned it off. Finally.

"Now, where were we . . . ?"

Between one blink and the next, I found myself on my back, his lips latched onto my throat as he playfully sucked where he had bitten me last night. For some reason, tilting my head back like that made a bit of a tickle form in my throat, so I was at turns giggling and coughing as he worked his way down my body. It was hard to be mad at him for allowing all of those interruptions when he so obviously wanted to spend his time with me.

And then someone knocked on the door.

He practically collapsed on top of me, groaning. I flailed a bit so he'd give me some room to breathe as he barked out a harsh, "What?!" over his shoulder.

Clarisse poked her head in the door, grinning when she saw us. Probably because she now had confirmation that I'd spent the night doing more than sleeping with Royce and she could collect on a bet. Or maybe because she was getting a good gander at his bare ass. "Ah, lovey, ye need tae come—"

Royce twisted around and gave her a look that stopped whatever words the Irish vampire was going to say in their tracks. Her eyes widened, and she nodded rapidly.

"Right, then. I'll just take care of that for ye, lad. I'll, erm, keep the rest of the wolves at bay, shall I?"

The growl that rumbled in his chest gave me the shivers and was all the answer Clarisse needed. She disappeared without another word, the door clicking shut behind her.

He levered up on his elbows and glanced down at me with a frown. "This is not quite how I anticipated my first evening with you would turn out."

"I'd hope not," was my dry response. "How about that shower? Unless you think we'll be interrupted there, too . . ."

A wicked twinkle sparkled in his eyes, his frown soon replaced by a sly grin. "Are you sure you wouldn't mind a bit of extra company? I'm sure I could arrange something." It didn't take long for my flat stare to coax laughter out of him. "I'm joking, Shiarra. For now, I plan on keeping you to myself. I'm not terribly good at sharing."

With that, he scooped me up in his arms, and carried me to the bathroom. He set me on my feet and started the shower, while I leaned my hip against the marble sink and enjoyed the view. The steam seemed to be easing the tickle in my throat, though my voice still came out in a more throaty whisper than I intended.

"I don't suppose you feel like telling me what your plans for me are?" At the look he gave me over his shoulder, I snorted. "I don't mean right now.

Duh. I mean like later tonight. Tomorrow. The day after that."

He reached out to take my hand and tug me with him under the spray of multiple showerheads. "There will be more than enough time to worry about that later. Let's focus on right now, shall we?"

His obvious ploy to get me to leave the subject alone was made more obvious by the sudden, intense kiss he used to keep my mouth busy. Unsurprisingly, it worked.

There wasn't much getting clean happening in that shower, but for the time being, I was happy to let that slide. Much like last night, Royce paid very close attention to the places he knew would make me stop caring about anything aside from the moment. Thoughts surrounding what to do about the police, the Ravenwoods (or whoever it was out for my blood), what had happened to Jack, what I would do about my family, and if Royce knew why I hadn't changed into a werewolf, were blown right out of my head. For a good long while, I *didn't* care, and was happy to let all of those worries melt away under the vampire's talented ministrations.

Like most good things in my life, it wasn't destined to last. Royce murmured a soft curse against my lips when a pounding sound came from somewhere outside the room. He put a little extra pressure on a spot that made me squeal in a very good way, but whoever was knocking wasn't going away.

Royce muttered a quiet expletive and straightened, holding me steady until my weak knees

were ready to hold me up on their own. "Wait here."
He gave me a parting kiss and a wolfish grin as he
opened the glass door. "Get lathered up; I won't
be long."

"Can't it wait? We still need to get cleaned up," I
said, reaching for him. He took my hand and kissed
my knuckles in a move that would have been
charmingly gallant if not for his nakedness.

"They wouldn't be interrupting if it weren't important. I'll get it settled quickly. You be ready for
me when I get back. I don't like to wait."

"Could've fooled me," I muttered.

In a flash, I was pressed up against the shower
wall, and I didn't need any more proof of his desire.
As my hands settled on his shoulders, he bit my earlobe lightly, sending a shock of pleasure down my
spine. He then whispered in my ear, making me
squirm in all the right ways. "Don't doubt for a
moment that you're mine, my little hunter. You've
been mine longer than you know. A few moments
apart will never change that, and I'll spend eternity
proving it to you if you need me to."

I would've answered, but I was a bit too busy
trying to pull him back to nibble on my ear some
more. I pouted when he drew back despite my
urging him to continue.

That earned another wicked twinkle in his eye
and a razor smile that made my heart do a funny
little leap in my chest. My cheeks burned at his next
comment.

"Be glad of my constraint, Ms. Waynest. If I had

waited much longer to drag you to my bed, you might not have survived my efforts to scrub every other partner you've ever had out of your mind. When I return, I intend to finish what I started. Be ready."

He turned away. I huffed and, with my newfound resolve not to be afraid of him, found it in me to slap his ass as a parting shot. My God, I had to be insane; he was going to *kill* me for that—

The look he shot me over his shoulder was dark and full of promise, a hint of fang visible in his grin. It was all the things he *didn't* say in that heated look that made me burn with a flash of desire. Much to my surprise, this left me breathless and quivering in anticipation instead of from holy-hell-I'm-going-to-pee-my-pants-before-I-die terror. He grabbed a towel to wrap around his waist and disappeared into the bedroom.

Maybe a bit disappointed, but no less enthusiastic for what would no doubt happen once he returned, I took my time picking out which product to use to get soaped up like he'd mentioned.

The shower was gigantic, and the selection of skin and hair care products looked like it belonged in a spa. Some of them didn't have labels, and I took my time enjoying taking in the unusual scents and rubbing the different oils between my fingers to see what would work best for what I had in mind.

I sat down on the marble bench that ran along the wall, closing my eyes and enjoying the warm spray as I rubbed some vanilla-and-something-scented shampoo into my hair. While I was massaging my scalp, something stung my eyes. Figuring it was just some soapsuds, I rinsed a hand off and splashed some water on my face. The sting didn't alleviate.

The tickle in my throat grew worse as I scrubbed furiously at my eyes. When I managed to squint them open, I spotted a mix of blood and black crud on my fingers being rinsed away.

Coughing, I pressed a hand under my nose. The warm wetness there was from another nosebleed, not the shower spray. Crap.

It wasn't as bad as it had been while I was hiding with the White Hats, but it was still nasty. I stuck my face under the spray and groped for a washcloth, scrubbing the residue from the corners of my eyes and around my nose.

A cold hand closed on my upper arm and yanked me back, another soon pressing against my jaw to tilt my head back. It hurt too badly to open my eyes, but I wasn't afraid.

Well, maybe I was a little afraid.

Shut up; you'd squeak like that too if you couldn't see who was grabbing at you while you were naked in someone else's shower.

"When did this start?"

Royce's voice was sharp, cutting. I wasn't expecting it and coughed a few times before stammering out a response. "Just a minute ago. I'm fine. Let go!"

He did release my arm, but only so he could cup my face in both hands this time. "Did this happen last night? Is this what happened before you came here?"

I nodded. He swore and crushed me against his chest. The combination of hot/cold from the shower and his body was suddenly discomfiting—almost more so than the pain under my eyelids and building in my sinuses—but didn't compare to the sudden fear that the vampire knew more about what was going on in my body than I did. Why else would he be clutching at me like I was his favorite set of pearls?

Between coughs, my voice shook with not a little fear. It was hard to say whether I was more afraid of this strange sickness, or of what Royce might know about it. "What's happening to me?"

"It may be your body still fighting off the lycanthropy virus. What I tasted in your blood last night—I assumed it would fade over time."

I still couldn't open my eyes, but I would have glared at him had I been able. Snarling, I punched his shoulder, though it was about as effective as hitting a stone statue. "You asshole! You knew there was still something wrong with me last night and didn't say anything?"

His grip shifted from my jaw to my upper arms, keeping me from twisting away or hitting him again. "Stop this foolishness. Do you know how unusual it is for someone to be both bound to a vampire—two vampires—and then infected with lycanthropy? I did not want to start you needlessly worrying about something that we may not be able to change. I don't want to meddle with your blood and can't be certain what side effects you will experience, because this *does not happen*. You are an anomaly, Shiarra. A very unusual anomaly, and all of the normal methods I would use to deal with human sickness do not apply here."

I would have plied him with more questions, but a more severe bout of coughing wracked my body. He helped ease me to the tiled floor as I bent double, a pulsing pain building in my stomach and sinuses. The cramping wasn't so bad, but the abrupt onset of the sinus headache made my head feel like it would split in two.

The water washed away the secretions of blood and whatever the hell the black stuff was. When Royce realized I was clutching at my head because of the pain there, he carefully moved my fingers and gently stroked over the parts where the pressure was the worst. He could probably see the black stuff under my skin, because he knew exactly where to rub. It helped, because the choking wave of crud that flooded out of my nose and mouth a minute later made the headache all but disappear. Though I was still coughing, breathing came much easier, and the stinging in my eyes, nose, ears, and throat was fading far faster than it had the night before.

The vampire gathered my trembling hands in his and pulled me to him, using the cloth I'd dropped to carefully wipe the stuff from around my eyes and mouth. Blinking a few times, then squinting at him through my lashes, I took in the angry knot between his brows and the way his jaw muscles had tensed. He wouldn't meet my eyes, but I could still tell his thoughts were racing by the determined way he stared at me.

I said his name, the sound mangled by the lingering crud lining my esophagus. Then cleared my throat, trying again. "What's happening to me?"

"You," he said, voice thick with what sounded like regret, "are no longer entirely human. Nor are you quite Other. This is some kind of transition. I cannot say how long this will last, or what the end result will be."

Tears—real ones this time—trickled down my cheeks, mixing with the condensation from the shower.

"I would not have asked you to become permanently bound to me until you had more time to adjust, but it is possible if you take more of my blood that it will keep you from succumbing to whatever this sickness is. I cannot promise it will work, but it may help."

Swiping my hand under my nose, I closed my eyes and bowed my head. I'd already known that I'd chosen a hard road, but I hadn't expected my descent into becoming less than human would include permanent servitude to the vampire. Or, at least, that it would come this soon.

While I would remain attracted to him for the rest of my life, no matter what I'd felt about him before, and while he could call me to his side or influence me in other ways if we were in close proximity, agreeing to being permanently bound was a whole new ball game. I wasn't ready to take a leap off the edge of that cliff.

"I can't, Royce. Not now. Not this soon."

He didn't say anything else, just held me, the two of us silent and unmoving as the water sluiced over us and washed the last remnants of the black liquid off our skin.

Chapter 3

Later, once I stopped leaking the black crap and the two of us had cleaned up—without the fun and games I'd been planning on, unfortunately—Royce gave me some clothing that he must have sent someone out to get for me. The sweater and designer jeans still had tags on them. I wasn't about to ask how he knew my bra or underwear size, but the underthings that came with the new clothes were far more silky and revealing than I was used to, and a shade of green that was a bit more daring than I would have chosen on my own. It looked better than I was expecting, but neither Royce nor I were interested in doing anything about that after the scene in the shower.

He brought me downstairs with him. Some of the other inhabitants of the building were waiting for us, watching with eyes that glittered like red gemstones in the dark as we passed. The atmosphere was a hell of a lot more sinister in here sans the night vision and superhuman strength granted by the belt. Royce looked back at me as a shiver crept down my spine when Wes fell into step behind us.

After that, Royce took my hand. It was creepy how he'd known something was wrong without even looking at me. The cool press of his fingers curled around mine was comforting, but didn't make me any less afraid of the crimson embers burning in the depths of Wes's eyes when I glanced at him over my shoulder.

No doubt the dread pirate vampire was still pissed at me for the cheap shots I got in during our fight last night.

Royce led me to Mouse's apartment. The door was open, and I did my best not to stare at all of the swords and daggers and other sharp, pointy objects the house guard kept in her living room.

"Analie. You remember Ms. Waynest, do you not?"

There was a young girl with mousy brown hair in the kitchen, furiously stirring something in a bowl. She used a flour-covered arm to move some stray strands of hair out of her eyes and gave us a sunny grin. "Sure. Hi, Shia."

I lifted a hand and gave her a halfhearted wave, wondering what all this was about. Analie was one of the three werewolves who were currently "guests" in Royce's home. I didn't know the specifics of how Analie had come to be the vampire's ward, but I knew it wasn't something she'd been happy about. The other two—Ashi and Christoph—had done something stupid and tried attacking the vampire to save her from his clutches. Since their actions hadn't been sanctioned by their alpha, they had been magically neutered by some collars that suppressed their ability to shift and gifted to Royce's household. When I was stuck recovering from the blood bond to Royce, I had met the three of them in passing, but I wasn't supposed to spend much time around any of them.

Royce ushered me before him, settling his hands lightly at my waist. It struck me as a strangely possessive move, but I wasn't about to complain. "I have some errands to attend to. Give her a sample of your new skills. Perhaps you two can keep each other entertained until I return."

That made me stiffen. "You're leaving?"

He leaned in to kiss my cheek. Analie, blushing, nodded and turned away from us.

"You're staying here," he said, cool lips lingering against my cheek. "I won't be long."

With that, his grip tightened in what I assume was supposed to be a reassuring squeeze, and then he pulled away.

Dismissed so easily. It served as a reminder of what I was now. Something I wouldn't ever be able to forget. Feeling a little sick, I sat in the chair Wes pulled out for me, not surprised when he settled down across from me. Royce nodded to Wes and left without another word.

Analie put the bowl down and shook her spoon at Wes. "Stop glaring at her." It wasn't until she said anything that I realized Wes had been giving me the evil eye. Which, when it's coming from a very old vampire, is pretty disconcerting. "If you're going to hang out in my kitchen, behave yourself."

Wes continued glaring at me a moment longer, then eased back in his seat, blinking the crimson glow out of his eyes. The crystalline blue that took its place as his pupils contracted and darkened was as chill as the red was hot, the sleek lines of his carefully trimmed goatee bristling as the muscles in his jaw tightened.

"I'll behave if she does."

"I don't have the belt," I said, suddenly tired beyond measure. "I'm no threat anymore. Not to you."

"No? You still stink of desperation and sickness under the sex. Did you think no one would notice?"

Analie's spoon jangled as she dropped it on the counter, her gasp lost in the sound of my indignant sputtering. I rose, the chair clattering to the floor. Before I could do anything more, Wes was in front of me—I hadn't seen him move—and his hand had closed around my wrist, preventing me from running off or falling as I jerked away from him. It wasn't until I felt warmth trickle down my arm that I realized he'd cut me, too.

"Look at it. You're filled with corruption. Tell me that isn't a threat."

It didn't exactly hurt—the cut he must have made with a fang or a nail when he grabbed me wasn't deep—but he was right. I didn't bleed red— I bled black.

"What's wrong?"

Wes and I both tore our gazes off of the dark trickle at my wrist to look at Analie. She didn't look afraid or upset, as I had expected. Just curious.

When Wes didn't answer the question, I realized he was waiting for me to tell her. Like I had any answers to give.

"I wish I knew," I said, pulling experimentally to see if Wes would let me go. His fingers tightened reflexively, then released me. "Royce didn't know. He said it has something to do with being bound by . . . by having vampire blood in me and the infection from a werewolf at the same time."

Now didn't seem like the right time to discuss how Royce had bitten me while we were doing the horizontal tango. I didn't doubt now that he must have known something was wrong, though I wondered as to his motivation behind remaining quiet about the illness he must have tasted.

As for Analie, the look she gave me was hard to decipher. She put the bowl down, absently licked some batter off of her thumb, and came closer. I didn't resist when she took my wrist, sniffing gingerly at the blood. Her nose wrinkled, and she quickly backed away.

"I doubt it will kill you, but yeah, he's right. That blood stinks of infection something fierce."

Bowing my head and pressing my fingertips to my temples, I did my very best not to growl something uncomplimentary at them both.

"Just stay there, keep quiet, and I'm sure we'll all get through this evening unscathed."

I put my hands down and gave Wes the most baleful look I could muster. He stared back, clearly unimpressed.

"Well," Analie said, her voice full of false gaiety, "you two can stay and keep me company. I don't mind. It's better talking to you guys than listening to Christoph and Ashi complaining about their collars again."

So Wes and I stayed at the table, listening with half an ear as Analie chattered about her cooking lessons with someone named Jacques. She occasionally pulled out a dish, utensil, or a spice and held it up for us to see as she made a point, and we nodded along, making obliging sounds at the right times, though I honestly have no recollection of most of the stuff she told us. My mind was too busy considering what might be wrong with me (aside from an obvious and complete inability to make good decisions) and what the rest of the night might hold in store for me once Royce returned.

After a while, I came out of my introspection

long enough to notice that Wes kept glancing at his phone, and was occasionally typing something on it. E-mailing or texting.

He shrugged at my questioning look and put the phone on the table. "Alec says he's had a change of plans and will take a little longer than expected. He'll be back as soon as he can." At my dispirited nod, he continued. "Don't look so glum. He's bringing your friend back with him."

That got my attention.

"Sara? He's picking her up?"

"Yes. So no running off while the master is out, eh?"

That wasn't a moniker I wanted to associate with Royce anywhere other than in my head, but the thought of seeing Sara again had me too happy to be upset about it. I grinned and leaned across the table. Wes jerked back from my touch, but I yanked him into an awkward, sideways hug anyway.

Analie, smiling, gave my shoulder a pat. "How about we make some cookies for them while we wait? Christoph and Ashi wanted more of these things Jacques showed me how to make. They're these cinnamon cream-filled pastries. . . ."

I nodded and rose to join her at the counter, hoping the mundane activities would keep my mind off of all the craziness going on and busy enough until Sara arrived that the passing minutes wouldn't feel like hours. Doing something so normal might also help distract me from little details. Things like my fellow chef's being a werewolf, our babysitter's being a vampire, that we were using a vampire's kitchen to make goodies for other werewolves who occasionally doubled as walking Slurpees for the vamps, and—say, what did a vampire need a kitchen for, anyway?

Chapter 4

A few hours later, Royce returned, and he wasn't alone. By then, I had tried somewhere in the range of forty to fifty different kinds of cookies and pastries Analie had made. Somehow she got it into her head that all my worries about what was going on internally could be smothered by sugar and chocolate.

And I'll be damned if she wasn't right.

By the time Royce entered the apartment with Mouse, Christoph, Ashi, Clarisse, and Sara on his heels, I was near ready to explode from sugar shock. I barely registered the others—seeing Sara for the first time in a month was enough to stun me into immobility. Which is quite something considering how much I had been vibrating from the sugar.

She looked fabulous. Not that she didn't usually look like every man's wet dream—damn her frizz-free blond hair, model-perfect body, blue eyes, and perfect skin—but whatever she'd been doing while I was gone really agreed with her. There was something different about her. A blush of health to her cheeks, a sparkle in her eyes, something not entirely tangible that I hadn't seen before. Even though she was currently frowning and glaring at me from where she'd stopped in the kitchen doorway, giving me a look like I'd kicked her favorite puppy.

The others (except for Mouse, of course) had been chattering away, but that died down when I stood and took a few halting steps toward Sara. That awkward silence probably would have lasted longer if I hadn't thrown my arms around her and hugged her hard enough to force all the air out of her lungs.

She stayed stiff and unyielding at first, but soon gave in and hugged me back as best she could considering how her arms were pinned. Her voice was a bit thick as she wheezed out a few words.

"Don't you ever run off like that again. You had me worried sick, you bitch."

All the regret in the world wouldn't bring back the lost time and resources or reverse the bad decisions I'd made over the last month. It had hurt to leave her behind when I had first abandoned her to Royce, but it hurt even more to know that she'd so easily forgiven me. I squeezed my own eyes shut so I wouldn't start leaking tears all over her. In the last thirty days, I'd already cried enough to last a lifetime.

"Much as I like seeing two chicks all over each

other, you're blocking the path to the cookies. Mind shoving over?"

Sara and I both made sounds that were a combination snicker and snort, pulling away from each other to give Christoph room to get past us. Mouse gazed after him with a look of mixed dismay and amusement, her hands on her hips. That was when I noticed that all the newcomers, save for Sara and Royce, had returned in clubbing clothes. The leather-and-chains look was pretty distracting now that I'd noticed it, though I did my best to keep my eyes above Ashi's and Christoph's belts. Holy *wow*, could those two pull off leather pants. . . .

Analie was more than happy to stay busy preparing plates of sweets. First one for Christoph, and then one for Ashi, too, once he pulled away from Clarisse's arm and slipped past Royce with a look of undisguised contempt.

Though I hadn't dealt with them much on my prior visits, their behavior didn't come as much of a surprise. The two were werewolves, though relatively harmless since the leather collars around their necks prevented them from shapeshifting. I had never asked for specifics—honestly, I hadn't even known what they really were until Christoph had told me last night—but the two were almost always hanging out together even though they didn't seem to like each other very much.

The pair wolfed down the cookies Analie gave them (ha—see what I did there?) as Clarisse and

Mouse trailed inside, taking seats at the table with Wes, while Royce leaned against the granite breakfast bar. Seeing as almost all of the seats were taken, Sara and I joined Royce, who pulled out stools for both of us. Sara and I each took a seat, grinning and leaning against each other like a pair of happy drunks. Though she was startled by it, Sara didn't protest when Royce positioned himself behind us, a hand on either of our shoulders.

Mouse's hands moved, signing something. Wes, Christoph, and Royce all nodded when she was done.

Wes then glanced in my direction and, for the first time all evening, didn't look like he wanted to throttle me. Instead, his facial muscles tensed, and the rest of his body went into that unnatural stillness I associated with a vampire experiencing a pang of guilt or discomfort. "You might want to advise them about what's been happening over the last twenty-four hours."

"Oh, give it a rest, love. This is just cozy—no time for that sort of talk," Clarisse said, her green eyes positively gleaming with mischief. "I don't suppose you'd reconsider, Alec? Just for a few nights."

"Reconsider what?" I asked.

"Something I'll discuss with you two later. Privately."

Clarisse pouted but didn't protest, though she was clearly disappointed that she'd be missing out on what I assumed was going to turn into some quality drama the minute Royce dropped whatever bomb he'd saved up for us. The others shrugged and kept quiet as Sara and I exchanged mystified, and slightly alarmed, looks.

The vampire's grip tightened on my shoulder, as he was probably sensing just how much I was bothered by his decision to wait to tell us whatever the heck it was he was hiding this time. "Try not to worry. I've found a way to keep the situation contained. For the most part, everything is under control."

Sara twisted around to face him, shrugging his hand off her shoulder. "Hiding things from us is not 'keeping the situation contained.' If whatever you're up to involves us, we deserve to know what's going on."

Mouse and Clarisse nodded, and Wes shrank down in his seat, while the trio of werewolves watched us with the kind of rapt attention I would expect them to devote to a good movie or daytime TV. Royce was not amused, and his clipped tones reflected that.

"Yes, you do. However, I had thought you might appreciate some time to relax and catch up with each other before discussing business."

While Sara wilted under the pressure of Royce's gaze—not that I blamed her, since he was pretty damned scary even when he wasn't intentionally being so—I didn't like the idea of backing down so easily. His words might have been thoughtful, but his tone was downright frosty, which told me he was more interested in putting it off than in telling us what was going on. Still, I thought it might be best to tread carefully since I didn't want to make him genuinely annoyed with us after all he had done.

"We appreciate it," I said, placing my hand over his on my shoulder, "but so much has already happened that we haven't had any time to relax as it is. If we know what's going on, at least we can come to terms with whatever else has gone wrong instead of incessantly worrying about what's coming next."

Sara was eyeing the way I touched him with undisguised speculation. No doubt she would demand to know what had happened between me and the vampire as soon as she could get me alone for a few minutes. Considering my phobia of vampires, and my prior obvious distrust of Royce, to say that times had changed was quite an understatement. Not a conversation I was looking forward to, but it wasn't something I was going to be able to put off for long.

Royce, for his part, seemed less than thrilled about the way everyone else in the room was watching him, just waiting for him to reveal the latest bombshell. For the moment, I felt too emotionally drained to be terribly worried about what he had in store for us. After all I had been through, there was little left to get worked up about.

"You two can't stay here."

Except for that.

"You both must leave the city. Tonight. I've made arrangements for you to stay with an ally of mine across the country."

I just looked at him.

"You know," he said, his tone turning dry, "I did try to tell you that it would be best to wait until we had more privacy to discuss this."

"Oy, lovey, are ye sure they can't stay another day or so?" Clarisse seemed exceptionally put out, which led me to believe she had a bet riding on our presence here. "Seems a shame to send them away seeing as they've both just returned."

Royce tilted his head down and lifted a hand to press his fingertips against the bridge of his nose. I got the distinct feeling he was as annoyed about the situation as I was, which was unexpected. After spending the last couple of hours thinking he was going to make a grab for any excuse to rid himself of me now that he'd finally had me in bed and tasted my blood, the thought that he would feel any sort of annoyance or regret over sending me away was beyond belief.

"Why do we have to go? I don't get it—I just got here."

He must have either read the hurt in my voice or felt it through whatever connection it was we now shared. His brow rested against my temple briefly, followed by the brush of his lips on my cheek. "I'm not doing this because I'm trying to get rid of you, Shiarra. If I could, I would keep you here, but it's too dangerous. Not just for you, but for the rest of my flock. Until I can remove the threats and guarantee your safety, it would be best for us all if you stayed with one of my allies. It's only temporary."

Christoph mumbled a question around a mouthful of cookies. "Where're you sending 'em?"

"Los Angeles."

Christoph choked on his cookie as Analie and Ashi both straightened and started talking at once. I couldn't make out a word since the three were talking over and shoving each other to get closer to us. Startled, Sara and I both shrank back, but there wasn't any place for us to go. Royce's grip on my shoulder tightened, keeping me from slipping off the chair.

His voice took on a note of command, a shiver tracing up my spine at the chill in the words. "Do not get your hopes up. She will not be contacting your pack while she is there."

Christoph and Ashi's faces fell, the twin looks of disappointment almost comical to see on the pair. Analie, on the other hand, looked close to tears, wringing her hands as her gaze flicked between me and the vampire.

"Please, I haven't seen Gavin in so long. Can't she just take him a letter for me? Maybe some cookies?"

As tough as the vampire's attitude had been a moment ago, the frosty edge was soon replaced by a far gentler tone than I'd thought Royce capable of. "Analie, it would be dangerous for Shiarra to meet with him without me there to protect her. You know how your pack feels about vampires. What do you think they might do to her if they knew she was staying with one of my friends?"

"Gavin wouldn't hurt her," she insisted, turning that pleading look on me. "Please, I know I'm asking a lot, but if I give you a package can you bring it to him? Please? I'll do anything to repay you, and I'll call ahead and everything so—"

"Analie," Royce interrupted, "don't disobey me in this. You can mail a package to him, if you wish."

"But I—"

"No."

She ducked her head and hunched her shoulders, backing away. Christoph gave her an awkward pat on the back, but she twisted away from us, gripping the counter so hard I thought I heard the marble crack. Mouse glared daggers in Royce's direction, which meant Sara and I were on the receiving end, too. We shared a look, uncomfortable meeting the mute vampire's accusatory gaze.

Royce did not appear troubled by any of this. He shifted to rest his hip against the counter in a casual lean. "Clyde Seabreeze has agreed to take you two in while I sort out matters here in New York. I do not want to risk either of your lives, which is why I am sending you away. The White Hats have become unstable with the loss of their leader—"

I cut him off, alarmed. "Wait, what? What happened to Jack?"

The casual shrug Royce gave did not fit with the words coming out of his mouth. "I upheld my end of our bargain. Since he was turned, the local White Hats have fractured into two factions: those who believe that not all of us are monsters, and those who still feel that every Other must be exterminated. There are quite a few who blame you for Jack's fall from grace."

Turned. That meant Jack had finally caved. He was a vampire now.

Chapter 5

"Jack, the crazy guy who kept threatening Shia at knife- and gunpoint to join the hunters, is a vampire now?"

Sara's incredulity was perfectly understandable. I was having a hard time coming to grips with the idea, too.

"Aye," Clarisse drawled. "He was so high and mighty until he knew he was faced with death, not in battle, but from a slow sickness eating him from the inside out. As with most people who choose to hunt us, he learned too late that his hatred was due to his envy, and so he bargained with the devil to become what he hated so much."

We all considered this, save for Analie, who was still pointedly giving us her back. Christoph looked uncomfortable, not meeting anybody's eyes, and Mouse was thoughtfully nibbling her lower lip as she watched him. Clarisse had put an elbow on the table and was cupping her chin, staring at Sara and me like she was expecting us to say something captivating at any moment.

The voice that broke the silence wasn't the one I expected. Ashi ran his fingers through his hair in a nervous gesture, shifting his weight from foot to foot as if he were about to bolt. "They never tell you what you're getting into until it's too late. Doesn't matter if it's vampires or werewolves. He's going to regret his choice, and a lot of people are going to suffer for it."

That seemed to break Christoph's tension. He scoffed, shoving the smaller man's shoulder. "Don't tell me you're regretting being changed. You know you were asking for it when you picked that fight."

"Yeah, well, even if I was, being stuck here was never supposed to be part of the deal."

Royce tilted his head, and I'd swear the look he gave Ashi held a kind of hunger that I'd only seen in the vampire when we were alone and he was thinking about bad, bad things to do to me. "Would you have preferred death? I had no need to spare your life then, nor do I now."

Whoa. Whatever was going on between these two was far more intense than I had previously guessed.

Ashi bared his teeth and settled into a fighting stance, meeting Royce's gaze. He wasn't giving an inch—despite the nervous sweat he'd broken into.

"Try to take me, leech. Just try."

"Och, that's enough," Clarisse said, shaking a scolding finger at Royce. I was more than a little surprised to see the older vampire bow his head, the hunger and tension he'd exhibited only a moment ago replaced by a small, mockingly contrite smile. A grudging concession, maybe, but he was willing to back down for her. "You know I've laid the claim, Alec. He's mine, now."

"As you say," Royce murmured, though his gaze briefly slid back to give Ashi a look that I interpreted as a warning. Ashi remained right where he was, stiff and unyielding in his stance, his raised fists only lowering a fraction. "Do try to recall that I am master here."

Ashi's lip curled. "Not mine. You don't own me. I'm not some stupid, broken house pet like those two."

Christoph and Analie whirled on Ashi, both of them growling—though Analie sounded a bit more like I expected of a werewolf. Christoph, on the other hand, made a sound more like a guttering wheeze.

Mouse rolled her eyes heavenward, and Clarisse put her head in her hands. "Here we go. . . ."

It was as if Ashi had no idea what kind of effect he'd created. He was still stubbornly glaring at Royce like he could hate him to death.

The vampire leaned forward, and I felt the cold breath of his whisper against my cheek, making me shiver. "Are you certain you wish to raise the ire of your packmates, Ashi? I shouldn't think I would have to remind you that you have few friends here."

Oh, God. I didn't even want to *imagine* what

kind of look must be on the vampire's face while he said that.

A fine tremble was visible in Ashi's arms, but he stood his ground. "I don't need their friendship. I need their respect."

"You lost it when you tricked me into coming here, you asshole." Christoph glared at the much smaller man, though I noted he didn't seem in any hurry to attempt any kind of physical confrontation. He kept some distance between them, edging almost imperceptibly closer to Mouse.

Ashi sneered, not breaking Royce's gaze. I thought maybe he was concerned that if he looked away, Royce might pounce on him.

I wouldn't put something like that past the vampire.

"If you weren't such a sucker for beer and football, you wouldn't have fallen for it, you imbecile."

Analie shocked me by socking Ashi in the arm, sending him stumbling to one side and crashing into the table. Mouse, Clarisse, and Wes scooted their chairs out of the way, but made no move to help Ashi, who was sprawled on the floor and clutching at his head. Hell, the vampires looked bored.

You know you have an exciting lifestyle when the novelty of werewolves fighting in the kitchen has worn off.

"It's *your fault* I'm still stuck here, you insensitive asshole!" Analie was verging on tears again—but there was a hint of fang and a not-so-subtle glow to her eyes that hadn't been there a moment ago. Hormonal teenaged werewolves. Gotta love 'em. "I can't even send Gavin a letter! I'm not going to see him for *years* because of you!"

Royce's fingertips dug into my shoulder. This situation was escalating to a very uncomfortable level in more ways than one.

As fascinating as it was watching this little drama unfold, I did not want to get caught in the middle of a fight between vampires and werewolves. Even if it was all verbal, this was way too messed up, even for me. I cleared my throat, drawing the eye of every supernatural in the room.

Peachy.

"Look, I know this is not my business, but maybe we can come up with some kind of compromise, huh? Analie, I'll take a letter to Gavin for you." The glow in her eyes seemed slightly less threatening, even though the wide grin she gave me was made with a mouthful of fangs. I wasn't sure if the twinge of fear twisting in my gut was from nervousness at the idea of meeting Analie's caretaker, or from the way Royce's anger suddenly became palpable. I hastily continued before Analie could say something else to break my heart and leave me feeling obligated to do another favor I probably couldn't afford. "It's not like it's a big deal. I don't have to stick around, just deliver it—right? I can drop it off and leave it at that."

Royce growled. Actually *growled*. And since he was still hovering over me, the sound vibrated uncomfortably against my ear, making me squirm.

His voice was cold and each word carefully enunciated. "Ms. Waynest, my arrangements to see to your safety by taking you away from all of the dangerous elements you have become a magnet for will be completely negated if you insist on carrying forward with this foolishness. You've already managed to raise the ire of the East Coast werewolves, the White Hats, and the police. Do you truly plan on tempting fate with the werewolves in Los Angeles?"

Annoyed, I twisted around on the chair to face him. "You know what? Yeah, I do. I don't need you to keep rubbing it in that I've screwed up my life. What do you think I spent the last month doing? For weeks, I haven't had a break from the voice in my head telling me nonstop what a fucking screwup I've been. I don't need you telling me, too."

A light touch to my arm drew my gaze away from Royce's. Sara was watching me with such concern that I was having a hard time holding on to my anger. "Shia, I know things have been rough on you lately, but maybe you should listen to him. You weren't here to see what it was like the last few weeks."

My gaze flicked back and forth between Sara and Royce. He didn't appear to be thrilled with Sara for butting in, but he wasn't gritting his fangs anymore either, so maybe her involvement in this conversation wasn't such a terrible thing. As badly as I wanted to hold on to my righteous anger, this wasn't the time or the place for it. Explaining my reasoning wasn't going to be fun, but I wasn't going to let this go so easily.

"I'm sorry," I said, my words as slow and measured as Royce's had been only a few moments ago, though for a far different reason. "This isn't something I can just let go. I've been a . . . a really terrible, thoughtless person for the last month. I've done some things that are going to haunt me for the rest of my life."

I'd hunted Chaz and other Sunstriker werewolves like they were dogs. I'd joined and aided a group of extremists who had no regard for the lives of Others or people sympathetic to their cause. I'd ignored my friends and family for the sake of revenge.

I'd killed someone.

"There's blood on my hands, and the only way I can wash it away is by being a better person."

"Soap and water takes care of that, you know," Christoph commented. Wes bopped him on the back of the head, prompting a watery smile out of me.

"I've done some really stupid things, guys. I need to feel better about myself, inside and out, and one of the ways I can do that is by repaying the kindness Analie has shown me. She's not asking for much, and it will be a start on my road to recovery. Am I making any sense?"

"No," Ashi said from his seat on the floor. His

dark brown eyes were narrowed, watching me with distrust.

Clarisse and Wes both shushed him, Mouse shook her head, and Royce cupped my chin in his palm to make me turn my head to look at him. The melancholy expression he wore didn't suit him, but it was an improvement over the irritation he'd been exuding for most of this conversation.

"I believe the fault in this matter lies with me. If you understood the danger you would be putting yourself—and Sara—in by contacting the Goliath pack, you wouldn't be so eager to do this."

I put my hand on his cheek, the tips of my fingers playing along his smooth skin as I studied his features. There were tiny creases like half-formed laugh lines around his eyes and mouth. His lips were thin but pliant under my caressing thumb. The tension in his jaw gradually eased under my touch, the muscles no longer visibly bunching up around his cheekbones and the line of his jaw.

It took me a little time to figure out how I wanted to express my thoughts without making myself sound like a suicidal lunatic.

"I'm not deliberately putting myself at risk this time because I have a death wish—I'm doing it because I need to prove to myself that I still have the capacity to do great good, not just great evil. There's no way to undo the pain and suffering and death I was responsible for, but repaying Analie's kindness and doing something to make her happy is a step in the right direction for me." I gave Royce a significant look. "I value my freedom and humanity. I need to do something to remind myself what those things are worth, and to earn them back."

My turning the vampire's own words back on him gave him pause. Though I could tell he was not entirely happy with the idea, he didn't seem up to fighting me over my choice anymore. He leaned in to press a kiss to my brow, his own words so soft that I caught some of the others in the kitchen leaning forward to listen in out of the corner of my eye.

"If there is one thing I have learned over my many centuries of life, it is that humans most often cause their own downfall by only seeing what their lives should have been, rather than shaping their lives into what they wish them to be. Your desire to be a better person is admirable, but I wish that you would have found some other task to start with."

"Yeah, well, when have I ever taken the easy road?"

Sara snorted. I gave her a look.

Royce breathed a sound that might have been a sigh or a growl, then urged me to stand. "As you wish. Analie, write your letter and prepare your package." He had to talk over her squeals of glee as he continued. "Ms. Waynest, Ms. Halloway, I need you to prepare your things. I've arranged for someone to drive you to a private airfield. My pilot will take you to California. You two will remain with Clyde Seabreeze while I make better arrangements for your security and safety upon your return to New York."

"And how long will we be gone?" Sara asked. The tone of her voice drew my attention back to her. She was hiding her anxiety well to anyone who didn't know her as well as I did, but she was twining a loop of her hair around her finger over and over. A sure sign she was worried about something.

Royce shook his head. "I can't be certain. Only as long as it takes for me to be sure you will both be safe and able to return to your loved ones. A month or two at best. Perhaps as long as a year."

That gave me a twinge. Worse, Sara paled, her already china-doll complexion going waxen. It occurred to me belatedly that I wasn't the only one who would be leaving behind people who were important to me.

While I would not be able to see my parents or brothers, Royce, or any of my other friends, Sara would have to leave behind her sister and her boyfriend, Arnold. Not seeing our friends and family for that long wasn't going to be easy, but the alternatives were to endanger all of Royce's people, jail, or death by rabid werewolves or White Hats.

Staying with Clyde wasn't appealing, but I'd take staying with the other vampire over dying any day.

Chapter 6

Royce sent me with Sara to collect what remained of our things in the room we had briefly shared before I went on my rampage. Sara had already packed away most of her stuff before she went to stay with Royce's ex-honey, the model and closet elf, Dawn Hartley. Her dogs were still with the elf, who had kindly offered to care for them until Sara returned to claim them.

Dawn was awfully chummy with Royce, considering they were no longer an item. Though I often did my best not to think about Others who didn't show any personal interest in me or butt their way into my life, I had to wonder what she had to gain that she would so easily accept Sara into her home.

Not that Sara had suffered for it. She looked great. Better than great. Healthier than I had ever seen her.

And she was pointedly avoiding looking at me as she helped me stuff some things into the duffel bag I had brought with me weeks ago. I hadn't had time to unpack before I went postal, so there was little for me to collect and put in the bag but some toiletries, the Rolodex I had left on the counter, and some clothing I vaguely recalled leaving in a pile on the bathroom floor that was now neatly folded in a stack on the bed.

"I'm sorry," I said, once the last piece of clothing was shoved into the bag. "I didn't think things would turn out like this."

Sara finally looked at me, her icy blue eyes having taken on the chill look she usually reserved for deadbeat clients. "That's the problem, Shia. You never think things through. You don't consider the consequences of your actions."

That stung. Mostly because she was right.

"We're supposed to be partners. You could have consulted with me before you ran off. What am I supposed to tell Arnold? Who's going to check on Janine? You know how unstable she is. . . ."

Sara's younger sister was a neurotic wreck. She would probably pitch a fit because Sara was leaving, but Janine was perfectly capable of taking care of herself. Even though I knew Sara was just bringing up Janine to make me feel even worse than I already did, I couldn't hold it against her. This whole mess was my fault, start to finish, and Sara was the one paying the price for my foolish decisions and behavior.

Grimacing, I rubbed the back of my neck and looked away, not wanting to face her while I spoke.

"I don't have an easy answer for you. If you want, I'll make the calls and give them the news. We can't take Arnold with us—if Royce wouldn't let him visit you here, I can't imagine Clyde would be any different—and Janine is probably safer not knowing where we're going. Maybe we can tell her we have an important case taking us out of town or something. It's close enough to the truth that she won't question it and won't make demands about visiting or following us, either."

My offer to be the one to break the news mellowed Sara out somewhat. She considered the offer, looking down at her hands as she toyed with the buttons on the cuffs of her long-sleeved shirt. When she answered, her voice had lost its brittle edge, replaced by resignation.

"Fine. Do it. Call Arnold first; explaining to him will take less time."

I nodded, zipping up my duffel and making my way out of the bedroom, Sara following close behind. Analie was waiting for me in the living room, her package already ready for me. Sara scooted past me to plop down on the couch, and I set the duffel bag down next to the door, accepting the small box Analie held out to me.

She shifted her weight from foot to foot, her eyes wide and imploring. "I wrote the address on the box. I'll call ahead so Gavin knows you're coming, but make sure you don't have any vampires with you when you go, okay? He's—we're—Goliaths, I mean—we're usually very careful never to have anything to do with vamps. Ever. As long as it's just you, and maybe Sara, too, you should be fine."

That sounded ominous. I wasn't the biggest fan of vampires either, but showing up alone at the home of a member of a rival Were pack wouldn't be the brightest idea. Maybe I could just leave the package on Gavin's doorstep and hightail it.

"Can you give him a hug for me, too? And Jo-Jo? Please?"

Oh, cripes. The puppy dog eyes the kid was giving me went straight to my heart, shredding it like a politician's phone records.

Sara's giving me a very significant 'do-it-or-we'll-be-having-words-later' look went a long way to help me along with my decision. "Okay. Yeah, I'll do it."

Analie squealed in delight and hugged me tight, crushing the box against my chest and prompting a twinge in my ribs. The little preteen Were was *strong*.

"Thank you, thank you, thank you!"

I gasped out something unintelligible in reply, and she let me go, dashing out the door and calling for Mouse at the top of her lungs. She was cute as a button, but man, she had no concept of her own strength.

Rubbing my aching ribs with one hand, I put the box on top of my duffel and continued on to the kitchen, using the phone on the counter next to a microwave. Sara called out Arnold and Janine's numbers for me from her spot on the couch, and I dialed the mage first. He answered after a couple rings.

"Arnold, it's Shia."

He didn't sound terribly surprised to hear from me. "Jeez, where the hell have you been? Sara and I have been worried sick about you."

"I know, I know. I was extraordinarily stupid, more so than usual, and I'm really sorry about that."

"I take it you've been saying that a lot lately," Arnold said. I could practically hear him grinning through the phone. "If that's the case, I assume you don't need me to rub it in, too."

"Yeah," I muttered. "Anyway, listen—"

"Hold up a sec. Did you end up turning Were? Did you shift with the moon?"

Train of thought derailed at the station. It took me a sec to get my mouth back in gear to answer him. "Um. No, I didn't."

"You didn't?" He made a thoughtful sound. I heard some rummaging and clattering through the phone, as well as a few low curses. Then a thump, and the sound of pages being turned. "Hold on . . . just a—here. Anything happen when the moon rose? Anything at all?"

"I didn't grow fur, if that's what you're asking. I coughed up some black stuff, and some of it came out my eyes and ears." It might have been absurd to have listened to it, but the belt had talked me out of putting my faith in the mage for finding a solution to prevent my potential lycanthropic infection. It hadn't occurred to me until he started asking questions that he might have information about what was happening to me. "Do you know why?"

"Black stuff. Huh. Consistency?"

I made a face he couldn't see. "Arnold . . ."

"Sorry, it's for science. This is important, Shia. Anything you can tell me about the symptoms—even the slightest detail—could make a difference."

"Ugh, I don't know. It was gross. It was mixed with blood, kind of thick and oozy. The first time, I had a nosebleed and a headache, then the stuff kept coming for what felt like hours. Earlier tonight it plugged up my sinuses and made it hard to breathe for a minute or two, then it all came out in a rush. What does it mean?"

"It means you've got some strain of lycanthropy that I need to do more research on. Sounds like something in your body is fighting it. Might be the vampire blood. Any chance I can get a sample?"

Well. Couldn't have asked for a better opening for letting him know about what else was going epically wrong in our lives. "I'm afraid not. That's kind of why I called you to begin with. I'm really sorry—again—that I'm not calling with good news, but Sara and I aren't safe yet. There are still people after us, and we're going out of town to lay low for a while."

"Can't say I'm surprised considering all of the people who are after you. I suppose it's better you two are somewhere safe until all this blows over. Where are you guys going, and for how long? Someplace I can visit?"

"We're going to Los Angeles until Royce settles things here. We're staying with some vampire Royce knows, so it probably wouldn't be a good idea for you to swing by unless we can meet somewhere other than the vamp's house."

Arnold didn't reply right away, waiting just long enough for the silence to grow ominous before he spoke. "Whatever you do, stay away from the werewolves out there. There are two primary packs that will pose a great deal of danger to you if they even get a whiff of your scent. The Amberguard pack might just kill you, but the Goliaths will kill and eat you. Not necessarily in that order."

That was . . . good to know.

Particularly considering that Analie had mentioned her pack name at one point. Gavin, the werewolf I was supposed to deliver the package to, was a Goliath.

Great. Just peachy keen.

"Hey, you've got my number. Just call me if you run into any trouble. I won't be there to help you two, but I might be able to talk you through any tough spots. And check in with me in a few days; I might have an answer for you about what the black stuff is and what it means."

For the first time, I truly regretted blowing off Arnold's offer to help me over the last month. He might have saved me a lot of grief if I hadn't listened to the belt and had contacted him before the sickness set in. Even though he'd as good as confirmed I was still infected, I wasn't afraid anymore. He had resources in his mage coven and access to potential solutions I couldn't have dreamed of coming up with on my own. The belt had well and truly warped my perceptions of what my options and who my friends really were.

"Thank you," I said, voice a bit thick. "Arnold, you're a lifesaver."

"Hey, what are friends for? Now put my girlfriend on. I want to hear her voice before she leaves."

I leaned over the breakfast bar and tossed the phone to Sara. She was quick to scoop it up and rise from the couch, heading with purposeful strides and a quiet murmur into the phone into the bedroom, shutting the door behind herself.

It seemed as good a time as any to find Royce and let him know we were almost ready to leave. The two of us needed to have a chat, too. This entire situation was driving me bonkers. After I had finally broken down and given in to my desire for him, we had to separate. The breadth of a continent would be between us, taking away any chance I had to get to know him as more than the embodiment of a fairytale nightmare and understand what I had committed myself to practically before it began.

No one was in the hall when I left the apartment, though I could see someone's booted foot and jean-clad leg sticking out, barely visible in the doorway leading to the foyer and outside. Whoever was on night watch was sprawled at the front desk.

I headed up the stairs, quietly padding my way to the third floor. The door leading into Royce's quarters was ajar, light spilling out through the crack. I nudged the door open a bit and poked my head in, glancing around for the vampire.

He wasn't in the main room with all its intimidating open space and eclectic collection of statuary. For some reason, I felt the need to tiptoe across the hardwood floors, my bare feet not making a sound as I made my way to Royce's bedroom.

The vampire was there, as I had suspected, though I was not expecting to see him seated on the edge of the futon with his elbows on his knees and his head in his hands. His voice, when it came, startled me.

"I don't think I have had so many of my plans go awry in centuries. Why is it that whatever you involve yourself in always takes so many unexpected turns?"

I bit my lip, hesitating in the doorway before settling down next to him. He lifted his head and folded his arms against his knees, glancing at me.

"One of the others has arranged to give you a cell phone to use to stay in touch with me while you are with Clyde. He would not have been my first choice, but there's little help for it now. If anything goes wrong, call me immediately."

I swallowed around the growing lump in my throat. "You expect things to go wrong? Why are you sending us to stay with him if you don't trust him?"

"He is one of the most powerful allies I have who was amenable to the idea of harboring you two while I make other arrangements," he replied. "It isn't ideal, but his debts to me are significant enough that he should make an effort to keep you safe."

That wasn't terribly reassuring. It wasn't until Royce ran his thumb under one of my eyes that I realized I was crying again. I'd promised myself I wouldn't do any more of that, but so many things were going to hell just when I'd thought I was getting a handle on life again that I couldn't help it. I didn't want to leave New York. I didn't want to leave my friends and family behind.

More than that, I didn't want to leave Royce. Not after all I had been through. Not after last night. Not after finally owning up to just how much I desired him.

"Try not to worry. You'll be able to stay in touch with the phone—though you should take some care not to call too often. Authorities are looking for you, which means we'll need to keep contact to a minimum until I can arrange for your return."

That was a hell of a blow. Logical as the statement was, my heart still ached at the thought of our impending separation. Only the knowledge that I wouldn't just be putting myself in a bad position, but that I might endanger Sara or his household, kept me from arguing to stay.

"You had a point, earlier. It's unfair of me to keep so many things from you."

And the hits just kept on coming. I frowned at him, having to clear my throat a couple of times before the raspy quality faded enough for my voice to be understandable. "Is that a roundabout way of telling me there's more bad news you were going to hold off on sharing?"

His wry smile didn't match the look in his eyes. "To a degree, yes. There are two things that may be of some interest to you. Firstly, I am sure you must have given some thought to what your family must have been doing in your absence."

Actually, I hadn't, and I was more than a little ashamed to realize this was the first time I'd given them more than a passing thought in quite awhile. Royce must have mistaken my stricken look, because he was quick to reassure me. "Your father had a mild heart attack, but he is out of the hospital and at home with your mother again. Your brothers have been paying them regular visits, and all four of them have been staying away from the press. Some of my people have been assigned to guard them at all hours, so you don't have any reason to be concerned about their well-being."

That was good to know. I let out the breath I hadn't realized I was holding, though my relief was short-lived.

"As for the other . . . I thought about keeping it to myself as I felt no need to alarm you or make you worry about yet another thing you have no control over. However, considering your current condition, it may be best for you to know that whatever this infection is, it may be a sign that you will find yourself drawn to run with the other Sunstrikers or perhaps force you into shifting should you be in their proximity during the full moon. It is part of the reason I think it a very good idea to send you away for the time being."

Tension drew all the muscles in my neck and back into sudden, painful knots. To think, if I had chosen to hunt with Chaz and the White Hats instead of come after Royce, I might not have been able to walk away from the pack after the fight.

Though I wished someone had said something to me sooner, I couldn't exactly blame Royce for keeping his silence. If he had said something about it while I was still under the influence of the belt, I might have rushed out to destroy what remained of the pack to ensure they would have no hold over me.

"I know that look," Royce said, drawing my attention off my clenched fists in my lap to meet his gaze. "No more running off. Things are under control now. We have a plan. Even if it isn't ideal, it is better than the other options available to us at the moment."

That he said available to us—not to me or to him—went a long way toward making me feel better about the way things were going. As Royce had said, it wasn't ideal, but it was enough for the moment. He accepted the hand I slid into his, twining his cool fingers with mine.

"I wish," he said, leaning in to press a kiss to my temple and breathe his next words in a husky whisper against my skin, "that I had more time to romance you properly now that you're open to the prospect."

"When I get back," I replied, tilting my head to reciprocate his kiss.

He leaned in to me, his free hand rising to cup my cheek. The other tightened around my fingers, pulling me close. While he held me tight, this wasn't exactly like it had been last night. There was a touch of desperation in the hungry way his lips slanted over mine. It was in the way he pressed against me, in the small sound he made in the back of his throat as my lips parted so I could slide my tongue along his and taste the mint he had used to cover the underlying trace of salt and copper from the blood he must have drunk, and in the way his fingers moved over my skin. Though he was possessive, we both knew this was our good-bye, and that it might be the last time we held each other for a year or more.

It was a bittersweet way to end the night, but in that too short span we did everything we could to say without words what we felt, fighting to fit in years of need and repressed desire before the break of dawn.

Chapter 7

The flight and our arrival were uneventful. Prior to the flight, Sara and I spent most of the day left to our own devices. The majority of the vampires were taking their day rest, or busy on watch, and the flight wasn't scheduled until late afternoon. I had hoped I might get to talk to my family or update the two cops who had helped me stay a step ahead of whoever in the NYPD was after me, but we were advised to keep the rest of our calls to a minimum until we were safely out of town. Royce couldn't spend much time with me since he was busy with his lawyers and some mess at his corporate office that he was trying to handle by phone. The last thing he managed to tell me before he sent me back down to Sara was not to put my trust in Clyde—which made me feel ever so much better about this trip we were about to take.

For a little while, Analie kept us company, telling us stories about her best friend, Freddy, and her caretaker, Gavin. The Goliaths didn't sound so bad when she was talking about them, but I was sure Sara and I wouldn't be as welcome as someone who had been born and raised into the pack—especially if we showed up at Gavin's place covered in the scent of vampires.

After hours of going bonkers with a combination of boredom and nerves, we were taken to a private airport. Though I knew little about planes, the one we were escorted onto was sleek, pristine, and full of so many gadgets and amenities that I was afraid to touch anything inside in case it might break. Sara was more at home, staying in her seat and reading a book while I prowled around the cabin.

A flight attendant came in at one point to see if we needed anything and tried to show me what a few of the doodads did, but it wasn't as fun to poke around with someone following me around and sounding like she was parroting off a sales brochure. Eventually, exhaustion crept up on me, and I did my best to nap while we sped in our little flying tin can across the expanse of the United States.

Once we drew close to our destination, the flight attendant explained we were about to arrive at the Santa Monica airport, and that Mr. Royce had made arrangements for our pick-up and transportation to our destination. I stared out the window as we approached, noting the nearby ocean and pier and all of the tiny buildings and cars looking like toy models from this height. As we drew closer, I grew more and more nervous. Eventually I pulled the shade over the window and clutched at the armrests of my seat, closing my eyes. Sara laughed at me, but I didn't care. Much.

The landing jarred us a little bit, but we arrived in one piece, so I couldn't complain. Once we were on the ground, I opened the window again, peering out. The plane taxied off of the runway and into a huge, whitewashed hangar, the big door sliding shut once the plane stopped inside. A few minutes later, duffel slung over my shoulder, Sara and I stepped onto the gleaming white floor, glittering with polish that reflected the lamps high above our heads.

A gentleman in a suit and reflective shades was waiting for us, gesturing that we should follow him. He didn't bother to wait to see if we did as we were bid. When I checked over my shoulder, someone else had grabbed the rest of our bags. Sara and I exchanged a look, then shrugged and followed.

He led us across the huge bay of the hangar, empty save for the plane we'd arrived in, and out through a people-sized door on the other side. An ocean-scented breeze whipped my hair around. Once I brushed it back, I was greeted by the sight of a sleek white limo. The man who had led us out was now holding the limo door and waiting for us, his expression clearly indicating he was bored and unimpressed with us. Though I knew he was impatient to get out of here, I took a moment to look around. This was my first time in Santa Monica, after all.

The nearby mountains were oddly brown and

dead—nothing like the vibrant greens of the Catskills. The sky was alive with a splash of strange oranges and reds, a sunset like nothing I'd ever seen back East. Palm trees were *everywhere*. Funny looking cacti mixed with some weird flowers that had long green stems, nearly as tall as I was, topped with spiky orange and dark purplish flowers, planted alongside the building, sprucing up the otherwise plain white structure. A touch of the wild in the otherwise carefully deliberate landscaping.

Sara entered the limo, and I soon followed suit. The man shut the door behind us, and I heard the luggage being tossed in the trunk. Despite the more than generous size of the passenger area, which probably could have fit half a dozen people comfortably, it was claustrophobic in the plush interior of that limo, and neither of us wanted to speak.

Soon, the driver got in, turning his head just enough to acknowledge our existence. "Mr. Seabreeze extends his welcome. He's hosting a party in your honor tonight. You'll be staying in the guesthouse. We can stop there first if you'd prefer to freshen up, but he was very insistent that he would like to meet you right away."

"I would rather meet him first."

Sara didn't see any reason to delay meeting our host either. "So would I. If we're going to be stuck here for a while, I want to know who and what I'll be dealing with."

The driver adjusted his rearview mirror to look

us over, probably not realizing we could see his features at that angle, too. I got the impression it was the first time he was really looking at us—and that he didn't approve of what he saw. His lip curled slightly before he turned his attention ahead again, starting the limo. "As you wish."

Though it wasn't my first time in a limo, this wasn't something I did every day. For Sara, this was old hat. She lounged back and watched with some amusement as I fiddled with all of the buttons and panels, discovering the hidden TV (how the hell do you get cable access in a car?), satellite radio, selection of drinks, and even something that tinted and untinted the windows. Special sunproofing for the vampire, maybe?

Soon, it wasn't the car, but what was passing by outside that drew my attention. It didn't take long for us to reach a ridiculously extravagant area, full of small but manicured-to-within-an-inch-of-the-property-line lawns with weird ornaments and excessive lighting, while the houses themselves, each one seemingly bigger than the next, looked like they belonged in TV shows or movies. Come to think of it, this was part of Los Angeles, so they probably *were* in TV shows and movies.

For the first time in my life, I was intimidated by buildings.

Sara did not appear concerned, but I was seriously reconsidering making that pit stop at the guesthouse to change into something more appropriate than jeans and T-shirts before visiting this

Seabreeze guy. Though with a name like that, I had the feeling I was going to have a very hard time taking him seriously, even if he was a very rich and important vampire who lived in a mansion.

I figured now was as good a time as any to let Royce know we'd arrived safely. Tugging the cell phone out of the pocket of my duffel I'd shoved it into, I scrolled through the few contacts already in the phone.

Someone had been quite thoughtful. Not only had they added Royce's cell, but they'd included Royce's head of security, Angus, as well as Mouse, Wes, and a few other familiar names, too. If I needed to reach anyone in a hurry, there were multiple ways for me to do it.

Royce picked up after a couple of rings, though he sounded a bit distracted until he realized it was me.

"Hey, just wanted to let you know we made it here in one piece."

"Good. Have you met with Clyde yet?"

"No," I said, glancing at the driver again, "not yet. We're on our way from the airport right now."

"All right. Call me immediately if he makes any effort to alter or renege on our agreement. And be careful, my little hunter. I want you to come home to me safely."

"I will," I promised. "You owe me a hell of a romantic evening after this."

He laughed and whispered a promise to do something to me once I got back that had me blushing so hard, I thought I might ignite by the power of my mixed mortification and desire alone. Cripes, I hoped to hell Sara hadn't overheard, though judging by the look she was giving me it wasn't totally unlikely.

She didn't ask, and I didn't say anything as I ended the call and shoved the phone back in the duffel, still hot with embarrassment. Rather than meet her gaze, I turned my attention to the world passing by. If we were going to be stuck here for weeks or months, I might as well get to know where we were going.

Not that watching the route we took was helping much. We were soon lost in a maze of houses. I would have no hope of finding my way around here without the help of GPS or a map. Few of the streets seemed to run in straight lines. Some curved with the landscape. It was strange and not a little unsettling to a girl who was used to the straightforward streets that ran in simple north-south-east-west lines in New York.

After a while, we were beyond the "mildly impressive and not a little intimidating" mansions and were now drifting past the "are people even allowed to live in these places" estates. The limo turned into a short driveway and pulled up to a manned security station. The driver said something to a guy in a uniform with a clipboard, and then we were beyond the huge, metal gates and prowling past a few fairy-tale homes that should have been—scratch that—probably were regularly featured on the covers of magazines like *We Have Better Homes & Gardens Than You.*

Thus, it was not a little disconcerting when we reached one that had a slew of expensive import and sports cars jamming the streets around it and sat somewhat above the others on a rise.

It was enormous. It looked more like it should be housing a slew of families, not a coven of vampires. Though there were curtains drawn behind all of the many windows, there were occasional flashes of what I thought might be a strobe light filtering around the edges on the first floor. Even from within the limo and half a block away, a heavy bass thump rhythmically vibrated under my feet.

Still, something about the place made it seem as if it were standing in silent judgment over the other homes, and finding them wanting.

The driver spoke up, drawing my attention off the small but carefully sculpted water gardens on either side of the long, winding driveway. Funny, I thought I'd heard somewhere that this part of California was in a drought.

"Your bags will be delivered to the guest house."

Guess that meant I had to leave the duffel in the limo. Not a bad idea. It would probably look pretty tacky lugging it around, and I didn't like the idea of wandering the halls of this particular master vampire's house with a cheap department store knock-off instead of a designer travel bag. I already felt out of place. No need to add to the raging insecurities I was already dealing with.

"Oh, and a word of advice, ladies."

Sara and I both gave the driver our full attention. I had the feeling we were going to need all the help we could get to fit in here. Clearly Clyde was not above flaunting his money.

Our chauffeur wasn't looking at us as he brought the limo to a smooth stop in front of the path leading to the brightly lit French double doors. One of the trio of armed security guards at the door came down the steps and opened the car door for us as the driver left us with some parting words of wisdom.

"Don't mention the hair."

With that cryptic statement, the two of us were left to face the security guard, who was doing a decent impression of a brick wall while he held the door and waited for us to decide if we were going to come out. Sara edged her way out first, accepting the guy's hand as he helped her to the curb. If he thought her "Yes, I Run Like A Girl—Try To Keep Up" T-shirt was a bit much, he didn't give any sign.

Once I was on my feet, I followed Sara up the steps and tried not to wince when the doors opened and blasted us in the face with electronica music. Yet another security guard roughly the size and dimensions of Mount Everest met us just inside. It was too loud for us to hear much of anything, but he gestured for us to follow him.

The place was just as grand and imposing on the inside as it was outside, though the furniture and artwork had more of that tacky-but-expensive look of red velvet and black satin rather than the carefully maintained Barbie's Dreamhouse architecture and landscaping outside. Like some exclusive S&M club, except with a bunch of famous people hanging out in the latest Hollywood chic instead of leather and chains.

Somehow, I managed not to stare. It helped that the strobe lights made it too disorienting to keep track of the security guard if I didn't keep my eyes locked on him, for the most part. Though I did take a peek when Sara tapped my shoulder and jerked her chin to the right. I squinted into the shadows, and nearly fainted at the sight of one of my favorite actors lounging on the couch, talking with a girl who was probably also famous, but it didn't matter because *oh, my God,* that was *really him.*

The security guard was more than a little annoyed that he had to backtrack and find us. Even more so when he had to resort to a firm hand on our shoulders to get us moving again. This was probably a good thing, because it reminded me to close my mouth and not look like the ragingly obvious tourist I was.

Some of Hollywood's finest were looking beautiful and carefree and having a great time dancing and drinking and rubbing elbows with vampires. It was difficult to tell which were the monsters and which were the real people, but if you looked hard enough, you could always spot the Others. It seemed that everyone here had a touch of that predatory mien, but only the vampires had that special glitter to their eyes.

Then again, that glitter could have been drugs. Not that it mattered. Everyone here was dangerous in his or her own way.

Sara and I were led deep into the house. We eventually reached a door where the guard had to punch some numbers into a security pad before he could open it. He motioned us into the stairwell, not following us down the rabbit hole.

Though the stairwell was well lit, and the walls here were a much more appropriate off-white, hung with the occasional framed photograph, being starstruck was replaced by that sense of dread and intimidation all over again.

For her part, Sara didn't seem concerned. She moved on the stairs like she was heading down to meet a business acquaintance. Taking a cue from her, I schooled my features into what I hoped was a pleasantly blank expression instead of one that said "dear-God-get-me-out-of-here."

At the bottom of the stairwell was a hallway that branched off into other rooms to our left, and a wide-open space directly ahead with floor-to-ceiling windows that overlooked the beach from the heights of a cliff. Or maybe we were on a mountainside. We'd gone through so many twisting, winding roads, I wasn't sure anymore.

"Ah, ladies, you made it," said a pleasantly deep male voice from our right.

I had seen pictures of Clyde Seabreeze before,

and even a couple of video interviews online. However, they lacked the impact of the real thing, who was currently—and very deliberately, I was sure—standing under a small spotlight a few feet away from a small group of men. One was lounging on some more artsy than comfortable looking couches, and the rest were hanging back in the shadows; probably bodyguards.

Of course, the first thing I noticed was the hair. It was dark—black—obviously dyed. It wasn't a good color for him, but that was like saying it wasn't a good color for Brad Pitt in his prime.

His gaze drew me in next. Clyde's eyes were . . . well, cliché as it sounds, a smoldering, dark blue. Come-hither eyes. Eyes deep enough to drown in. I remembered at the last second to look away, and, much like whenever David Bowie came on screen in *Labyrinth*, soon found myself staring at what was obviously framed by his too-tight pants and the tails of the shirt he hadn't bothered to button.

"Mr. Seabreeze," Sara said, and with far more grace than I could possibly have mustered, "it's a pleasure to finally meet you."

"Oh no, the pleasure is all mine."

The two of them were very cool and polite with each other considering he looked like he'd walked off the set of some romance novel photo shoot. I debated opening my mouth, but the words *package* and *balls* were dangerously close to the tip of my tongue. Instead, I mutely offered my hand when he approached to give us both a polite, welcoming handshake. I imagine my vow of silence was probably for the best—for all of us.

"Ms. Waynest," he said, smiling in a way that told me he knew *exactly* what I had been staring at a moment ago, "I am thrilled to finally meet the girl who stole the heart of Alec Royce. I must admit, I never thought he'd request that I be the one to offer sanctuary to one of his own, but I am delighted that I could be of service."

I'm sure my blank look spoke for me. His smile became a little more genuine, and he spread his arms, bowing his head in a theatric move reminiscent of an orchestra director.

"You must forgive me, I have forgotten my manners. Ladies, may I introduce you to Fabian d'Argento, master of San Francisco."

A man who was sprawled as if he had been placed *just so* on the couch inclined his head to us. "Delighted," he said, clearly not.

Like Clyde, Fabian was lovely to look at but undoubtedly far more deadly than you would think based upon appearances. I had once mistaken Royce for a lackey; had I not just been introduced to the two, I might have easily assumed the same of Clyde and Fabian. Though they were both pale, and perhaps unfairly good-looking, they did not give off any dangerous vibes. Their ability to pass as human and my instant attraction to them was what made them dangerous, particularly since, as both were masters of their respective cities, they must have been ancient. The old ones always seemed to be devious and strong enough to lay the smack down on anyone who got in their way.

"Fabian, this is Shiarra Waynest and Sara Halloway. Alec has sent them here to visit for a time."

The other vampire finally looked mildly interested, one brow quirking. "Is that so? You pair are private investigators, yes? I understand Ms. Waynest has caused quite a stir back East."

I cleared my throat and looked away. "Yes, we are, and that's why I'm here. Why we both are."

"Fascinating."

After an awkward pause in which the vampires carefully studied the two of us, and with more interest than I liked, Sara stepped forward. "It's very kind of you to extend us your hospitality, but we're both very tired and hungry after that flight. Is there anything we can do for you, or would it be possible for us to get settled in?"

She had always been more direct than I was. Though I was dismayed to see that Clyde was watching us with the intense interest of one who is formulating devious plans and won't be afraid to use them.

"Just a moment, before you go. I was just discussing with Fabian a little . . . problem I have been dealing with. You say you are PIs?"

Sara and I nodded, though I could tell she was just as wary as I was. This did not bode well for us.

"Excellent. Then I must insist upon your assistance with this matter. Perhaps you can help us determine who—or what—has been directing the zombies infesting the area."

Sara's mouth dropped open, as did mine. She recovered her voice more quickly than I did, probably thanks to her internship and few months spent as a practicing attorney in her parents' company after she graduated law school.

"Zombies? Please tell me you're joking."

Clyde's lips twisted into a smirk. "I'm afraid not. I don't believe you would be in any danger. The creatures have only been attacking the vampires of my bloodline—they have not harmed anyone from other lines or with a pulse. If you wish to remain here, you can pay your way with your investigative skills. Find me their maker, and I will consider that adequate payment for your stay."

Sara straightened, folding her arms and assuming the haughty ice-queen look she had perfected in her college debate classes. I was still struggling with the whole zombie thing, let alone the rest.

"As we understand it, Mr. Royce has already negotiated the terms of our stay. We'll be happy to take on the job—for our usual fee."

I had to hand it to her. She was much better under pressure than I was. Then I realized what she was saying and grabbed her arm. "Hold on a second. Sara, can I talk to you for a minute?"

The vampires both appeared intrigued by Sara's reply. Fabian leaned forward on the couch, a gleam in his eye, and Clyde held out a staying hand. "Oh, no, Ms. Waynest. No need for that. I accept your terms. Considering your circumstances, I assume you would prefer payment by cash rather than a check. In the morning I'll have one of my people fetch a deposit and a file with the information we have collected thus far."

That wasn't exactly what I had been going to talk to Sara about. Rather, I was worried about what the hell we were getting into, chasing zombies around a strange town on behalf of a vampire we barely knew. Royce's parting reminder not to trust Clyde wasn't going to do us any good if we tied ourselves to him in a business relationship. Having him as both our host and client was guaranteed to get awkward somewhere along the line—but it looked like it was too late to do anything about that.

"Thank you again, ladies. I'll have someone escort you to the guest house. Tomorrow evening, one of my drivers will be made available whenever you are ready to search for the source of this infestation." One of the security guards who had been hanging back in the shadows stepped forward, though he stopped in his tracks when Clyde held up a single finger. "I must warn you—there are certain parts of the San Fernando Valley which are off-limits to my people. You would do best to remain as close to the city and coastal region as possible."

"We'll keep that in mind," I said. Though it made me uncomfortable to say the next part aloud, I didn't want to give the vampire the idea that he could keep us completely under his thumb while we were here. "However, I can't promise that we won't spend some time in other parts of the Valley. We may have to follow leads or interview people who aren't part of your network."

Sara nodded. "As long as you let us do our job without interference, we'll do our best to keep things discreet on your behalf."

"Touché," he murmured. "Well, then. I'll see that you are adequately compensated for your efforts."

With that, he turned his back on us and joined Fabian on the couch. Clearly we were dismissed. Judging by the hand Fabian was quick to place on Clyde's inner thigh as he leaned in to whisper something, this was a good thing.

The security guard walked us out. The last glimpse I got of the two involved glowing eyes, extended fangs, and hands in interesting places.

Chapter 8

The guard who walked us out led us through a maze of hallways and rooms filled with people who had wandered to the fringes of the party. What felt like an age later, we were taken out a side door, stepping onto a brick-inlaid patio surrounded by palm fronds and vibrantly colored flowers. The change in temperature was intense, like stepping out of a food locker and into a sauna, making my skin feel tight and uncomfortably dry.

I wasn't sure how Sara could stand the heat in that long-sleeved shirt of hers, but she gave no visible sign of discomfort. If anything, she was lost in thought—probably considering the mess she'd just thrown us both into by agreeing to help Clyde.

We walked around the Olympic-sized swimming pool, stepping around a group of people huddled together, passing a joint back and forth. Most of them looked familiar to me, but we didn't linger, and it was too dark for me to be certain which stars

I was spotting. On the other side of the pool, we went through a gate, down a set of steps cut into the steep slant of a hillside, and into another fairyland of twinkling lights, manicured garden paths, and burbling fountains.

Nestled against the side of the hill was an elegant miniature of the mansion. It put me in mind of those doghouses that were perfect replicas of their owners' homes I once saw on some TV show about how the rich and famous spent their money.

Despite how minuscule this place was in comparison, it rivaled the size of my parents' home back in New York. Though my two brothers and I had all moved out years ago, my parents had no plans of becoming snowbirds and migrating to Florida once my dad retired. They loved that house, and someday it would be passed down to Mike, Damien, and me.

That thought gave me a jolt. The last time I had spoken to my father, he had made it perfectly clear he no longer considered me part of the family. That made my stomach churn with anxiety I had managed to bury away while dealing with all the other problems on my plate.

Great. Now that I no longer had worries about turning furry when the moon was full, I could move on to wringing my hands over my family problems.

It would have to wait until I was alone. The security guard who led us up to the front door took a few moments to explain that we were the only ones staying in the guesthouse for the time being but that staff would come in and out regularly to clean, cook for us, handle our wardrobe—which I took as veiled condemnation of our current attire—and that other guests from the party might end up staying here as well.

He then gave us the code to the keypad that unlocked the front door and let us in. Our bags were already waiting just inside the entrance, next to a table with spindly legs and gold onions at the feet. There were sprigs of freshly cut jasmine and honeysuckle spilling from an ornate marble vase, and the scent permeated the place like a sickly sweet perfume.

I turned to ask the guard which rooms we could stay in, but he was already striding back to the mansion. Shaking my head, I shut the door and glanced around, noting that this place was decorated like some grand hotel lobby—lots of marble and gold shine designed to either intimidate and awe those who hadn't grown up around money, or set those who had at ease.

Sara, being the latter, was not as impressed with our surroundings.

She gestured at the bags, and I soon had a frown that matched hers. They were both open.

No wonder the chauffeur had urged us to leave our bags. Perhaps Royce had underplayed just how strained his relationship with Clyde truly was. The master vampire of Los Angeles might have thought well enough of our skills to offer me and Sara a job, but he obviously didn't think we were totally above board.

Funny, considering I thought the same of him.

We knelt by our stuff, checking for anything missing. The phone was gone. My Rolodex wasn't missing anything, but I had no doubt somebody had gone through it. Nothing much important was in my bag—clothes, mostly—but the thought that someone had been poking around my underwear and had taken the phone was enough to send my blood pressure spiking through the roof.

If Clyde wanted to play hardball, fine. We'd play hardball.

"You have the detectors?"

"Yeah, one sec." She dug around in her purse, pulling out two small, black boxes. They bore a resemblance to a walkie-talkie, but they both had a red-tinted lens near the top. She tossed one to me. "You get the wireless, I use the lens finder?"

"Sure."

She did a slow turn, studying the decorations and artwork hanging on the walls, peering through the lens.

She found what we were looking for first. "Camera's over here," she said, pointing to a vase sitting on the mantel in the room beyond the entrance. No doubt the camera had a decent view of anyone who might enter or leave. Sara had something similar in her house, and I'd helped install one just like it in her sister's apartment a couple of years ago.

We both moved closer to check if it was a make we were familiar with. Judging by the way the pinpoint gleam of the lens matched the dull shine of the rest of the series of small, dark stones circling the base of the vase, whoever had made the piece knew what he or she was doing. Not well enough to hide it from someone who made a point of supplementing her income by selling similar gadgets on a regular basis and knew enough to carry a bug detector at all times, but it was a clever touch if you were a paranoid master vampire who wanted to keep tabs on unexpected—and unsuspecting—guests.

"Do you think the bedrooms are bugged?"

Sara shrugged. "Wouldn't put it past him. I doubt he expects us to do anything stupid while we're here, but we might as well play it safe. Check around before you shower or change your clothes."

We wandered around, exploring our new temporary home, getting a feel for the place. Most of the lights were already on, and we discovered the place had a full kitchen, fully stocked wet bar in the living room, a small sauna and exercise room, half a dozen bedrooms, and a sizeable dining room with an impressive set of china on display. Like the entrance, the rest of the place was full of delicate, gold-trimmed, expensive things—and a number of additional cameras that were hidden nearly as well as the one aimed at the front door. Even the matching furniture appeared to be more for display than comfort. The one personal touch was provided by enormous vases of gardenias, their scent overpowering every room.

Sara chose one of the bedrooms that looked out

over the garden and walkway leading up to the main house. I took the one across the hall from her, preferring the view of untamed hillside and a sliver of the ocean beyond. The hills might have been dry and dead, but it felt more natural than the man-made wonderland out front and suited my dark mood.

Sweeping the room for bugs turned out to be a damned good idea. I found no less than three in the bedroom and another one in the tissue box on the vanity in the bathroom. Finding them was a pain in the ass, but disabling them took no time at all, as they were wireless; all I had to do was toss a cloth over the lens or turn them toward the wall. The alarm clock beside the bed had an SD card. Popping it out and flushing it down the john wasn't totally necessary, but it still made me feel better.

After we dragged our bags into our respective rooms, Sara sat down next to me where I had exhaustedly slumped onto a bed. I wasn't sure if it was the travel catching up with me or how draining it was to realize just how deep a hole I was currently in. Across the country from all I had ever known and loved, under surveillance by our host, and stuck doing a job that would no doubt get us in even deeper trouble than we were already in. The only bright side was that I was sharing this impromptu adventure with the only person I had ever been able to count on. Sadly, she was probably ready to throttle me. When I glanced over at her, she was looking down at her folded hands, not at me.

"Sara," I said, then hesitated. What to say to her?

She darted a look at me, then back down to her hands. One slid up to twine a few blond strands around her fingers. "The business is probably in default by now. I haven't been able to reach Jenny, but our rent should still be paid. I asked Janine to take care of it while I'm gone."

Damn it. Sara must have contacted Janine directly after she had hung up with Arnold. I'd forgotten to make that call. Running a hand down my face, I mumbled against my palm. "Cripes. I really am sorry. For everything. This is all my fault. It's like I fuck up everything I touch."

"Don't say that."

"Why not? It's true. It's my fault Others became interested in the business, and in you, and my fault H&W is as good as gone. My fault we're across the country as guests to some strange vampire. My fault my dad disowned me."

"Hey," she said, her voice sharp enough to draw my wide-eyed gaze over to hers. "Don't start that. He loves you, and I'm sure he didn't mean whatever he said. We'll get through this. We always do. If things get too weird here, you know Janine has some property she bought out here. I'm sure she wouldn't mind if I borrowed the beach house."

Beach house. I'd forgotten about Janine's home-away-from-home in Malibu. Sara and I had spent a week "borrowing" the house for a vacation getaway a few years ago. We spent most of the time sipping margaritas on the deck and watching dolphins pass in the waves as the sun tinted the surf unreal shades of red and orange. That didn't sound like such a bad time to revisit.

"What happened with Rob, anyway? What did he say to you?"

I cringed and looked away, not wanting to face the concern etched in the fine lines around her cornflower blue eyes. Though I was no longer as torn up over it as I had been at first, it still hurt to think about. "Dad was pissed because he saw the article that said I might have been infected. That's how he found out I was contracted to Royce. I had never told Mom or Dad. He didn't know. Didn't even suspect. Said I wasn't a Waynest anymore, and that I should never come home again. I should have said something—"

"Oh, stop. There's nothing you could have said that would have made it okay. Just give him a little time. I'm sure he'll get over it."

I gave her a look.

"Okay, maybe not over it, per se, but he'll learn to live with it."

That prompted a humorless smirk out of me. "Yeah, I suppose. He can't stay mad forever, right?"

She scooted over to put an arm around me in a hug. Though the memory of my father's voice, thick with the cigarettes and whiskey he never touched save for when he was stressed, replayed over and over in the back of my head, I didn't feel like reaching for my guns and hunting Chaz to the ends of the earth anymore. All I felt now was that I was getting far too old for this shit.

Sara's fingers tightened briefly on my shoulder. "We'll handle this somehow. We'll find a way to make it right. H&W isn't gone, it's just on hiatus. Until then, *stop it*. Don't worry about what you can't change. By the time we get back, he should have cooled off."

I wished I could believe that.

"*Shiarra.*" The force behind her voice made me cringe. "If you start listening to nothing but death metal and wearing all black, we can't be friends anymore."

That drew a choking laugh out of me. It took me a few moments to regain my composure enough to answer her, and killed most of the melancholy mood in its tracks. "I'm sor—"

"Enough! You've already apologized plenty of times. Let's move on. As long as we're here, we've got a job to do. I'm not going to go zombie hunting with you if you're just going to mope around the whole time listening to angry girl music and dripping with mascara. Are you with me or what?"

My laughter this time was far less strained. Sara soon joined in, the two of us giggling like madwomen until my ribs and diaphragm ached too much to keep it up. She rubbed under her eyes with her palms, still snorting like she did when she really lost it.

Her eyes were a little red when she glanced at me, her lopsided grin telling me she had needed that emotional release almost as badly as I had. She was usually better at hiding her inner turmoil than I was, but she had to be hurting if her usually cool and collected façade was cracking. She no longer had a mom or dad to turn to for comfort. All she had was her sister.

Well, there was also Arnold, but both of them were three thousand miles away. She'd have to make do with me.

I slid my arm over her shoulder and held her, the occasional hitch in my breathing betraying my suppressed laughter. Though I knew I should have been more solemn in that moment, Sara had done me the favor of pulling me out of my funk. It would be only fair for me to reciprocate.

"You know," I said, as conversationally and with as straight a face as I could muster, "I'll bet, when you get back, the sex with Arnold is going to be fantastic."

Sara nearly choked, covering her mouth with a hand as she looked at me. This time the tears really were from mirth; I could see the curve of her lips between her fingers, and she was trying her best to smother her laughter. I gave her an innocent look, widening my eyes and batting my lashes. That earned me a halfhearted punch in the shoulder, which got me laughing, too.

Giggling between words, she gave me a mock glare. "Damn it, now all I'm going to be able to think about until we go back is hopping in the sack with him. Man, you have no idea how great it is with a mage."

"Once you go magic, you never go back?"

She snorted again and shoved me as I waggled my brows. "Something like that. Though you're one to talk. Finally knocked boots with the vampire, huh?"

The heat in my cheeks was sudden and intense. Sara's exaggerated leer didn't help. I coughed into a hand, avoiding answering her.

"Yeah, yeah. You can dish it—"

"—but I can't take it. I know."

Smiling, she rose and stretched, closing her eyes as she got on tiptoe and arched her back. Guess I wasn't the only one feeling a bit sore after being cooped up in the plane on the way here. When she was done, she patted my knee and then headed for the door. She paused there, hand on the knob. "Get some sleep. We'll meet with Clyde tomorrow, start working this case, and stay busy so we don't have to worry about what's going on at home. Sound good?"

I nodded, rubbing the back of my neck. With a flash of pearly teeth, she was gone, her own door soon clicking shut quietly behind her. I rose to shut my own door and start getting ready for bed.

My family might be a mess, my business in the toilet, my love life a shambles, and my neck on the line with the cops, White Hats, werewolves, and who knew what else—but I had a job to do. We wouldn't forget our friends, our families, our commitments, or our enemies, but we would be safe, and far enough away that the people hunting us would most likely lose interest or forget about us given enough time. Arnold would protect the rest of our friends and family. Royce would fix the mess and make it safe for us to return. I hoped.

On the bright side, I no longer felt the pressure of outside forces pushing me around. Even though I wasn't thrilled about hunting zombies, Sara was here, and the two of us could solve this case together. We'd make Clyde pay through the nose for our services, which should put us on track to salvaging H&W Investigations, and it would most likely keep us busy enough to forget all the worries we'd left behind in New York.

For now, that would have to be enough.

Chapter 9

Though Sara and I both woke up long before the sun went down, nobody came to give us any idea what we were expected to do. In the late morning, while the two of us stumbled around the kitchen in search of breakfast, a lady with skin tanned dark from hours in the sun and dark, silky hair swept up in a neat chignon, had bustled in and introduced herself as Florencia, the resident cook. We were supposed to ring her on one of the internal phone lines if we were hungry.

I wasn't totally comfortable with the luxury of having a cook at our beck and call, but Sara had been very gracious, thanking her and asking for what I assumed by the sound was a Spanish dish. The foreign words rolled off her tongue as she conversed with the cook, leaving me feeling foolish for taking French in high school. When Florencia turned to me, I gave Sara a helpless look. She laughed and told the cook—in English, making me feel doubly foolish—to give me an omelet and a pot of coffee, thanked her again, and then led me to the kitchen table.

Outside of a restaurant, I had never had such fantastic food. Florencia explained as she cooked that she had gone to culinary school and intended to open her own restaurant, but that working for Clyde had given her the opportunity to earn the capital she needed to finance the venture.

"Three more years of this," she said, flipping the omelet in the skillet with the kind of practiced ease I had only seen in movies and TV shows, "and I should have enough to start Mama Flora's. I have my eye on an old restaurant near the pier. If the market holds steady, I'll have everything I need, and Mr. Seabreeze has promised to help with the negotiations and decorating."

Sara and I congratulated her, though we both raised our eyebrows at her blithe mention of Clyde's promise. Though he was clearly the type to showboat, if he kept his word and was truly so good to his faithful employees, perhaps he wasn't quite the mercenary we had assumed.

Royce had proven to me that not all vampires were evil, mindless beasts, and that they were capable of being compassionate. We hadn't had the opportunity to get to know Clyde, so considering he had been backed into a figurative corner due to this zombie infestation, it was possible we had thus far only seen his worst side. Granted, I was pissed about the cell phones being confiscated, but not entirely surprised.

At first, Royce had also been a bit of a manipulative dick, which was part of why it had taken me so long to see that he wasn't such a bad guy. I imagined it might be the same with Clyde. We were nothing special to the vampire. Just another couple of "dumb humans"—only good for food or entertainment, if that much. He didn't respect us yet, so he saw no reason to treat us as anything other than pawns. Now that I had played the Other games of dominance and grandstanding for a few rounds, I was confident I could find a way to show him that Sara and I had teeth.

Close to noon, we were munching on some snacks while we hung out in the den with the big screen. As we were trying to get into daytime TV, someone showed up with a depressingly thin file folder containing the information Clyde was willing to give us about the zombies, and an envelope delightfully thick with cash.

After storing the envelope in one of Sara's bags, we opened the file on the sprawling kitchen table to see what was inside and spread everything out. There wasn't much. A list of missing and dead vampires, a few blurry pictures, and a couple of handwritten notes describing what surviving human servants had seen. Though it took some doing to figure out what the shaky scrawl spelled out, we had a rough picture of the situation before long.

Though they were, of course, frightened and

disoriented by what they had seen, their stories were clear enough. Most of the descriptions involved great numbers of the walking dead—and there was no doubt that's what they were, considering the way the survivors wrote of stink and rot—shoving them aside to reach their vampire masters. The accounts didn't include the handwritten notes of what happened after. The pages were missing, or had been deliberately removed. Instead, there were a couple of photos clipped to the back of the folder, standing mute testament to the massacre that must have taken place.

I'd never seen a body torn apart before. Though I'd been in the room while a pack of werewolves had torn apart a vampire and a mage, feasting on their remains, I had kept my eyes closed so I wouldn't see anything I'd never be able to unsee.

And now, nightmares of those pictures—the chunks of missing flesh, the shredded flaps of skin, and the gleam of white bone set in a pool of crimson—would haunt me for the rest of my days.

Sara grew very pale next to me, but we both somehow managed to keep from barfing.

We quickly shoved the pictures and accounts of the survivors back into the folder, then moved on to the note-covered maps. If not for all the assurances in the folder that no one but vampires had died, I would have said to hell with the case then and there.

Instead, we soldiered on, spending about an hour going over maps of Los Angeles that had notations about where the bodies of dead vampires had been discovered. We needed to get to know the lay of the land and the places we would have to explore. Though all the attacks had occurred within LA County, no two had happened in the same place.

When she saw what we were doing, Florencia gave us some help figuring out where we were and the limits of Clyde's dominion. His territory, though it included major cities like Santa Monica, Los Angeles, Beverly Hills, and Hollywood, was quite a lot smaller than I was expecting. Considering Royce controlled multiple states, it was a bit anticlimactic to find out Clyde had such a small amount of land to call his own. When we asked about the areas that fell outside of his purview but were still in Los Angeles County, Florencia didn't have any answers.

The one common thread we could see was that many of the attacks took place close to properties Clyde owned on the fringes of his territory. Whoever or whatever was controlling the zombies appeared to be situated somewhere just beyond the borders. We couldn't be sure since we didn't know this area like we did New York, but hiding that many decomposing bodies meant they had to have a damned good place to store them in this heat to keep any neighbors from finding them. My guess was a morgue, a climate-controlled warehouse, or perhaps they were kept somewhere outside of the city—maybe in the Angeles Crest Forest?—until they were needed and then transported wherever the next attack was supposed to take place.

There were problems with each of those theories, but until we had a chance to examine some of the locations of the attacks in person, I had the feeling that we wouldn't be able to narrow this search down any more than we already had. More than anything, I wanted to know what the survivors' notes didn't say. Who were Clyde's enemies? Who in the supernatural community around here had the kind of power it must take to command a small army of the walking dead?

Arnold might be able to help with that end of things, though I wasn't sure how much he'd know about Others in California.

Sara and I decided to put off further speculation until after we'd spoken to Clyde. We spent the rest of our day mostly bored and occasionally shuddering when the memories of those pictures resurfaced during our discussions about where to start our search.

The most likely place appeared to be near Burbank and Glendale, where three attacks had occurred close together.

Shortly after sundown, I had a nosebleed tinged with the black stuff again. It was far less intense than it had been back in New York, and most of it was in my nose and throat instead of everywhere else, but it was still awfully unpleasant. Sara helped me to the bathroom and sat with me while I spat out ropy strings of blackish liquid, washed it from the corners of my eyes, and blew it out my nose. It was disgusting, yes, but nowhere near as painful as it had been the other times. There wasn't as much of the crud as there had been that first night, or even in the shower with Royce the night before last.

Sara said nothing as she held my hair off the back of my neck while I washed the crud out of my mouth, though I know she must have had questions. She knew I'd tell her when I was ready.

Unfortunately, it was going to be awhile before I could bring myself to explain. She might have been my best friend, but the memories of those hours of helplessness, of pain and blood and knowing I was no longer quite human, were too close.

Before I could help her come to terms with it, I needed to do something about that myself.

Not long after I finished cleaning myself up and we returned to the kitchen, a knock on the door frame startled us. A new security guard—a woman, one I didn't recall seeing last night—was examining us with dark, narrowed eyes.

"Ladies. Clyde would like to see you now."

Sara and I exchanged a look before rising and following the guard to the main house. I was annoyed to note she was quite a bit taller than me, so perfectly beautiful and graceful with her high cheekbones and sleek, braided hair that I knew she must have been another vampire. Her dress was like that of the security guards I'd seen last night, though she had guns holstered on either hip. Her deadly grace reminded me strongly of Mouse, though there wasn't much other resemblance.

We entered through the door near the pool deck. She took us through some hallways to a room full of weird paintings and strange sculptures and told us to wait.

There wasn't any place to sit, so we just stood awkwardly, staring around the room. Separately, the pieces were just . . . well . . . weird. Together, they made a strange kind of sense. The swirl of colors and clashing styles made me dizzy, so I made a point of focusing on one piece. Of course. It had to be a Warhol.

My feet were starting to hurt by the time Clyde swept into the room, a bevy of buzzing sycophants trailing in his wake. His hair was a different color this evening, no longer black, but a deep chocolate color with frosted tips, making for a striking, punk-rocker look that fit with the bare chest and draw-string leather pants slung low on his hips. He waved a hand airily and the people surrounding him backed off, mumbling reassurances about his hair, his clothes, something about appointments and a TV spot, and a few other things I didn't quite catch.

As the others backed away, he snapped his fingers at the security guard who had escorted us. She froze, hovering near the door.

Once he was across the room, he turned to face us, and I could have sworn that his eyes were a solid black. Like fathomless pools of pure hunger sucking me deep into a cold, lonely place.

It might have been the space between breaths or an eternity before he looked away, his attention fixing on a granite statue of a robed angel with sweeping wings, the tracks of tears permanently etched across the cheeks of that androgynous face. Air seeped out between my teeth in a hiss as tension ran out of me. Gut instinct told me we were on the verge of experiencing something very nasty by his hands if we didn't watch our step. Made me wonder just how well that little charm around my throat—the one that was supposed to prevent vampires and magi from messing with my head—was working.

"Good evening," Clyde said, his voice smooth as silk and completely at odds with the way he had devoured us with his eyes a moment ago. "I wished to see you before you begin your search. Do you have any questions about what you saw in the file you were given? Were you able to glean anything useful?"

Sara and I exchanged a look. As badly as I had wanted to snark at him about taking the phone, now clearly wasn't the time.

She stepped forward, and I let her lead. She was better at verbal sparring than I ever was; a necessary skill I would need to hone if I was going to be spending much more time around these strange vampires.

"Yes. We think we know where to start, but first we'd like to know who you think might be behind this. Or any enemies who might have more information? They won't know us, so they might be willing to let something useful spill if they don't realize we're working for you."

He threw back his head and laughed, the sound booming through the room loudly enough to make me flinch. When the sound tapered off, he rubbed a faux tear from the corner of his eye. "My, you *are* direct. How refreshing."

Sara was unmoved. She folded her arms and gave him an "I'm waiting" look. I did my best to follow her example, though I don't think I looked nearly as convincing or intimidating as she did.

"I have no enemies, my dear. If I knew who it was, I would have taken care of this matter myself."

He added a charming smile at the end of that statement with just a hint of fang showing. It was a pose Royce often took when he was trying to see if he could use his nature to scare me into dropping information he could use, make me react in some calculated way, or distract me from asking vitally important questions.

Though Sara was taken aback by Clyde's answer, I wasn't impressed. "You're the master vampire of Los-freaking-Angeles. Don't tell me you don't know where your enemies are. There's no way you could be this arrogant, and hold a city of this size for so long, being completely ignorant of the whereabouts of the people who have a bone to pick with you."

Clyde stared at me, his dark blue eyes briefly flashing with embers of red in the pupils. His expression remained stony and unwavering for a very long moment—and then he smiled, making no effort to hide the fangs that peeked out from behind his lips. "My, my, Ms. Waynest. I do believe I now see what potential Rhathos must have sensed in you." It had been a long time since I'd heard someone refer to Royce by that name. The last one to call him that was Max Carlyle. It put me on alert since I doubted anything good could come of it. "It's a pity you won't be staying here long. I suddenly find I would like to know more about that clever tongue of yours."

Heat instantly suffused my cheeks, but I refused to be cowed or swayed by the posturing of this overconfident, conceited ass.

"Don't change the subject. You know as much about me as you need to. What I'm interested in are your enemies. And don't pretend you don't know what I'm talking about."

"If you want us to work for you and solve this case," Sara cut in smoothly, tempering my harsh words, "then you need to give us what we need to do our jobs effectively. Like our phones, and the information we've asked for, and far more politely than you deserve."

Clyde leaned against one of the angel's stone wings and steepled his fingers, his eyes narrowing as he regarded us. It was rather obvious he was weighing his options and deciding what information would be safe to divulge—but at least he was considering telling us what we needed to know. Progress.

"Locally, there are two groups that may have

information about this mess, and whoever is behind it. There is a section of the city of Glendale that I do not hold dominion over—another vampire named Jimmy Thrane calls himself its ruler."

Another vampire running a portion of the city? That didn't sound like good news, and Royce had made no mention of it before I left. No wonder Clyde looked and sounded like he'd just bitten into a lemon as he spat out that tidbit of information.

That sense of hunger emanating from him was growing again, somehow both magnetic and repulsive at the same time. The fine hairs on the back of my neck were rising, a sense of dread becoming a growing pit in my stomach. Sara didn't appear to be handling it much better, if the pallor and flutter of her eyelids were anything to go by.

"Aside from Mr. Thrane, if you are willing to run the risks inherent with making contact with them, we have a local branch of White Hats in town. Undoubtedly they will have information I cannot provide, but either the White Hats or Mr. Thrane's band may see you as a threat. They may even attempt to take you and use you as leverage against Mr. Royce or me. If you don't heed my warnings, and either of you end up in the enemy's hands, I will not go out of my way to save you."

"We can take care of ourselves," I said, hoping it was true.

"Good," he replied, jerking his chin toward the door and the woman waiting nearby. She'd been so quiet, I'd forgotten she was there, waiting in the shadows. "Trinity will see to your transportation needs. Report to me when you return."

"And the phone?" Sara asked. More daring than I was willing to be right now.

"If it appears you are in need of it, then it will be returned to you. Now do your jobs. I'm not paying you to question me."

I bit my tongue to keep from saying something sarcastic in reply. My refuge in snarky humor might help keep me sane in terrifying situations, but right now didn't seem to be the best time to bait Clyde.

As much as I wanted to go running back to hide under the covers of my borrowed bed, we needed to get this over with. And while I had every intention of meeting the rival vampire ruler, Jimmy Thrane, my first order of business would be to introduce myself to the local White Hats.

If anyone might have a burning desire to get rid of Clyde, it would be the White Hats. If I was lucky, they might know who in the supernatural community was after him, too.

Chapter 10

Trinity didn't say a thing when I told her we wanted to go to the nearest known White Hat hideout. She led us to a waiting car, then took her place behind the wheel. Sara and I sat in the back together, making note of the routes she took, comparing them against one of the maps Sara had tucked away in one of her jeans pockets.

We took expressways I had only heard of in movies—the 405 and 101—that were packed with an ungodly amount of traffic. Somehow we kept moving at a decent clip, and it took a little under an hour to reach North Hollywood.

Sad as it was to say, this part of town reminded me more of home. The apartment buildings and businesses were not as polished and pristine as the ones in Santa Monica. Here and there, streetlights were out. There appeared to be an uncommon number of auto repair shops and liquor stores in relation to the few apartments and homes we passed along the way. The only greenery was provided by scrubby-looking bushes or the occasional scraggly palm tree.

The heat made it hard to breathe. I hadn't noticed it right away, but now that I was outside, the dry air made my skin feel tight and my nose feel like it was on the verge of a bleed.

Trinity pulled into a small parking lot, then twisted in the driver's seat to regard us. She did not appear amused, her tone flat and bored. "Obviously, I can't follow you two inside. How long would you like me to wait before I assume they've killed you so I can head back?"

I blinked. Sara made a little coughing noise.

"Um," I said.

The vampire grinned, exposing extended canines that gleamed in the meager streetlight, matching the flicker of red in her eyes. "Just a little joke." Sure. Judging by the look in her eye, our sudden, stark fear was the source of her amusement. "If you do not return in, say, half an hour, I will come inside looking for you."

I did not envy any White Hats who might try getting in her way if it came down to that.

"Thanks," Sara muttered, opening her door and stepping out with the kind of swift grace that bespoke her discomfort. She could move fast when she had good reason.

Following her out, I ran a nervous hand through my hair, brushing some stray curls out of my face as I took in the club. It didn't look like much: a rundown hole-in-the-wall with a flickering neon sign and some incongruously cheerful country-and-western music spilling out to mingle with the sounds of traffic on the night air. I might not have thought anything of The Brand except that it had a white neon cowboy hat flashing under the name. To advertise their presence so obviously, either these guys had bigger balls than the hunters in New York or they were horrifically stupid.

I was willing to bet on the latter, though I kept that thought to myself.

A guy in a wifebeater, jeans, scuffed cowboy boots, and a leather vest leaned against the wall next to the entrance. He watched us approach with interest.

"*Hola. ¿Cómo está?*"

"*Muy bien, gracias,*" Sara replied. "*Me llamo* Sara."

He gave her a wide grin, his teeth a white slash against dark skin. "*Mucho gusto. Encantado. Me llamo* Jesus." He glanced at me, then abruptly shifted to English with only the barest trace of an accent. "I take it you two aren't from around here."

Sara shook her head. "In town on a visit. We're here for business."

"Who are you here to see?"

She looked at me, and I shrugged before pointing a single finger at the sign over our heads. "I guess that depends on whether your sign is advertising a certain type of business."

Jesus frowned and pushed off the wall. "You two shouldn't involve yourselves in White Hat business. It's not a game."

"We never said it was," I replied. He towered over me, but I held my ground, tilting my head back to meet and hold his gaze. My nose was about level with the shoulder holster not very well hidden by his vest. "There's something bad going on in this town. We thought some of your people might know who's behind it."

"What kind of bad? What are you talking about?"

I didn't give an inch, not even when his chest brushed up against mine. "Someone's using a forbidden type of magic. Messing with the dead. Who might know about that?"

He stared down at me, dark brown eyes crinkling at the corners as they narrowed, his frown deepening. Eventually, he turned his head away and spat. "*Sí. Los muertos* and the *brujo*—I have heard of this magic. Go into the back room and speak with the man in the red jacket. He might know who is behind it."

Though I didn't understand it all, I was glad he was giving us a pass. I gave a last glance to the car, dark and mostly hidden in the shadows at the back of the lot, before moving inside.

Once my eyes adjusted to the darkness beyond the front door, I took in all there was to see. The place looked like a real rat trap. The scarred bar was being manned by a guy who looked like he could most likely wipe the floor with anyone, human or no, who tried to mess with the patrons. A couple of guys in biker leathers gave us bleary-eyed leers over their shoulders, as we edged past the bar and a stage taking up a good portion of the floor to an unmarked door that presumably led to where the White Hats gathered.

Nobody said anything or tried to stop us, but it

was a bit strange to have the suspicious stares of everyone in the room on us while Shania Twain poured out of the stage speakers. It didn't seem like the right kind of music for a place like this, but then again, it wasn't my place to be pointing out the inconsistencies.

Sara led the way into the back room, which, unlike the bar, was comfortable. Overstuffed chairs and couches were spread in a loose circle around the room, laptops and other gadgets mixed with the papers and guns spread over the low table in the middle of the room.

About half a dozen of those seats were occupied, and the people sitting in them looked up sharply on our entrance, two or three of them reaching for guns as Sara and I both raised our hands and jerked back.

"Don't shoot! We're unarmed!"

Though the guns had drawn my attention before I could register any details about the hunters, the flash of red as one of the men stood up caught my eye. "Shiarra? What the hell are you doing here?"

My mouth dropped open. "Devon? What the— wait, what are *you* doing here?"

He laughed and stepped around the table, waving at the other hunters to put their weapons away before sweeping me up in a tight hug. I was too shocked to do anything to reciprocate right away, and he'd done a pretty good job of pinning my arms.

"I thought you were dead! After what happened to Jack and the rest—"

"No way," I squeaked out, short of air thanks to his grip. "I thought maybe *you* were dead since you—"

"—and all those werewolves! And the stuff in the paper, and—"

"Yo! My man, you mind letting her loose long enough for me to say hello, too?"

I grinned up at Tiny, who had slipped behind Devon while we were babbling at each other. Almost the moment Devon let me go, Tiny swept me up in a hug that made my feet leave the ground and ribs twinge in protest. Meanwhile Devon greeted Sara with a bit more decorum, shaking her hand.

The two hunters had disappeared sometime after I allowed Royce to bind me to him by blood. They hadn't liked the idea, though they both had known that I didn't have much of a choice at the time. It was either take the vampire's blood, or risk being called to that psychotic prick, Max Carlyle, against my will. Max had slipped me some of his own blood during one of my bouts of unconsciousness as his prisoner. Thanks to being bitten against my will, unconsciousness had been frequent enough that I sometimes wondered if all my bad decisions of late had stemmed from brain damage related to lack of oxygen from the blood loss.

Planting a wet kiss on my cheek, Tiny squeezed all the air out of my lungs and then set me back on my feet, careful to help me catch my balance before he let me go. Devon clapped me lightly on the back, facing the rest of the room. "Guys, you'll never believe who this is. You remember the chick I told you about who was working with Jack and that leech in New York?"

The other people in the room gave tentative waves, though they looked more bemused than unwelcoming. I was sure my expression betrayed just how baffled I was, too. Devon and Tiny had never told me where they were going, and this was one of the last places I had expected to run into them.

Trinity was waiting for Sara and me outside. We couldn't afford to dawdle. As much as I wanted to catch up with the hunters, I didn't think it would be wise to let Clyde know I had ties to them, or vice versa.

"It's really great to see you two, but we don't have a lot of time. We're actually here on a job, and we have a couple of other places we need to check out tonight, too."

Devon and Tiny exchanged a look I couldn't quite decipher before Tiny answered me. "Let me guess. Something to do with Clyde Seabreeze and the vampires who have been showing up dead, and the zombies shuffling around town?"

Sara coughed. "Well, yes. Should we even bother asking how you know?"

Tiny gave a derisive snort, pulling away to collapse into one of the bigger couches, sending up a puff of dust. "It's our job to know. There's some new big bad in town, and he doesn't play by the same rules as the others."

Well, this was an interesting development. I thought about some of the places bodies had been found, dredging my memory for names of unfamiliar streets.

"Do you guys know anything else about him? Where we can find him? We were going to check out some place off of Magnolia in Burbank next—"

Devon shook his head and gestured for Sara and me to take seats. Though I didn't want to offend the White Hats, we didn't have enough time to hang around and play nice. Not unless I ran out to tell Trinity to wait for us a little longer. I didn't like the idea of annoying her, so maybe we'd come back here some other night—without our vampiric babysitter.

"You're not going to find him there," Devon said. "I can see you guys don't have much time to talk. The short story is that he's not from around here. He showed up in the last week or so, and zombies have been sighted all over LA County. We're pretty sure he's been storing them in the Angeles Crest, but it's impossible to say for sure. The guy comes and goes seemingly at random. We've run into him a couple of times when we were out looking for particular targets at known vampire haunts. I'd call it luck that we happened to see him at all, but it's not going to do you much good."

"Why's that?"

One of the other White Hats responded, leaning forward as he toyed with the safety on his gun. "He's one of those magi who can fade. Looks like most any other guy on the street, and you forget what he looks like as soon as you walk away. The harder you try to recall the details, the faster they slip away."

"Yeah, we've all seen him at least once, and none of us can agree on a solid description," one of the others chipped in.

"We just know he's a guy who's sometimes surrounded by zombies. Aside from that? Can't tell you much. We can't decide if he has dark skin or pale, what color his hair is—nothing."

Fading. That was a new term to me, but I could see where it could come in handy for a mage. Must be some kind of defensive mechanism some of them had developed to blend in. Considering what type of magic this guy did, it made a whole lot of sense for him to use some sort of passive forgetting spell that made peoples' memories of him fade like that. Too bad it would fall under the category of black enchant, since it directly messed with an unwilling subject's mind, and was therefore even more illegal than raising the zombies.

At least we knew we were looking for a man. That narrowed it down, if only by roughly fifty percent of the population of greater Los Angeles. Sigh.

The charm I was wearing might assist me in spotting and remembering the mage if we ran into him, but unless Arnold gave her something to counter that kind of magic, Sara wouldn't know if she was looking at him. Even if she did, later on she wouldn't know which guy I was talking about. This would be a heck of a manhunt.

Biting back a frustrated growl, I turned to Devon.

"I do want to catch up with you, but our ride is waiting outside, and I don't want her to come in with guns blazing. Can we meet up later? I'd like to talk and maybe see if I can help you remember some details about this mage."

If Devon was disappointed, he hid it well. His smile was sweet and sincere, and he reached out to give my shoulder another squeeze, which this time felt more intimate than a simple expression of platonic friendship thanks to the way his thumb brushed over my collarbone.

I gathered the twinkle in his eye was from the knowledge that his touch was making me blush.

"Yeah. Seeing as you're in town, we'll have to make some time to get together."

Coulda-woulda-shoulda's rang dim alarm bells in the back of my head. The hunter had previously expressed some interest in seeing me as more than a friend. Since I was technically seeing Royce now, it wouldn't be kosher to lead Devon on.

Luckily, I was saved from having to say something awkward about my love life in this room full of staring, judgmental hunters by Tiny's booming voice. "Yes, we will. Let me give you a number. . . . Hold on. . . . Here." He thrust a scrap of paper with a phone number scrawled on it at me. "Call us when you're ready to get together."

"We will," Sara promised, me nodding as she pushed me toward the door. "Thank you for your help!"

"Yes, thanks!"

"Anytime," Devon said, watching us go with hooded eyes.

Chapter 11

Trinity didn't say anything until Sara and I were both back in the car. She glanced at us in the rearview, the reflection of red in her eyes hinting at her agitation with something—maybe us? Or was it the proximity of the White Hat hideout?

"Good to see you're still alive. Were the White Hats not home, or did you get what you came for?"

"We got what we needed," Sara said, her tone carefully neutral.

Trinity turned her attention ahead, the glitter of crimson no longer visible from my angle in the backseat. "That's good. I'm sure Clyde will be thrilled to hear all about it." The not-so-veiled threat in what she didn't say made me glad we'd cut things short with Devon and Tiny. If Sara and I had hung around much longer, Trinity or Clyde might have grown suspicious that we were plotting against him. "What's next on your agenda, hmm?"

"Can you take us to any of the places where these attacks took place?" I asked.

"You sure that's what you want? They've all been cleaned up, so you won't see much."

"Yeah. You never know. You guys might have missed something."

Trinity made a derisive sound in her throat and started the car. "I sincerely doubt that, but if that's what you want, then that's where we'll go. Did you have a particular destination in mind?"

Sara and I looked at each other, then simultaneously shrugged, never mind that Trinity couldn't see it. "How about the one in Sun Valley? That's close to here, isn't it?"

She made another sound, this time more like a choked laugh. "Interesting choice. Buckle your seat belts. It won't take long to get there."

Though she was right, the area seemed to go from bad to still bad to oh-God-where's-my-pepper-spray territory. Graffiti was sprayed on a number of the walls, shards of broken beer bottles scattered on the blacktop of empty parking lots shone with the glitter of fallen stars, and most of the windows on the houses and apartments were protected by iron bars—in some cases, even on the second and third floors.

When Trinity stopped at the side of the road in front of a 24-hour Laundromat, for a long moment, I wasn't sure why. Then she tilted her head to look at us, her braid sliding across the slick leather of the seat.

"Well? What are you waiting for? I don't want to be here all night. Go take a look. It happened over there."

I took a look where she was pointing. There was a sign for a . . . *carnicería*? Whatever that was. Judging by the signs in the window, it must have been the Spanish term for a deli or butcher shop.

It felt like Trinity's eyes were boring holes in my back as I slid out of the car and started walking toward the shop. I was sure she must have known how uncomfortable she was making me, but she was staying in the car and out of our way. That would have to be enough.

Sara came around until she was beside me, the two of us moving in tandem as we approached the shop. The hours posted in the window said it should have been open now, but the lights were off and a "Closed" sign was visible behind the streaks on the glass front door. Though I hadn't made any special effort to breathe through my nose, the scent of dead things—worse than old, congealed blood, *much* worse—instantly coated my throat and tongue.

Sara stopped as I did, her brow wrinkling with concern. "You okay?"

I coughed and spat, trying to get the taste out. "Cripes, you don't smell that?"

She sniffed, then lifted her shoulders. "Smells like you'd expect this close to a butcher shop. Maybe something went bad?"

"Really bad."

We tried the door on the off chance someone

might have left it open, but of course the thing was
locked. Both of us cupped the glass and peered
inside, trying to see past the coat of dust and glare
from a nearby streetlight.

There was a dim glow coming from the display
case next to the register and from some fridges in
the back with sodas and beer. The track lighting on
the ceiling and above the board behind the counter
with prices painted on it was turned off. The racks
of snacks and junk food didn't seem to be out of
order, and aside from some chips in the paint, what
I could see of the flooring, counters, and two tables
inside was clean. If the attack had occurred inside,
there was no sign of it from where we were standing.

Still, that smell led me to believe that there was
more to see here, something we hadn't found yet.
Stepping back from the window, I took a few short,
sniffling breaths through my nose, just enough to
get a whiff of that decaying stuff again. It wasn't
coming from the front.

Sara followed me as I alternately sniffed and
gagged. The looks she was giving me made me
wonder just how weird my expression must have
been. I couldn't help the way my nose scrunched
up, my eyes watered, or how my mouth was twisting,
like I had bitten into a not-quite-ripe lemon. Whatever was giving off that odor was *rank*. Like bad
meat in a plastic bag under the summer sun, left
to bake until it burst.

There was a light illuminating the side of the
building between the Laundromat and the *carnicería.*

Roaches scuttled out of our path and disappeared into crevices as we moved closer to the source of that smell. It appeared to be coming from close to the Dumpster flush against the wall, next to an exit from the butcher shop.

I couldn't get any closer. My nose had started running, and my eyes were watering so badly that I could barely see. Taking her cue from the wave of my hand in the general direction of the trash, Sara kept going while I turned away to retch by the sidewalk.

When I managed to lift my head and blink the worst of the sting from my eyes, I saw some of the people in the Laundromat giving me dirty looks as they sorted their colors and folded their undies. Awesome.

Scrubbing the back of my hand against my mouth, I turned, watching as Sara crouched and poked at something on the ground. With her bare hands? Yuck.

Suddenly, she rose, almost tipping over her high-heeled boots. Once she regained her balance, she strode back to my side in a hurry.

Once she reached me, she didn't look at me, placing her hands just under her ribs and taking a deep breath. She stared at, but I had the suspicion did not see, the used car lot across the street.

"Your nose didn't lie. There's a piece of zombie back there. I think it's a finger."

Oh, God.

"It moved when I touched it."

Oh, *God*.

"Let's get the hell out of here."

Though I felt like making like Sir Robin in that *Holy Grail* movie, now wasn't the time to run away. "We can't leave without knowing what else happened here. Maybe someone in that Laundromat saw something. Which way did they go when they left? How did they get here? There's got to be something more that we haven't found yet."

She nodded, but did not look particularly enthusiastic. We headed to the Laundromat, the people inside who hadn't thought much of my behavior suddenly quite studious in their folding activities. One guy grabbed the remainder of his laundry in his arms and fled out the door opposite the one we were entering. He probably knew something, but I wasn't in the mood to chase unwilling witnesses.

We went toward a lady leaning over the lower half of a Dutch door, watching one of the TVs playing from a wall mount across the room. She barely looked in our direction when Sara and I stopped in front of her.

"Excuse me," I said, giving her a little wave. "Hi, there. Can we ask you a few questions?"

She tore her attention off the TV and looked me up and down. "*No hablo Inglés.*" Back to the TV.

Sara wasn't deterred. She shot off some Spanish in rapid fire, and the older woman looked at her with surprise. They jabbered back and forth a bit, the lady becoming agitated before long. There were a lot of hand gestures and grabbing at the little gold cross around her neck.

After tonight, I was going to invest in a Spanish-English dictionary.

I gave Sara a pat on the back to indicate she should keep on with it while I moved to interview some of the other people hanging around.

There wasn't much more to be learned from the others. Everyone I asked either didn't speak English, hadn't been around that night, or had only heard, not seen, what had happened. The noises they described were pretty par for the course considering it had been a zombie attack. Moans, groans, and screams had sent most of them diving for cover or calling the cops. They didn't know what had made the noises, but they assumed it was shady business involving Others.

Sara startled me a few minutes later with a hand on my shoulder. The guy I was talking to eyeballed her cleavage like he hadn't just been involved in what I considered to be a serious discussion about whether zombies that shamble versus the ones that run are more dangerous. He'd seen some of the ones that had attacked the vampires in the alley, though he had no recollection about where they'd come from or how they had left. Must have been some of that mage "fade" mojo, no doubt.

"I've got something. Let's go," Sara whispered.

I waved a good-bye to the guy, who failed to return the gesture. He was too busy gawking over Sara, who didn't appear to notice his attention.

She kept her mouth shut until we were outside, slowing down a bit to mutter her findings to me under her breath before we returned to the car. "Looks like that mage knows how to cover his tracks. Rosalie said she saw the guy, looked right at him in fact, and that he tried to cast a black enchant on her to make her forget. Her family is a line of magic users, though, so she just pretended it worked and hid before he could figure out his spell didn't work.

"He's young, early twenties maybe, and wears stylish clothes. Pale skin, dark brown hair, tall and skinny. She didn't get close enough to see his eye color, but she did spot a tattoo of a pentagram on his palm when he was casting at her. The zombies were brought here and taken away in a U-Haul, driven by a second man she didn't see very well and couldn't describe."

"Not bad," I said. "Don't suppose she happened to catch the license plate, too?"

Sara smirked, moving around to the other side of the car. "Sadly, no. She did say the truck had a picture of the Golden Gate Bridge on the side, so that narrows it down—slightly."

For a moment, I thought we might have the case in the bag—but then I groaned and slapped my palm on the roof. "Shit, no. We can't call their home office to ask about rentals without using our PI license. Or call the cops and ask them to do the legwork for us. Damn."

"Maybe not," Sara replied, getting in and leaning across the seat to continue, "but I'm sure Clyde has connections, and we know enough to narrow down the search. With the guy's description, and knowing about the truck, we should have enough info that Clyde could figure out who it was more rapidly than we could."

Trinity tapped her nails on the steering wheel, not bothering to look back at us as I slid in beside Sara and buckled up. She took off almost as soon as the "click" of the seat belt locking sounded. "I take it you two found something?"

"Yeah," Sara said. "We'll tell Clyde when we get back. I don't like repeating myself."

Trinity didn't say anything, the plastic covering the steering wheel squeaking under her fingers. Touchy.

I sincerely hoped Clyde would appreciate the work we had done and what we had found out for him. Hopefully he'd consider it enough and wouldn't expect us to continue digging.

But knowing my luck, and considering the vampire's behavior thus far, whatever we did for him would never be enough.

Chapter 12

"That's a good start," Clyde said to Sara as she finished telling him about what she had learned from the lady at the Laundromat, "but I need you to *find* him."

Clyde's expression had remained stony as we each told him what we had found out. I noted a brief clenching of his jaw as he took in the details about the necromancer when Sara described him, but otherwise, there was no sign that the vampire was in the least affected by what we had to say. Though it was a tell, I wasn't sure what it meant yet. He either already knew who the mage was, or he had a suspicion confirmed. Regardless, it just meant he hadn't told us everything, which was something I already knew.

Sara shifted in her seat, a sign she was uncomfortable. It was a small miracle she'd been able to get as much information as she had out of that woman. Clyde probably didn't realize we'd struck what was the private investigator's equivalent of a gold vein, or maybe he just didn't care.

I wasn't all that surprised. Trinity had led us straight to Clyde as soon as we returned. The room we were in now was one we had passed through the first night on our way to see him. Well-lit and without the strobes, it was almost homey. There were numerous overstuffed chairs and couches, and the artwork on the walls, which hadn't been there the night of the S&M-themed party, was of fields and horses and English countryside scenes.

He had placed himself in the center of it all, sprawled on a leather couch that matched the red silk-screen wallpaper. Fabian was seated on the other end with one leg thrown casually over the other.

Once again, Clyde wasn't wearing a shirt, only this time he had on stone-washed jeans that weren't so tight that nothing was left to the imagination. His followers—minions—whatever they were—had taken seats around him, some of them taking notes, others on the phone or tapping away on laptops, and a couple on the floor in front of Clyde, touching him and probably giving him the occasional compliment to stroke his ego. Or something else. Who knew, right?

I couldn't help but wonder if every time he arranged to see us, he prepared in advance to pose in such a way that he would look devastating. If I hadn't seen Royce do much the same every now and then, I might have been more impressed, but his posturing was getting old very fast.

As much as I wanted to call him on it, and ask him why he didn't just use whatever connections he must have in the LAPD to track the necromancer down, it didn't seem like a good time to push him. Maybe it wouldn't hurt to ask, but I already knew how he was going to answer.

"Clyde," I said, quickly amending my words after seeing his expression, "Mr. Seabreeze, we don't have access to our resources out here, and we can't use our PI licenses or announce our presence to local authorities. It would defeat the purpose of our coming here. Is there any way you can ask the police to look into this with the information we gave you? We've got a getaway vehicle description—a rented van. With that kind of information, they'd probably find this guy a lot faster than we can."

"I don't want the police involved in my affairs. There's little they can do against a magical menace like a necromancer. If they were to find him first, they would inevitably die, and thus draw more bad press down on Others. I can't allow it."

His answer cemented my earlier theory that he knew who was behind this. From all I knew about him, he loved being in the spotlight, and he would undoubtedly have jumped on the opportunity to come across as the "victim" of some kind of hate crime if the culprit had been human instead of Other. This was something deeply personal, an affront to Clyde's power structure and tenuous hold on this city.

I needed to get in touch with Royce as soon as

possible and see if we could come back to New York or if there was somewhere else we could go. This place was more dangerous than where we'd been, if not in the same way, if Clyde was bringing down this kind of heat on himself.

As much as I wanted to come back with a smart-ass reply, I put on my best professional face and tone, bearing in mind that pissing him off would be unwise. "Okay. I'm not saying this to make you upset, but do you realize we have no way of following the leads we were able to scrounge up? It's a dead end."

His blue eyes gleamed, and I detected a hint of fang in his humorless smile as he leaned closer to me. "Really? No, Ms. Waynest, it hadn't occurred to me."

His sarcasm was really unnecessary. It took every last shred of willpower I had to keep from saying something snarky in return.

"I chose to use you for your investigative skills. If you are too incompetent to do the job, I'm sure you can find someone else to take you in."

"No," Sara said, stepping forward. Some of the other vampires in the room leaned in, their own eyes taking on a touch of red. "No, we'll figure it out. We're just going to need more time."

Fabian rose from his seat beside Clyde, his eyes sliding over us in a way that nearly felt like fingers crawling over my skin. Creepy. I got the idea this was the first time he felt like we might be bringing something useful to the table, and that he also didn't like it. There was something about the aura he was projecting that made me wonder what his stakes were in this.

"You've discovered much in a short period of time. I think perhaps you underestimate what you can do for us. Find the boy, and you will be suitably rewarded."

Clyde shot Fabian a look that I interpreted as "shut the hell up." He then sat up and rested his elbows on his knees, giving Sara and me a smile that might have been endearing if he had kept his fangs to himself. "Continue your search as long as necessary. Use any of my resources you need to— but stay away from the local police. You wouldn't want to be discovered and extradited back to New York, now, would you?"

Sara and I both shook our heads.

"Good. Give Trinity the details. I will see if I can have one of my people find out who rented that van and what the reported destination was supposed to be, though I am not sure the information will help you much. You two keep doing what you're doing. You're on the right track."

Interesting. Clyde (and maybe Fabian?) had to know more than he was saying, but clearly wasn't going to tell us what that was. At this point, I suspected he didn't want to find out *who* was killing his people—he already had that information and wasn't of a mind to share—he just wanted to know *where they were.* Maybe to test how good we were at our jobs, too.

If we found the necromancer, I had little doubt Clyde would try to kill the guy, but I also wondered what had started this mess and why they were both working so hard to fight each other while going unnoticed. The mage was covering his tracks, and Clyde didn't want the cops involved. For Fabian to be here, I had the feeling something big was going on that meant Clyde had bitten off more than he could chew, and he needed the help of an older, more experienced vampire to make the Big Bad go away.

As for why they were so hell-bent on keeping things secret, it was possible old habits died hard. Others had kept their existence secret for hundreds, if not thousands, of years. The decade or so that had passed since Rohrik Donovan and the Moonwalker pack had revealed that werewolves and vampires and magi and who knew what all were living alongside humanity wasn't nearly long enough for most people to get used to it. The bulk of the supernatural community—the ones who had been around before their big reveal to the bulk of society—might have been experts at hiding their inter-Other wars from people, but somehow that didn't seem like a good enough reason.

No, there was something deeply personal going on. But what?

The investigative part of me was itching to twist Clyde's arm to work more out of him, but it wasn't the time. Sara and I excused ourselves, and Trinity escorted us back to the guest house. If I was ever going to deliver that package of Analie's, we'd need to figure out a way to travel without our babysitter. Maybe tomorrow I would see about having Clyde let us take the car without a driver. It was unlikely he'd allow it, but we could always ask.

Trinity hovered in the door once we were inside, frowning at us. I raised a brow in question.

"You two should be careful."

Sara smirked, tossing her purse on the first step and leaning against the banister. "We're doing our best, but I have the feeling your boss doesn't care. You know something we don't?"

Trinity backed out of the door, lowering her head. I wondered if she was trying to keep what she was saying from being picked up by the security camera, or if she actually felt bad about how Clyde was treating us.

"You're doing better than I thought you would," she said. "Still, it's worse than you know. I can't tell you, he'd—I just can't. But trust me when I say you don't want to be around when he finds out where this necromancer is staying. It'll be bad—for all of us."

With that, she turned on her heel and fled. We didn't even get a chance to tell her the details about the van.

"What is it about vampires and cryptic statements? Is it physically impossible for them to say what's on their minds?" Sara asked.

I laughed. "Yeah, something like that. You should have seen Royce when he finally admitted that he was hiding things from me. Never thought I'd live to see the day."

"Yeah, well, you almost didn't. How are you feeling, anyway? Arnold told me he's still trying to find out what's going on with you."

That made me cringe. I hadn't thought Arnold would talk to Sara about my problems, but I shouldn't have been too surprised. They were dating, after all.

Sara must have gathered that she'd hit a sore spot. She clapped me on the back and then started up the stairs. "Don't worry too much. Once we get out of here, I'm sure Arnold will find a cure."

Being reminded of the illness didn't make me feel much better. Though Sara had sat with me while I was spitting out that black crud in the bathroom, I wasn't sure exactly how much she knew about what was wrong with me. I didn't want to face the idea that I was part lycanthrope or part vampire or whatever I might be. It had to pass. Whatever it was, it *had* to work its way out eventually. The pain had lessened, and I wasn't growing fur in weird places. It *had* to be working its way out of my system.

Lowering my head and rubbing my fingertips over my eyes, I did my best to put it all away in the back of my head. Worrying about the infection on top of what Clyde was hiding, where we were going to turn for clues now that we had to follow what was essentially a dead end, and what was going to happen if Sara and I blew the lid on where the necromancer was hiding, was just one problem too many. Oh, and let us not forget that I was obligated to figure out how to get Analie's package to a bunch of werewolves that *might* eat me if I showed up smelling like vampires.

If I could, I'd avoid thinking about the infection the entire time I was here, and maybe even after I got back to New York.

Denial. Not just a river in Egypt.

Those pleasant thoughts in mind, I trudged up the stairs after Sara, wishing I could call my mom and dad and see how they were doing. My dad might not speak to me, but my mom—maybe she wasn't biased against me for being involved with Others. Not to mention my brothers. Mikey hadn't seemed surprised or upset by my involvement with the Others and had even offered to represent me in court if it came down to that. It was good having a lawyer in the family.

Damien, on the other hand, had probably found out from the papers if my dad hadn't told him first. I would have to find another disposable phone, or maybe see about borrowing one from somebody outside of Clyde's retinue to see how they were doing. Not knowing was killing me, and even with Royce's assurances that he'd been doing what he could to take care of them—discreetly—in my absence, it didn't make it any easier to cope with not having heard my mother's voice in over a month.

As I changed my clothes and crawled into bed, I had to fight the urge to cry. Someday this would all be over. I could hug my mom again. I could tease Damien about his crappy taste in movies, and Mike about never getting married.

I could tell Dad what an asshole he was for trying to disown me, and then show him that I wasn't so different from the little girl whose bruised knees he had kissed better.

It was a long, lonely time before I finally managed to get to sleep.

Chapter 13

The next day wasn't much better. No one was available to drive us around town, and no one showed up to give us orders or any hints as to what we should do next. Sara and I met in the kitchen around noon, and we took some time to consider our next move. Though I didn't like the idea very much, I thought it might be best to get Analie's gift for her caretaker out of my hands first thing. After that, we could pay a visit to the other vampire master, Jimmy Thrane, to see if he might have any information on our necromancer friend or his zombie sidekicks.

Sara and I spent some time plotting out our route for the evening while Florencia cooked for us. The kitchen smelled awesome, and we both thoroughly enjoyed the meal of tacos and fajitas she made for us. The meat for the tacos was incredibly tender, more so than any steak I could remember having before.

"Florencia, that was great," I told her as Sara and I helped her clear dishes from the table. "What was that meat you used for the tacos?" I wondered if it was a local thing, or maybe a cut of meat I could request from the local delis at home.

"*Lengua*," she said, smiling.

"Cow tongue," Sara translated for me.

I did my best to keep my expression neutral and managed not to barf once it really settled in.

Note to self: Ask about the ingredients *before* eating anything else in this town.

After we cleaned up, Sara and I hung out outside for a while, taking in some sun. The light was nearly blinding, but I didn't mind. The heat and fresh air were welcome. Inside that air-conditioned house felt claustrophobic and a little too much like I was constantly under watch. Something to do with the security cameras hidden all over the house, no doubt.

With little else to do after I put Analie's letter and care package near the front door, we spent the remainder of our time until sundown watching bad daytime TV. We had no computers to surf the Internet and no books to keep us occupied, but the old school Godzilla movie marathon on some cable channel kept us from going completely bonkers while we waited for Trinity to come get us for our next round of Find-the-Necromancer.

Once she arrived and we told her where we wanted to go, she started laughing at us.

She kept right on laughing until she realized I was serious.

"You're insane," Trinity told me. "Completely unbalanced if you think I'm going to take you into the heart of Goliath territory."

"Then give us the keys and let us do it ourselves," I said, holding out my hand.

"Oh, no. Clyde would kill me if I let you two run off somewhere without someone to keep an eye on you."

"Then take us. Your choice. You can take us, give us the keys, or we'll call a cab. We have a job to do, and I'm not going to let your cowardice stop us."

That made Trinity's eyes gleam with irritation. "If you had even the slightest idea what you were getting into—"

"How do you know we don't? Look, make your choice before I make it for you. I'll be happy to tell Clyde you're preventing us from following up on a lead—"

She growled, a deep, threatening sound that never should have come from a human throat. With a sharp gesture, she indicated we should follow her.

What a great way to start the night. Expelling a breath I hadn't realized I'd been holding, I picked up the letter and package and fell into step behind the vampire, taking Sara's hand when I felt her groping at my wrist.

I kept forgetting that she wasn't used to dealing with the bluster the monsters dished out. And I needed to remember that I no longer had the belt to give me tips and an extra physical boost if it came down to a fight. Whatever might happen, whether Trinity or some other monster took it into his or her head to beat the crap out of me or turn me into dinner, I would need to be a little more careful. There was no one here to save me if I bit off more than I could chew, and I had no superhuman strength or speed to help me. Hell, I didn't even have my guns or stakes or anything else to protect myself if I ended up in a fight.

The car ride was tense and silent, no one interested in talking about where we were going or what we would do once we got there.

Once Trinity pulled off the freeway, she took us down some side streets and beyond a number of apartment buildings and small shops until we were in what I suppose could be considered suburbia. The houses were a lot like the ones around my parents' house on Long Island, albeit with a lot more cacti and palm trees.

When we pulled onto Gavin's street, Trinity parked the car at least four or five blocks from the address we were looking for.

"Go do whatever the hell it is you came here to do. I'll wait. If you're not back in time for me to get to shelter by sunrise, you can stay here and rot."

I shook my head and slid out of the car, not bothering to dignify her snarky comment with an answer. Sara followed my lead. With any luck, I'd drop off the box and be out of this part of town within the hour.

I tucked it under my arm and stalked down the

street. Though Sara was taller than me, with much longer legs, she had to lengthen her stride to keep up with me.

"So," she said, arms swinging at her sides, "when this is over, are you writing a new and improved version of *How to Win Friends and Influence People*?"

My lips quirked. Sara always knew the right thing to say to defuse my anger. "Yeah, yeah. Sorry, I know I haven't been doing a good job of managing my temper."

"It's not me you need to apologize to. Though I can't say that she wasn't asking for it. . . ."

"Okay, I'll say something when we get back to the car. Let's just get this over with, shall we?"

She nodded. I kept an eye on the numbers on the houses. It didn't take very long to find the house; it had some plastic toys on the postage stamp-sized lawn and a light on over the front door. Paint was chipped and peeling in places, but it was clean, and the lights were all on. A carefully tended flower bed ran along the front of the house. Even from the street, I could hear the sound of cartoons coming from inside.

Sara stayed a few steps behind me while I went up to the door and knocked.

Then knocked again. Louder.

After the third time, my fist was stinging, and a little kid who couldn't have been more than six or seven years old opened the door, blinking up at me with wide blue eyes from under a fan of shaggy, dirty-blond tendrils.

"Hi," I said. "Is Gavin—"

"*Gavin!* Someone for you!"

Man, that little boy had a set of lungs on him. He turned around and raced off in bare feet, disappearing around a corner.

I stood in the open door, shuffling my weight from foot to foot. When I looked over my shoulder at Sara, her expression betrayed just as much confusion as I felt. So I turned my attention back to the hallway with child-height crayon scrawl all over the walls and waited.

Then the Viking came into view.

I don't toss out that word lightly. He was wearing nothing but a towel around his waist—oh, *my*—and every last inch of what was visible was covered in hard, ropy muscle. His blond hair was even more of a shaggy mess than the kid's, wild and untamed, framing a chiseled face that had the ghost of a beard emphasizing a sharp jawline and killer cheekbones.

Then his blue eyes flashed gold, and his mouth was full of fangs as he stalked forward.

If there is one reaction I have perfected these last few months, it's not to freeze when danger rears its head. Instead, I dropped the box, scrambling back to the street and grabbing at Sara to drag her with me as he stopped in the doorway, fingernails that had grown into talons biting into the wood.

"Vampire's whore! What are you doing here? Get off my property!"

Sara and I both started babbling and pointing

at the box. I don't think either of us made any sense, and to this day, I'm not even sure what came out of my mouth. Something along the lines of "oh-my-God-please-don't-hurt-me-the-box-the-box-the-box," I think.

His growl was thunderously loud, and it was at that moment that I realized all other sounds on the street had ceased.

Oh, there might have been traffic from a few blocks away, but all of the TVs had turned off, no dishes clanked, and no murmur of voices could be heard. Even the kid's cartoons were off. Like the whole block was holding its breath, waiting to see what would happen.

He kept his eyes on us as he crouched down, touching the top of the box. I wasn't about to tell him that he was flashing us, and most likely the neighbors across the street could see, too, considering his impressive . . . um. You get the picture.

His talon-tipped fingers found and slightly tore the letter on top. He picked it up, raising it near eye-level, and started to read it, every once in a while his eyes flicking back to us.

Then I think he must have realized it was from Analie. He stopped looking at us and hunched over the paper, clutching it in both hands, his gaze devouring her scrawl. I thought I might have detected tears at the corners of his gold-colored eyes, but I couldn't be sure.

Still holding the letter, he used one of those claws to slice open the tape holding the top of the box together. The kid—I hadn't even heard him creep up behind the guy—leaned around Gavin's impressively muscled arm to peer at the box. "What's that, Gavin? Are those cookies?"

"Yeah—yes. Analie sent them for us. Go back inside, Jo-Jo. I'll bring them to you in a minute."

The kid clapped his hands and bounced back, saying Analie's name in singsong as he rushed back into the house, racing some invisible opponent.

The Viking lifted his head and stared at Sara and me with wet eyes, taking a moment to focus as if he had just recalled we were there. The gold color faded into an icy, pale blue, his fangs retracting and—you know, I can't be sure, but I would swear that his hair stopped bristling quite so much around his face, too.

"You brought this all the way from New York? For me?"

Sara and I both nodded. We were still clutching at each other, and I wasn't sorry for that at all.

"From Analie."

It was a statement, not a question, but we nodded again.

He didn't say anything. He just crouched there, clutching the letter, staring at us.

I cleared my throat. "I guess we'll—ah—we'll just be going—"

"No."

Ha, that was funny. For a second there, I thought he said no.

"Come inside. I want to talk to you."

Oh. I hadn't imagined it.

The Viking stood up, towering in the doorway, his towel slipping lower on his hips. Feeling a tad ill, I lifted my hands, not quite sure if it was meant to be a negative gesture or a please-don't-hurt-me supplication. Sara and I stumbled back, fetching up against a big oak tree shading the yard and some of the street. He moved toward us, and the bark cracked under my fingertips as I clutched at the tree.

He stopped when he was close enough to touch, both of us gaping up at him like we were staring down Death come to claim us.

Then he engulfed us in a hug. I'm pretty sure I left a chunk of skin behind on that tree when he pulled us away. I didn't start screaming and flailing because, much like Analie, he didn't seem to have any concept of his own strength when he crushed us against him.

The only reason I knew I wasn't about to die was because the six-foot-plus terrifying werewolf warrior wearing nothing but a towel was crying all over us.

God*damn*, my life was getting weirder by the day.

Chapter 14

Sara and I awkwardly patted him on the back, staring at each other with wide eyes across the expanse of his—I'm not going to lie—*very* impressive shoulders. His bare skin was hot and prickly with the crisp golden hairs covering his arms and chest. A few minutes later, his crying tapered off, and he straightened up, still clutching us against him.

"You'll have to—have to excuse me," he said, sniffling. "I haven't seen Analie in so long. Come inside, please."

It wasn't a request. He probably could have picked us up and carried us, but he just half-pulled, half-dragged us along, marching us toward the house.

He finally let us go once we reached the door, giving us a not-so-gentle shove that sent us both stumbling inside as he bent at the waist to scoop up the box. We both turned our backs as soon as we saw the towel was slipping. I gave Sara the side-eye, and she was blushing just as furiously as I was sure I must have been.

"'Scuse me a minute, you caught me just out of the shower. Go have a seat in the kitchen"—he gestured vaguely deeper inside the house—"and I'll be right with you. Oh, would you mind taking this?"

I took the box as he handed it to me, making a heroic effort to keep my eyes above the level of his chest and not on where the towel had been a second ago but wasn't anymore.

Wow.

Oh, wow.

Sara and I fled in the general direction he had indicated, and he disappeared around a corner. The house wasn't terribly big. We passed an open archway that led into a living room. Jo-Jo was parked in front of the TV, but he was watching us over his shoulder with bright golden eyes. Just past where the kid was sitting was a big kitchen table, surrounded by enough chairs to seat a small army of hungry kids.

I set the box on the table, and Sara followed my lead and sat next to me. Jo-Jo crept in after us, peering from around the divider between the kitchen and the living room. Sara chewed her bottom lip and stared at the ceiling.

Gavin appeared a few minutes later, this time clad in a pair of jeans, padding into the room so quietly that his presence startled me. The guy was big, but he moved like a ghost. Sara and I mutely watched as he pulled out some mismatched glasses and small plates, setting them before us, with a setting for himself and another for Jo-Jo, who hadn't yet decided to join us.

He then poured us each a glass of milk, and then pulled out one of the containers with some of Analie's cookies inside, popping the lid and holding it out to me.

"Oh, no thank you, I—"

That earned me a capital "L" Look.

"—I would be delighted, thank you, um, yes."

Yeah. I took the cookies. And so did Sara, though we both put them on our plates and didn't start eating them until Gavin sat back and shoved one in his own mouth, watching us as he washed it down with half his glass of milk. We quickly followed suit, though I wonder if Sara, like me, didn't so much as taste the confection thanks to the flood of fear swamping my body with adrenalin.

Gavin placed the glass down on the table with a heavy *thump* and leaned forward. "Tell me about Analie. How is she doing? Is the leech taking care of her?"

I swallowed. Hard. Then again to get the remaining crumbs out of my throat. My voice still came out in a croak. "She's doing great. She's taking cooking lessons from the guy who runs Royce's fancy French restaurant, *La Petite Boisson,* and she's getting tutored through her school lessons by one of the local Weres. She talked about you a lot." At least, while I was listening. Don't even think it—I already felt awful for not paying more attention to the kid and her troubles. "She misses you."

Gavin finally looked down, breaking that fierce eye contact, and toyed with one of the cookies with now blunt, human fingernails. "I wish I could have been there for her. Could have taken her place so she wasn't in the clutches of that . . . that monster."

Though I had often thought as much of Royce, I didn't think now was the time to contradict Gavin. He was clearly high-strung where vampires were concerned, so debating their merits when he had first addressed me as a vamp's whore probably wasn't going to get us anywhere.

And I'll bet you thought I couldn't be tactful when necessity dictated.

"She might be stuck for the time being, but she's not suffering. He's given her clothes, food, shelter, and schooling. I think she'll be okay for now. Look, she even made these cookies we're eating."

I took another bite, this time dimly recognizing the taste of chocolate on my tongue. Gavin mechanically followed my lead, then shook his head and looked down at the confection in his hand. "Really? She made these?"

Nodding, I gestured for him to finish it off. He did so in silence, his brows moving around like he couldn't decide whether he should have an expression of shock or scowl at the cookie. Most likely the idea that Royce might put Analie to work doing something productive had never occurred to him.

Had I been in his place even a month or two ago, I might have thought the same.

The confusion eventually gave way to a scowl, but his eyes were misting up again. His manly-man persona was shattering under the weight of all that grief, I guess. "She was like a daughter to me. If I ever see Christoph or Ashi again, I'm going to kill them. When you go back to New York, you tell them that."

Sara and I both nodded rapidly, leaning back in our chairs.

"Yeah. Tell them that. I'll rip their throats out and eat their fucking soulless hearts."

Cripes. His eyes were going gold, and his nails were starting to look distinctly talon-like again. Had to remember that I was here to redeem myself and not because I had a death wish.

"Gavin," Sara said, her words coming out in a rush—anything to distract the werewolf who was barely holding control over his shapeshifting— "we're really sorry about what happened to Analie but we'll make sure she knows how much you miss her. Do you want us to bring anything back for her? A letter or something?"

That got him out of it. The hair bristling around his neck and jaw settled with an audible rustle, though his eyes remained a bright golden color. He muttered something I didn't quite catch and pushed back from the table, then dug around in one of the kitchen drawers. Once he found a pen and notepad, he hunched over the counter, his back to us as he scribbled away.

It felt like it took forever. My stomach was doing uneasy flip-flops as I watched him. He didn't do anything overtly ominous, but the words of wisdom that had been imparted to me by Arnold made me leery of trusting that he was going to let us out of here without doing something to make us pay for our freedom. Reminding myself that I was doing this on Analie's behalf and to be less of a shit-stain of a human being wasn't helping much. That thought seemed so very farfetched and out of place now that I was in the presence of a Goliath. His shirtless back was like a map to nowhere, traced out in a pattern of scars from battles long past.

Being around other werewolves hadn't prepared me for this. He had no qualms with making a show of his Other nature. He'd very nearly shifted right on his front lawn. Maybe because he had mistaken me for something other than human.

Unless he thought by my scent that I wasn't human anymore. Which was an unhappy thought I was going to stick with all that other crap in the back of my mind that I was not going to think about right then, like what my bills and credit must look like, and what my landlord might have done with the stuff in my apartment.

Analie damned well better appreciate this.

He turned back to us a few minutes later with a small stack of notepad paper, each page filled margin to margin with his scrawl. Shoving the papers at Sara, he looked back and forth between us.

"You'll make sure she gets this?"

"Absolutely. We'll put it in her hands as soon as we get back," Sara promised.

"Good," he replied. "If you don't, and I find out about it later, I will hunt you both down. You understand?"

Sara's eyes went wide and round, so you could see the whites all the way around.

A touch to my arm made me jump, and I banged my knees on the underside of the table. Grimacing and rubbing what would no doubt be a bruise later, I twisted around to face Jo-Jo, who was holding a grubby piece of thick, crayon-covered paper and looking up at me with wide golden eyes. There was something strange about these werewolves, even beyond the obvious. I had never heard of any type of Were pack where the children could show signs of their Other nature before hitting puberty.

Even so, his expression betrayed a fear and nervousness that tugged at my heartstrings. What must he have heard about vampires and the people who worked for them to look at me that way?

"Can you give this to Analie?" He held out the paper to me.

Gavin "ahem"-ed, and Jo-Jo tilted his head the other way, looking up at his caretaker. Gavin's tone was all patience, even and steady, nothing like how he had addressed Sara or me. "What do we say?"

Jo-Jo had to think about it. "Please and thank you?"

"Not to me."

Jo-Jo turned back to me and held up the paper, earnest and clearly worried that he'd offended us. "Please and thank you?" he repeated.

I had to suppress a laugh. Other or not, he was adorable. I took the paper and set it aside, then nudged my plate of cookies closer to him. "You're welcome. Don't worry; I'll make sure she gets it. You want one, kid?"

His whole face lit up, and the gold flooded out of his eyes in a weird spiraling motion, like it was sinking down the drain of his pupils, to be replaced with a more natural pale blue color. He grabbed a handful and shoved a full one in his mouth.

"Manners, Jo-Jo."

The kid choked a bit on the cookie and offered me another mumbled "thank you" before rushing off with the rest somewhere deeper into the house, a door slamming behind him.

Gavin smiled after the kid, the expression betraying a softness I was barely able to reconcile with the fearsome warrior who had very nearly given me a heart attack less than half an hour ago.

Then he reminded me why I should be scared when his heavy gaze slid back to meet mine again. The humorless grin, showing a row of pearly, pointy teeth, wasn't needed for emphasis, but that didn't stop him from showcasing growing fangs for our benefit. "You've done me a great favor by bringing me this. You'll do me a bigger one by leaving now and staying out of Goliath territory for the rest of your stay. Yes?"

I gave him a jerky nod, pushing my chair back. Sara was far braver than I was, holding out a pleading hand.

"Please, before we go, have you heard anything about a necromancer in town?"

Gavin's grin faded, replaced by a scowl. "Yes. We had to destroy quite a few of his creations before he realized we weren't going to let him hide in our part of town. The stink of those abominations is still in the air just a few blocks from here. Why do you ask?"

Sara looked to me expectantly. Gavin soon did the same. He didn't appear ready to tear my throat out just yet, but telling this werewolf we were working for vampires might get us eaten. Then again, we were bringing Analie his letter, so maybe he wouldn't. Without a doubt, lying to him would be worse. From what I had gleaned from Chaz and Royce, most Others could smell a lie at ten paces. Also, he was the closest thing we had to a lead right now, and risking pissing him off was a bit better than upsetting the guy who was giving us a place to hide.

"Well," I hedged, choosing my words carefully, "we have a client who is trying to find him. The guy's been doing some bad stuff around town, and the person who hired us wants it to stop. If you can point us in the right direction, you won't ever have to deal with him again."

"Let me guess. Your client is Clyde Seabreeze."

There wasn't any way around it. I nodded, bracing myself for his reaction.

He considered us, rubbing the stubble on his chin. The mixture of irritation and disgust was apparent, but he wasn't as peeved as I had expected.

"I suppose it's a little late to warn you ladies about putting your trust in, or working for, the Shadow Men. I want you to stay alive long enough to get my message to Analie. If you mess with a necromancer, that probably won't happen."

"Oh," Sara said, "we're not planning on tangling with him directly. We're just supposed to find his hideout and let Clyde take care of the rest."

Gavin growled, the sound a thick rumble that rattled the dishes on the table. "Don't believe that for a minute. He'll find a way to make you do his dirty work. They always do. You really think a leech is going to willingly put himself into spelling distance of a mage who controls the dead?"

I hadn't thought of that. Now that Gavin mentioned it, I wasn't going to be able to stop thinking about it, either.

Shit.

"Normally I would say to hell with the Shadow Men, but I have the feeling this mage is even worse. This probably won't help much, but check the towns along the 210 freeway between Sylmar and Sunland. Pay attention to the more rural, back-road homes up in the hills. There's a stench that follows him, and he might be trying to hide it. If you have a Shadow Man with you, he or she will probably be able to scent it out once you're in the right area."

This was far more than I had been expecting. "Thank you so much, Gavin. For everything." I held out my hand, offering a parting shake, but he looked at it like I was trying to give him a dead rat. My cheeks burned with embarrassment, but I was determined not to let his rudeness get to me. Much. "We'll make sure Analie gets your letters."

He gave us a sparse nod, then hooked a thumb in the direction of the front door. "I'm sure you two can see yourselves out."

Man. And he'd reminded Jo-Jo of his manners.

Sara and I had a lot to think about on our way to Jimmy Thrane's place.

Chapter 15

"Ma'am, I really don't think we should be here."

"Your objection is duly noted," I said, not bothering to look back over my shoulder at Trinity. This time she had decided to leave the car to follow us into the alley that was supposed to lead to the entrance to this Thrane guy's hideout.

Trinity had an expression of pure shock on her face when she saw Sara and me walking back from Gavin's place. We could see her bulging eyes and open mouth through the windshield. She honestly must have expected us to die or end up held hostage or something once we set foot on Goliath territory. I didn't know whether to find her reaction funny or take it as an insult.

By the time we'd reached the car, she had gotten a handle on her surprise and wrangled her expression into something more neutral. Then, once we told her we wanted her to take us to Thrane's place, she had barked out a laugh.

"You two are insane. First the Goliaths, now that ridiculous pretender? Do you have any idea how crazy that guy is?"

Sara huffed, folding her arms. "Do you have any idea how crazy it is that we're being asked to find where this necromancer is hiding without the help of police or other authorities to track him down? Stop judging our methods and let us do our job. You have a better idea of where we should be looking? We're all ears."

Trinity shook her head and started driving, not saying a thing.

Even if she was of the opinion that Thrane was nuttier than a fruitcake, it didn't deter me. I had been dealing with more than enough weirdos since I had arrived in Los Angeles. The addition of a few more didn't seem like such a big deal.

Clyde might have thought he was the Master of All He Sees and Then Some, but the reality was that he couldn't be everywhere at once, and to have a slice of land in the middle of what was supposed to be *his* Valley—territory—whatever—belonging to another vampire meant that he didn't have as tight a grip on his holdings as he would have liked us to believe. Plus, three of the attacks had taken place on the borders between Thrane's and Clyde's territories, which meant that Thrane might know which way the necromancer went, might have seen something useful, or maybe would be willing to help us if he was also losing people.

Granted, now that we'd stopped in front of what—

according to Trinity's sarcastic explanation—was supposed to be Thrane's base of operation, I could see why Clyde had appeared more annoyed than worried when he mentioned the "Master" of this borderline slice of land between Burbank and Glendale. The neighborhood, though not as nice as the one where Gavin lived, or as nasty as that armpit in Sun Valley we'd stopped in, wasn't real impressive, mainly small businesses sandwiched between apartments and old houses.

At first I thought Trinity must have been kidding. The place was nothing more than a run-down sports bar with dirty windows that obscured a dimly seen television mounted in the corner. There was a sign above the nearly deserted bar proclaiming they had a weeknight special on Budweiser and hot wings. Tucked away in a dark alcove on the side of the building was the door Trinity said led to Thrane's hideout. It was so narrow that I would have mistaken it for the location of the building's circuit breakers.

Sara and I approached the place together, wrinkling our noses at the padlocked Dumpster only a few yards away from the entrance to the vampire's hideout. This was *nothing* like the splendor I had seen vampires use to sequester themselves from humanity's prying eyes. If I hadn't gotten a nod in the affirmative when I gave Trinity a dubious look over my shoulder, I never would have guessed that Thrane lived here. It was either a terrifically clever front, or terribly sad.

Sara stepped aside, and I knocked lightly on the

door. A muffled voice came from the other side. "Password?"

Nonplussed, I looked at Trinity, who shrugged. Confused, I said, "I . . . don't know?"

"Close enough."

The door—was that piled-on insulation held on with duct tape?—opened, revealing a guy wearing track pants and a T-shirt slung over his shoulder. His skin was frightfully pale, and his hairy stomach protruded a bit over the top of his pants. He grinned broadly at Sara and me, flashing fangs. "Ladies, ladies, ladies! Call me Mac-daddy." He paused, then added thoughtfully, "Actually, if you're here to see me, you can call me anything you want."

Sara and I both hastily stepped back—probably a bit too quickly, considering the tragic look of disappointment that crossed his features—before a pleasant, feminine voice called out from the shadows behind him. "Mac, who is it? Get out of the damn door and let them in."

He got out of the way, disappearing into the dark. This was no more reassuring. Particularly as a third voice called out to us, this time another woman. "Are you just going to stand there all night?"

Terrifying as the thought of walking into that dark pit was, we weren't going to accomplish anything by standing in the alley. Sara fell into step behind me as I marched with what I hoped was a brave and dangerous expression into the vampire den.

If I'd thought the outside was bad, the inside was . . . bad.

A set of narrow, rickety wooden stairs sans railing led down about four feet into a cramped, narrow basement with a high ceiling. Fluorescent track lighting made everything take on a sickly, dim color. Someone had salvaged a large strip of puke-orange shag carpeting and laid it down on the bare concrete in the center of the room. The walls were beige and covered with posters, and there was a bulletin board that, at a glance, contained charming announcements like "Jason is a fag" scrawled in heavy permanent marker on scraps of paper between the job postings and concert flyers.

Though my own furniture in my apartment—cripes, did I still have anything of my own anymore? My landlord had probably dumped all of my crap out on the street by now. Ahem, back on track—though my own furniture *was* or *had been* of Ikea-level quality, it looked like the mismatched couches and chairs in this sprawling basement lair had gone a few rounds with their local Salvation Army store.

And lost.

Miserably.

The vampires didn't look much better.

Some wore jeans and T-shirts. Some wore stuff straight out of a Goth fashion magazine. One wore a pizza delivery shirt and cap, obviously either just coming from or leaving for a job.

Now I understood why Clyde was so obviously disgusted when he mentioned this Jimmy guy.

"Mr. Thrane?" I asked the room in general, not sure which one of the vampires to address. There wasn't much of a structure to this pack of misfits that I could pick up. The stuffy, musty scent and strangely echoic quality of the space, added to the cold due to the lack of body heat from the vampires, gave the impression of being at the bottom of a grave.

A frat boy's grave, maybe, but a grave, nonetheless.

The vampire lounging on the couch in the back nodded, touching the brim of his top hat. It was the only article of clothing he had on that was in good repair. Once he moved his hand, I could see a tattoo or something under one of his eyes.

"Ma'am. Might I ask why you're calling on us this fine evening?"

Well, at least he was polite. Sara, who had the look of rigid, forced politeness she often assumed when dealing with a client who made her uncomfortable, introduced us.

"Mr. Thrane, my name is Sara Halloway, and this is Shiarra Waynest, my business partner. We're private investigators. We wanted to ask for your help and see if you might have any information that might lead us to a resolution of some difficulties for a client."

"Wow, right on. Real private investigators?"

I glanced at the guy who had earlier been identified as Mac, giving him a look. He shrugged and grinned.

Thrane was not as impressed. "Fascinating. Really. But I would very much like to know how you two have heard of me and what you think I can do for you."

My turn to field the questions. "We heard that you're the ruler of some territory outside of Clyde Seabreeze's control. If that's the case, you may have information about who has been behind the murders and disappearances of Clyde's people."

Thrane's reaction was not what I had expected. At all. His fangs extended, and his eyes blazed red as he shot to his feet, pointing an accusatory finger at me. "You're working for that . . . that . . . *usurper?*"

Sara grabbed my arm so tightly, it went numb. The other vampires didn't seem very impressed, watching us with bored expressions. Once my heart crawled out of my throat and closer to the region it belonged, I squeaked out a few words.

"We—uh . . . yes?"

As suddenly as the anger had risen, it was gone. He blinked, and his eyes were normal again, the fangs retracting as he airily waved a hand at us. "Poofty von Metrofaggen can go find someone else to play his games. I'm not interested."

"Jimmy," one of the girls stage-whispered, her eyes comically huge in her heart-shaped face framed by inky black curls. "Jimmy, those are *humans.*"

I have never seen so many vampires so intensely interested in me at the same time. Talk about unnerving. Every one of them went deathly still—and I *mean* deathly—as their unblinking eyes locked on to us. It was like being stared at by a room full of china dolls. Hungry china dolls that are thinking about eating your face.

As the tension in the room skyrocketed and I contemplated throwing Sara over my shoulder and making a run for it, Thrane gave a long-suffering sigh, and the tension eased out of his body. He ran his hand over his face before giving the rest of his flock pointed looks.

"Yes, they are. And they are not for you."

The disappointment radiating from the other vampires was palpable.

"Aw, c'mon, Jimmy! We're hungry," one of them whined.

"You know," I said, edging back toward the door, "I think we're good. We'll find someone else to interview. Thanks for your time!"

Sara and I might have bolted if there hadn't been a vampire standing in the stairwell, barring our way out when we turned around.

At that moment, I could have kicked myself for being so stupid as to think I could waltz into some strange vampire's den without weapons or a way out. The only person who knew we were here was Trinity, and Clyde had made it perfectly clear how he felt about Jimmy, and about Sara and me exploring parts of Los Angeles beyond the bounds of his territory. Considering Royce was across the country, our chances of being saved were next to nil.

This was not good.

The other vampire glanced at me and Sara, then to Thrane, though he sounded far too excited considering the news he had to impart. "Cheese is dead."

Thrane looked from us up to the vampire on the stairs. "What?"

"Cheese is dead," the other guy repeated. Was it my imagination, or did he smell a bit like barf?

"Why is Cheese dead?" Thrane demanded, stepping around me and Sara. It seemed we'd been momentarily forgotten. Considering this new vampire was distracting the others from wanting to eat us, this wasn't altogether a bad thing.

"He got caught in the sun. Everyone was talking about it at the Sundown."

One of the others behind us snorted. "How the hell do you get caught in the sun?"

"I don't know; he just did. The police were sweeping him up around noon, apparently."

"I knew it was a bad idea to let him in," Thrane grumbled. "I swear, seventeen is like the magic number. No one that age lasts past a week." He looked over at the most sensibly dressed of the female vampires in the room in her slacks and button-down shirt, her reddish-brown hair swept up in a ponytail and her arms akimbo. "Why did I even let a vampire named Cheese join up?"

"You thought it was funny," the girl replied.

"Why is that funny?" Thrane wondered.

"Because you're an asshole," Mac muttered.

"Oh, yes. You two were going to be the best of friends. You remember why, don't you? You get it?"

Mac rolled his eyes. "I get it."

"'Cause it's Mac . . ."

"Thrane. I get it."

"A-a-a-a-and . . ."

"I get it."

"Cheese!"

The other vampires cracked up. Mac put his head in his hands.

"Well, only one thing to do. Everyone, stand up. Sta-a-a-a-and up." Thrane gestured at the others, pointing to each in turn. "Elly, Leewan, Megan . . . come on. Up we go."

Everyone stood up. Even Mac, once he finished cursing Thrane out under his breath. Sara and I stood where we were, awkwardly shuffling from foot to foot.

Thrane removed his hat and held it to his chest. "We are gathered here tonight to mourn the passing of one of our own."

"We're gathered here to hang out," the one he'd called Leewan mumbled.

Thrane pointed at him. "I can kill you."

Leewan fell silent.

"Cheese was our friend," Thrane continued. "He was our *brother.* Except to Janice, who wanted to boink him. Because otherwise that would be *wrong.*"

The girl I assumed was Janice closed her eyes, probably not in grief.

"Cheese lived a full life. It is with a heavy heart that we bid him farewell and hope that beyond this second death, he will find peace." Thrane wiped an imaginary tear from his eye. "Good-bye, Cheese."

"Good-bye, Cheese," everyone murmured.

"Hey, who wants to see if they're a cold fish or a passionate lover?" Elly called, having picked up a *Cosmo* in the middle of the service.

Everyone else's hand went up. My mouth dropped open, and I'm pretty sure Sara was gaping, too.

"Mac goes first," Elly decided.

Thrane turned back to us while most of the other vampires put their attention on Elly and her magazine.

"That was a moving speech," the girl in the nice clothes told him.

"Why, thank you, Shannon."

"You're welcome, Mr. Thrane."

"So, hey," Mac called out from across the room, "are we going to eat these people after we're done with the questions or what?"

Many red-tinged eyes were quite suddenly, very hungrily, focused on us. Again.

Chapter 16

As cold hands settled on our shoulders, Sara made a high-pitched sound, and I jumped about a foot in the air. Thrane had moved behind us, and I could hear the edge of amusement—and hunger—in his voice. "Now, now, children. What do I always say?"

"Never without a contract, and never without consent," the others droned. They sounded like kids in a classroom reciting some inane tidbit of trivia off of a chalkboard for their teacher.

"Very good! Next week, we're going to rehash the 'Your Donor is a Human, Not a Cow' and the 'Technically You're Still Human, so Have Some Humanity' talks."

That pronouncement was met with a chorus of groans.

Thrane's fingers tightened, and I tilted my head to look up at him, the tendons creaking in my neck with the movement.

"Now, I am sure you investigators have a great

deal of investigating to do, yes?" Thrane didn't wait for our reply. He started pushing us back in the direction of the door. "All right, then. You just go on about your business, and we'll pretend you never came here. Out of the way, Brendan."

Though Sara and I both stumbled some on the way, we soon got our bearings and moved under our own power again. Brendan, the vampire who had announced Cheese's death to the rest of the group, hopped off the steps and wandered over to where Elly and the others were doing their magazine survey.

"Please," I said over my shoulder, hoping this wasn't yet another dead end, "this might concern you, too. We're trying to find a necromancer."

Thrane came up short, nearly causing us to stumble again since he never let us go. He growled, the low rumbling echoing strangely in the room. Sara was pushed toward the stairs, while he spun me around to face him.

I finally got a good look at the tattoo under his eye. It was some kind of stylized Egyptian symbol. It added an extra level of creepy to his grin, which was already forced and predatory.

"Necromancer, you say?"

"Y-yes," I stammered, really wishing he'd take his hands off me.

"As in, the guy who has been toting zombies around town? That necromancer?"

Sara and I exchanged a look. Maybe this wouldn't be such a waste after all.

His fangs extended as I watched, my eyes widening. "What do you think, people? Sounds like Very Bad Things are going down in Froofty McPrissypants's territory."

The girl he'd addressed as Shannon shook her head. "Better not, Jimmy. Just let the necromancer take him out."

Thrane thrust a finger in the air dramatically. "We shall move in and strike while he is weak!"

Shannon smirked. "Uh-huh."

"Muster our forces. We book a cab and arrive at midnight!"

"Or, you know, we could go do karaoke."

One of Thrane's brows shot up. He was clearly intrigued. "Oh, better idea. Muster our forces. We go next door!"

Shannon's eye roll made it clear that his antics were nothing unusual to this crowd. Or to her, anyway. "Aye aye, chief."

Man, Trinity wasn't kidding when she said this guy was crazier than a shithouse rat. Thrane patted me on the shoulder, and I cringed. "You know, as much as I would like to help you ladies, I'm afraid I would enjoy seeing the usurper's kingdom torn out from under him one piece at a time far more. You're welcome to come join us for karaoke night once the mage is done dealing with that pretender."

"Please," Sara said, "we're asking for your help. If

we don't find that necromancer, something bad might happen to us."

"My dear, I am terribly sorry to hear that," he replied, tipping up the brim of his hat with his thumb as he bent to go eye-to-eye with her. "If only there were something I could do. But alas, your bad taste in clients is not my problem. Now, if you'll excuse us, karaoke music calls."

Fucking hell. He was hiding what he knew. Yet another grandstander—just what I needed.

Something stirred in me, deep down, making the hair on my arms rise and my fingers arch into claws. It felt like my vision was changing, growing sharper and picking up more details. Whatever was going on, it made Thrane uneasy enough to pull back from me a couple of steps, his predatory grin easing into a frown.

"Look," I said, my tongue feeling strangely thick in my mouth, "I have had it up to fucking *here* with you goddamned showboating, vain, ostentatious *assholes*! You know something about this guy, and you're deliberately keeping it from us. Do you *want* us to die? Because if we do, it'll be on your head!"

"Damn, lady," one of the other vampires said, "no need to Hulk out. Calm the hell down."

My glare shut him up pretty quick. He backed off, turning his gaze away. I didn't know what was wrong with me, but my temper hadn't gripped me so hard since the last time I was wearing the belt. Heat and rage simmered in my veins—and I liked it.

When I looked back at Thrane, a snarl curling

my lip, he raised his hands and also took a step back from me. "Ma'am, I'm sorry if I offended. Truly."

"About time somebody was sorry," I snapped.

"Shia, don't," Sara said. "Let's just get out of here."

As much as I would have liked to have left these weirdos behind, I stood my ground. There was no way I was walking out of here with nothing to show for it. Though there was a little voice in the back of my head that seemed to believe I might be over-reacting, I wasn't ready to let this go. Not yet.

"Well?" I demanded of Thrane.

He shook his head, taking another careful—very careful—step back from me. "We don't have much information. Sometimes he comes to our neighbor-hood. I've seen him here once or twice before, but we don't bother each other. He hasn't made a move against my people, and I would prefer not to garner his attention. Fair enough for you?"

Some part of me felt tempted to swipe at him with my nails. Thought that I could take him in a fight.

There was just enough common sense left in me to remember why that was a bad idea. Visions of how quickly Max and Royce moved, how viciously they fought, swirled in my head as I closed my eyes and clenched my hands into tight fists at my side. After a few deep breaths, I relaxed enough to reopen my eyes and give him a response.

"Fair enough. Thank you."

Thrane nodded, the other vampires edging over

to his side or behind him. Most of them looked nervous. Maybe even a little afraid. Of me? That was an interesting change of pace.

"Not to put too fine a point on it, but it's become a bit crowded in here. Shall we . . . ?"

When he gestured, I took the hint. It was long past time for us to get the hell out of there. Aside from the danger the vampires presented, there was something wrong with me, too. I needed to get out, clear my head, and get ahold of myself.

Sara led the way, bounding up the stairs two at a time. I couldn't really blame her for wanting to rush out. Yet she stopped at the door, blocking the exit.

I started to ask her what was wrong, but the words trailed off as a foul stench wafted into the room. All the anger faded away like smoke on the wind as that combination of death and rot invaded my nostrils like a physical assault.

The vampires behind me started complaining— some of them blaming Brendan for the stink—but then Sara was stumbling back into me, and I didn't have time to worry about where it was coming from.

Bloated, discolored fingers with long, jagged nails were grabbing at Sara's shoulder and arm, dragging her out through the door. By the time I got over my shock enough to reach for her, she was gone.

"Sara!"

She screamed, and I heard wet thumps—she must have been fighting back. Thrane was trying to haul me back while I was tugging at his grip on my collar to get free and chase after her.

"Get out of the way! We need to shut the door!"

"Let go!"

He did. I charged up the stairs and out, though I skidded to a stop at the sight before me, barely registering the sound of the door slamming shut and locking behind me.

Zombies had converged on the alley, dead bodies in various states of decomposition shuffling about aimlessly, save for a few that were still crouched over a red puddle and pile of body parts stained with thick, blackish blood. Trinity. I recognized her kitten heels on the dismembered leg being munched on by one of the monsters.

Sara was struggling and gagging in the arms of a dead man who towered over her, his lips bluish-green and peeled back from yellowing teeth, sunken, milky eyes staring at nothing in particular. He didn't react to the thumps against his forearms and shins as she beat at him, and it was no wonder why. I doubted there were any nerve endings left to feel anything in that walking corpse.

Some of the zombies turned in my direction, all gaping mouths and hollow or desiccated eyes. My back thudded against the door.

A few started shuffling toward me, their feet dragging and arms slowly rising as they approached.

"Stop, stop, stop! Those are humans, you bleeding idiots."

The zombies stopped exactly where they were, frozen in place. A few feet away, one tipped over on its side, losing its balance since it still had one foot in the air. It kept the pose even when it fell with a wet smack onto the pavement.

Another was close enough to me that its shriveled, mummified fingers were only inches from my throat. I couldn't stop staring into the empty, gaping holes of its eye sockets, every breath coming short and sharp, too rapid for me to manage a scream.

"Morons. All of you. Back up, you lot. Bring the other one over here."

The ones closest to me shuffled back, some of them voicing what sounded like annoyed moans.

A man soon stood before me, his hands on his hips and his brilliant green eyes narrowed with irritation. He towered over me, nearly Chaz's height, though he was skinny as a rail. I thought that might be an Armani suit draped on his lanky frame. Whatever it was, it wasn't off the rack.

He gestured angrily at the zombies, shooing away the ones blocking the path of the zombie still clinging to Sara, so it could set her down next to me. She smelled *awful,* and I didn't even want to know what that was it had left behind in her hair. The stink grew worse as she clung to me, one leg hooking around mine as she grabbed at me and simultaneously tried to crawl under my skin and shove me in front of her.

I couldn't blame her. I was pretty freaked out, too, though I was currently a bit too scared to do more than stand there staring stupidly at the necromancer.

Once the zombies shuffle-walked their way into a

rough semicircle around us, some of them dripping some black liquid from hands and mouths, the guy regarded us with a frown. He slid a long-fingered hand through his dark brown hair, settling some of the gelled spikes against his skull. "Well, this is a new development. I don't suppose you two were here with that fruit fly pretender, were you?"

Neither Sara nor I could figure out what he was talking about. We were a little too worried about having our entrails ripped out through our throats to consider it.

"For the love of Crowley, will you two stop looking at me like that? They're not going to hurt you."

Sara made a high-pitched keening sound. I think I might have gibbered something, but I'm not sure what.

"Right. Excellent. You know, just do me a favor. When you get back to that do-me queen, Clyde, you tell that asshole that I'm coming for him next. Got it?"

We both nodded, fingers digging into each other's skin and hair. That might have been blood or something else trickling over my fingers by her cheek. Didn't know, didn't care.

He sighed, and moved closer, lifting his hand. "Yeah. Of course you got it." I had time to notice that his palm was tattooed with an intricate design of a star in a circle with a few other smaller symbols inside, very similar to the design I had seen burned into the floorboards at Arnold's apartment, before he pressed his hand against Sara's temple. "Sleep."

Her body was a sudden deadweight against mine, dragging me down to the ground as my weak knees gave out. He knelt down, his bright, nearly glowing eyes boring into mine, sucking me into a cold, lonely place.

"That goes for you, too. Sleep."

My vision grayed at the edges and faded to a pin-point. It felt like all of my strength flooded out of my body as I slumped over, my cheek resting on the dirty alley floor. It might have been my imagination, but I thought he might have touched Sara's arm, brushing his fingers over her sleeve.

Before long, the necromancer rose and dusted off his pants legs, striding purposely toward the mouth of the alley. He snapped his fingers, and the zombies trailed after him in a slow shamble, leaving us alone with what remained of Trinity in a black-and-red-stained pile a few yards away.

Then everything went black.

Chapter 17

". . . stinks, man. Are you sure we have to help them? We're never going to get enough karaoke spots for all of us if we don't leave now."

"Shut up, Leewan. Pick that one up."

"Damn it, why do you get to carry the pretty one?"

The "pretty one"? Meaning Sara, not me. Awesome. Duly noted: Leewan was an asshole.

"Because I'm the boss of you. Now *be quiet* and get the other one."

Cold, strong fingers slid under my arms, and the sensation of being dragged across the concrete woke me up a bit more. I couldn't bring myself to open my eyes yet.

Pavement heat soon changed to a grave-like chill, and Leewan's grip shifted as he picked me up off the ground. "Cripes, they stink. You sure you want to bring them into the hideout?"

Thrane didn't answer him. I squinted my eyes open as Leewan grumbled under his breath, taking the steps with a gait so jarring, my teeth were rattling. He glanced down at me as I groaned, giving me a fangy grin.

"Wakey, wakey!"

I gave him the most irritated glare I could muster under the circumstances. "Anyone ever tell you you're an asshole?"

He shrugged and dropped me. I wasn't expecting it and voiced a little shriek that cut off as soon as my butt hit the couch, some of the air knocked out of me as my spine connected with the arm. *Owww.*

"Every day, but for you, I've trotted out an extra side of—"

"Leewan!"

Leewan looked up, frowning, then abruptly skittered out of Thrane's way with inhuman speed, giving the other vampire room to place Sara with a little more care on the cushions next to me. She was still out like a light. Thrane dusted his hands off and glanced at me.

"Normally I don't care much for anyone who threatens me and mine, but seeing as you got attacked by zombies on my doorstep, I figured I'd offer you two a hand."

"Yeah, right, Jimmy. You're just hoping the blonde will give you her number."

Thrane glared at Mac, but didn't dispute it. He turned back to me. "The gang knows they're not allowed to eat you. I'm going out. You can stay here until your partner wakes up. Bathroom's over there if you want to clean up." He hooked a thumb in the direction of a door with chipped, peeling paint and a black and yellow "Caution: Hazardous Area, Authorized Personnel Only" sign tacked on.

Some of the other vampires got off the couches and floor cushions to follow Thrane out of the basement and into the night. He started belting out "Panic Switch" by the Silversun Pickups once he reached the top of the stairs, spreading his arms wide and tilting his head back like he was howling the song to the heavens.

Half of the ones following him soon picked up the song, too, the pack of singing vampires disappearing into the night, the sound not quite fading entirely as the door slammed shut behind them.

I wondered if maybe I was dreaming. Really weird dreams as a result of the mage's dark magic or something.

"Don't mind Thrane," Shannon, the girl in the nice clothes, said, glancing at me over the top of a very outdated magazine. "He's not totally right in the head, but he means well."

Lifting my hands to rub at my temples, I leaned forward, doing my best to ignore the twinge in my back. "That's great. I don't suppose you have any idea what the hell happened out there?"

She shrugged and tossed the mag aside, lifting her legs to cross them at the ankles and let them dangle over the side of the couch Thrane had been on when we first got here. Her dark eyes examined me with curiosity, her lips quirking upward. "You going to be able to make it back to wherever it is you're staying?"

"I have no idea. If the car is still out there, maybe, but we're not from around here so I don't know if I can find my way back without directions."

"Clyde's place in Santa Monica? I can write it down for you."

I nodded thanks, scrubbing my palms over my cheeks and doing my best not to start crying. Across the country from my friends and family, lost in Los Angeles, and stuck with a bunch of lunatic, fringe-hobo vampires. If I saw Clyde again, I just might throttle the guy for putting me in the middle of his mess. That's assuming he hadn't been murdered by zombies by the time we got back to his place.

Sara groaned and shifted, bringing a hand up to her temple. ". . . The fu . . ."

I patted her shoulder and scooted forward, getting a bit shakily to my feet. Shannon rose far more gracefully than I did, rolling to her feet and offering me an arm. Waving her off, I headed to the bathroom, hoping washing some of the zombie bits off of me and splashing some cold water on my face would help me get over whatever the mage had done to mess with my head.

My trembling fingers slid up to my neck, closing around the gold chain there. I tugged the charm out from under my shirt, glancing down. The black and gold rectangle the size of my pinky nail was still there. Why the hell hadn't it blocked the necromancer from messing with my head? The tiny runes etched into it still had a dim glow. What the hell was wrong with it?

Whatever. I'd ask Arnold the next time I talked to him.

The bathroom was tiny. A toilet was sandwiched between a leaky sink and a shower stall, and the towels hanging over the stall and from a rack were threadbare. At least it was clean.

I ran some cold water and cupped it in my hands, splashing my face. It didn't do much to wake me up, but at least I felt a bit cleaner. The smell of zombie was probably going to stick with me until I showered, and that wasn't something I was about to attempt in this nuthouse.

By the time I was done, Shannon had some directions for me and Sara was looking groggy but awake. She got up from the couch and rushed into the bathroom as soon as I got out of the way, and the sound of running water soon followed.

"Thank you," I said to Shannon, giving her a wan smile.

She returned the smile and handed me the paper. "Anytime. Sorry if Thrane or any of the others gave you a scare. If you end up stranded in our neck of the woods again, just call me and I'll take care of it."

I nodded, lifting a hand to rub at my eyes so I wouldn't lose it. My emotions were too much in flux for me to control myself right then.

As soon as Sara was done rinsing her face (and I hoped to God managed to get out whatever the heck that had been in her hair), we thanked

Shannon once more and headed back out into the night.

The area still stank of zombies. No one had called the cops, which didn't surprise me too much considering the quality of the neighborhood. What remained of Trinity was a pile of parts and meat in a puddle of black and red congealing blood. The car sat unmolested at the mouth of the alley.

When we tried the doors, they didn't open.

The keys were somewhere in that mess.

Sara and I leaned against the car and contemplated walking back to Clyde's. All twenty miles or so, mostly uphill.

In the end, I lost our impromptu game of rock-paper-scissors and had to fish around in the mess for the keys. The squishy feeling was the worst part. Though I couldn't say I was too torn up about Trinity's fate, this was quite possibly the most disgusting thing I had ever done.

My fishing resulted in $0.87 in change, a cell phone that still worked despite being liberally doused in goo, and the car keys. The clicker didn't work until I smacked it against my palm a couple of times; then it unlocked the car. We found some napkins stuffed in the glove compartment and used them to wipe off the phone and the keys.

As badly as I wanted to get away from Thrane's hideout, I wanted to get away from Los Angeles even more. As soon as Sara was done cleaning the phone, I dialed Royce's cell, pacing in front of the car. She leaned against the hood and watched me, eyes wide and arms wrapped around her ribs.

It didn't take him long to pick up. "Hello? Who is this?"

"It's me. Royce, please, you've got to let us come back."

"Ahh," he said, dropping his initial guarded tone. "Why aren't you calling me from the phone you were given? You're lucky I picked up; I usually screen my calls."

"It's Clyde's fault. He had someone go through our stuff as soon as we arrived. They confiscated my phone, and this is the first time I've been able to get my hands on one when I didn't have one of his people breathing down my neck."

He voiced a low growl that still managed to carry over the line. "I see. That was not part of the arrangement I made with him."

"When can Sara and I come back? Can you get us a flight tonight?"

"I'm afraid I can't do that yet, Shiarra. There are still problems—"

"You have *no idea*, Royce. None. Sara and I were just attacked by a fucking necromancer."

He made a sound—maybe a cough—before replying. "You—are you certain? An actively practicing necromancer in Los Angeles?"

"Well, gee. He only had some glowing green eyes, some weird star-shaped tattoo thing on his palm, and, oh yes! Directed some zombies around. Come to think of it, I'm not sure."

"Sarcasm won't help matters. Where is Clyde? I'll speak with him about it."

It took an awful lot of effort not to scream at the phone. I was getting the idea that maybe my emotional state was a bit more raw than I had initially gathered. Before I might say something I'd regret later, I took a couple of breaths and counted to ten in my head. Then answered him.

"He's the asshole responsible for our running into the mage. He told us that we had to find the guy if we wanted to continue to stay with him. We can't do this, Royce. Please, forget talking to Clyde—can you send us somewhere else? Anywhere but here?"

"Unfortunately, not on such short notice. Pulling you out of there now would be an insult to Clyde's hospitality, and the only other person I'd feel you might be safe staying with has been experiencing difficulties with Max Carlyle recently. I don't want to send you out of the country or I might have placed you in Luxor with my eldest." He cursed softly, the sound barely carrying over the line, then quieted. I wasn't sure what to say in reply. The growl that came next was somewhat distorted, but he was obviously displeased with this turn of events. "Damn Clyde. He was paid well to keep you safe. If I'd had any idea . . ."

"Don't coulda-woulda-shoulda," I said. "I've already done enough of that for the both of us. Can you please just try to think of something?"

"Yes," he replied in a hiss, his anger palpable even

through the phone line. "I should have destroyed him when I had the chance. . . . For now, try to stay out of trouble. I didn't want to bring you back here until I had matters with the police in hand, but it seems I have little choice. Give me a day or two to smooth things over with Clyde and make arrangements. Can you manage?"

As much as I wanted to get in the car and start driving back to New York *right that minute,* that wasn't a good idea. Hopefully the necromancer would stay away for another couple of days.

"I'll do my best. Sorry to—you know, I'm—"

"Don't. Don't apologize. This was my error. It was a snap judgment, and I should have gathered more information about what was going on in California before I sent you there. Just stay safe, and try to be patient. I'll get you out of there."

"Thank you," I said, giving Sara an exaggerated nod to answer her questioning look. "I found an old friend. Maybe we can stay with him until it's time to go home. Or go to Sara's sister's place—"

"No. Not yet. The complications of insulting Clyde are too numerous for me to go into right now, but trust me when I tell you it is a bad idea. Let me call him. Just stay with him for now. I'll get you out of there as fast as I can."

We said our good-byes, and I hung up, shoving the phone into my pocket. It would probably come in handy later.

"We have to stay here for now," I said to Sara,

moving around the car to take the driver's seat, "but he's going to get us out as soon as he can."

She pushed off the hood and kicked the nearest tire with a curse, then got in the passenger side. "Seriously? Why can't we just get out of town right now? Stay at Janine's place in Malibu?"

"We can't risk upsetting Clyde. Some vampire political bullshit."

She cursed again, but more quietly, resigned. "What are we going to do? I don't want to go back there. What if the necromancer follows us or shows up while we're there?"

I tilted my head against the headrest, closing my eyes. There were no easy answers—though an idea occurred to me. "Maybe we can pretend like we're still on the case for Clyde, but slip away and hang out with the White Hats for a while. Devon probably wouldn't mind having us around."

Sara snorted. "White Hats. Since when did they become the better option?"

That got a small laugh out of me. With a resigned sigh, I opened my eyes. Time to go face Clyde and see what he thought of this mess.

I handed her Shannon's directions, my fingers tight on the steering wheel as I stared at the street ahead of us. Having a meltdown would have to wait until I was somewhere quiet and alone. The temptation to drive somewhere—anywhere—else was eating at me like a cancer. I put the car into drive and peeled off, tires squealing, as I made for the freeway.

"This sucks," she whispered.

My answer to Sara, when it finally came, was as much for me as it was for her.

"You're telling me."

Chapter 18

After a few wrong turns and a little bit of trouble from the security guard at the gatehouse guarding the entrance to Clyde's community, we managed to make it back to the vampire's home in one piece. I parked the car as close to the guest house as possible, intending to hold on to the keys and make use of it later—hopefully without a babysitter the next time we went out.

Though I knew Clyde needed to be informed about what had happened to Trinity, I wasn't looking forward to being the bearer of bad news. Without her around to let him know we were coming, we were going to be dropping the bomb on him with no advance warning. Who knew how he might react?

When we got up to the house, the security guards let us in, asking about Trinity and exclaiming about the stink clinging to our clothes. Since one of them was the guy who had led us to Clyde the first night we showed up, I didn't think it would be such a bad idea to tell him what was going on.

"We were attacked. She didn't make it."

The guy gaped. "Are you—she's—wait, but then why are you—"

"Alive?" Sara spread her hands. "We're not sure. But we really need to talk to Clyde. Is he around?"

The security guard held up a finger for us to wait while he turned away and muttered into the speaker of his earpiece. He waited, then said something else. Nodding to no one in particular, he took off at a trot, gesturing for us to follow him. "Come on. He's going to meet you in his parlor downstairs in a minute. After you talk to him, I'd like the whole story, and some directions so I can find whatever is left of Trin."

"You're going to need a garbage bag," I muttered, though I followed him without protest. Now wasn't the time to start annoying the other guards. Not if we wanted to be left to our own devices. I was starting to formulate a plan for how we might lose any tail Clyde was intent on keeping on us while we continued our "investigation" on his behalf.

Soon we were back in the room where we'd first met Clyde. The moon was still mostly full, this time gleaming over the ocean, casting a glimmering reflection over the waves. The lights were low, and Clyde was shirtless, pacing in front of the windows. Fabian was sprawled on one of the couches, also shirtless, watching us with narrowed eyes as he stirred some thick liquid in a bowl on the floor with a finger.

They both made faces when we arrived, though neither commented on the scent of *Eau de Zombie* that clung to us like cheap perfume.

"Well," Clyde said, not bothering to look at us, "I hear you have some unpleasant news for me. Care to explain why you returned without your body-guard?"

I frowned at him, though he wouldn't see it considering how he was so busy pacing like a jungle cat and staring out the window. "We didn't have enough plastic baggies to bring all of her back with us. Sorry."

That jarred him. He stopped, one hand on the glass, and tilted his head to look at us. The moonlight cast an eerie reflection on his eyes, making them appear colorless. Lifeless. Like the zombies. The thought alone made me shudder, but there was no point in being worked up about it. Royce would get us out of here soon—I hoped—so maybe Clyde's problems wouldn't seem like such a big deal once we figured out how to keep out of his way until then.

"You ran into Gideon." At our blank looks, he clarified, the strange lack of color in his eyes being replaced by the glimmer of red. "The necromancer. Did he kill her?"

Sara and I both nodded.

"Damn it, Fabian, can't you reason with him?"

Well, this was a new development. We both looked

at Fabian, and I'm pretty sure Sara was exhibiting as much shock as I felt.

The other vampire lifted his finger and sucked off the liquid he'd been stirring in the bowl, the look he gave Clyde so heated that I'm shocked the guy didn't burst into flames then and there. I suspected that the stuff Fabian was playing with was blood, but either way, this didn't feel like the right time to be interrupting these two. The air was charged with some kind of bad juju, and I wasn't too sure sticking around to find out why was such a good idea.

"I'm afraid not. He's quite incensed. I did tell you this might become a problem."

Clyde hissed, leveling a finger at Fabian. "You did not tell me he would start picking off my people, one by one."

"How was I supposed to guess that he would take it so personally?"

Clyde shook his head, turning those red eyes back on us. "Tell me what you've learned, and make it quick."

I stepped forward, letting Sara use me as a makeshift shield so she wouldn't have to meet his burning gaze. Even if the charm wasn't at full strength, if Clyde lost his temper, I was in a better position to defend myself against it than she was, however marginal that "better position" might be. My mind was racing, wondering just how much Clyde had kept from us, and just what kind of test not

telling us what he knew about the necromancer—
like his name—had been.

"We have narrowed down the list of possible
cities where he might be staying, but that's about it.
He must have known we were in the area somehow.
We were interviewing Jimmy Thrane." Clyde bared
his fangs at that, but didn't interrupt. "Trinity chose
to stay behind and wait outside. When we came out,
she was already dead."

In pieces. Many, many pieces. And considering
how he had reacted to Thrane's name, I wasn't
about to tell Clyde that we had gone to visit one of
the Goliath werewolves, either.

He resumed pacing, clenching and unclenching
his fists as he did so. This was not the image of a
master vampire in control of his empire. Even so, he
was dangerous. Perhaps more so than before. The
veneer had been stripped away, leaving a shadow of
a monster, frightened and backed into a corner,
ready to lash out at any convenient excuse.

"I received a call from your master this evening,"
Clyde said, his voice cutting. "You do not appreciate being hired to help me, I assume. He says you
wish to leave."

Well, yeah. No kidding. However, I didn't think
that would be a wise response. Nothing appropriate
was coming to mind—so Sara stepped in, her voice
tremulous and wavering.

"It's not that we don't appreciate your hospitality, but we miss our own homes and families. Our
friends. All the things we left behind."

That reminded me of my idea, and I was quick to jump in, forcing a measure of enthusiasm into my voice. "As long as we're here, we're still on the case for you."

Sara and Clyde both shot me a look. It was uncomfortable to be on the receiving end of those mixed signals, but I pressed on.

"It would help if you were a little more open with us about what's going on—" Fabian's black stare felt like a physical blow. I took a hasty step back, bumping into Sara in the process as I rushed out the rest. "If you can be, that is. We've got some friends who might be able to tell us more about where this guy is. Anything else you can tell us would help, of course, but we've triangulated the area where he is most likely staying and can probably find him with more time. As long as we're left on our own to search, of course, since it seems like he'll kill any of your people who are with us."

Please, God, don't let him realize why I don't want him to send any other vampires out on the road with us.

Clyde studied me for a time. Though I was expecting him to be the one to answer me, it was Fabian who spoke up, his voice rich with condescension. "You ladies may think you're fooling him, but you do not fool me. If you believe you can hide from Gideon, you are quite mistaken."

Sara cleared her throat, her voice coming out more steady this time. "Would you mind telling us what else you know about him aside from his name? We might have been able to move this investigation along faster if you'd come clean from the start."

Fabian's eyes flickered, but he favored her with a lazy grin. No fangs. No threat. Not yet.

"He was my lover."

Oh, that was not a happy thought.

"We wish to keep this amongst ourselves, you understand. It is a private affair, not a matter for the authorities. If we can find him, then I may be able to speak with him privately. If not, then he will continue this ridiculous assault—"

"Ridiculous? He's killed some of my oldest and most skilled progeny!" Clyde sputtered, his voice taking on a slight lisp around the extended fangs. "You can't possibly think that this matter—"

"May I finish?"

Clyde glowered at Fabian, but quieted. By this point, it was becoming quite clear to me who was wearing the pants in this relationship.

"As I was saying," Fabian continued, turning his attention back to Sara, "he most likely believes that Clyde worked some form of magic to make me tire of him. Though it is far from the case, Gideon won't understand unless he hears it directly from me. And as I don't fancy him using his magics to overpower me in the process, I want to know where he is hiding during the day so that I might seek him out and prevent him from casting anything truly nasty before I can get in my say.

"Are you satisfied with this, or would you prefer"—he ran his tongue over a fang in an all too suggestive motion—"more details?"

"No," I said faintly, "that's quite enough for us."

Now that I had a better understanding of what we were after and why, I wished they had said something about this mess from the start. I might have changed the way I went at this case. Not by much, but maybe Sara and I would have looked at the behavior of the necromancer in a different light.

Then again, maybe not. The vampire murders were still pretty insane, even if it was the act of a jealous lover instead of a power grab.

Love was a potent motivating force, and people did all kinds of crazy things in its name. Look at what had happened with Helen of Troy. An entire city under siege, gone to waste, and a war remembered thousands of years later, all because of the abduction of a single woman.

Max Carlyle had done something similar, planning for who knew how many centuries to displace Royce as the master of New York and utterly destroy his empire. All because Royce had killed the woman Max loved.

One had to hand it to the Greeks. They thought big when it came to the destruction of their enemies.

"I'll assign you a new bodyguard tomorrow," Clyde declared, stalking over to the couch to kneel next to it, his hand drifting over Fabian's arm, which had resumed stirring the bowl once more.

"Perhaps a human one. I don't care for the idea of you two running around town with no protection. Even if Gideon would not hurt you, there are others who would."

Though I was thankful for his offer, I couldn't help but wonder what he had to gain by keeping us alive. Maybe Royce had threatened him with some form of dire consequence if he continued to use us to deal with the necromancer on his behalf, or if something terrible happened to us.

Clyde glanced at us over his shoulder, his eyes once again an icy blue. He had gained some control over himself, finally, though he was still clearly upset. "If you are going to continue your search, then we need to rethink how you will be going about it. I am not certain yet if I want to continue to use your services. We'll discuss this again tomorrow."

We were obviously dismissed. Sara shook her head and tugged on my arm, pulling me away, but Fabian held up a staying hand.

"Ladies, do not fret. You are still human yet, and Gideon does not trouble himself in the affairs of those who are not of Other blood, aside from doing his best to maintain a measure of secrecy about his presence and his actions. If you do continue your search, then knowing that may be of some use to you."

I offered him a wan, humorless smile. "Thank you, Mr. d'Argento. We'll keep that in mind."

He nodded, his own smile sly and secretive. I had

a bad feeling that Fabian had his own agenda and was planning something unpleasant for Clyde, who was currently quite interested in exploring Fabian's bare chest.

I didn't envy the vampire. Either one of them.

Chapter 19

When Sara and I got back to the guest house, the first thing we did was shower. Well, second thing for me. First I stored Jo-Jo's and Gavin's letters in my bag so I wouldn't forget them whenever it was time to leave. I didn't want to cause the family of were-wolves any more grief than they'd already suffered.

That task out of the way, I spent a lot of time scrubbing and scraping and dancing around the little globs of ick that came out of my hair. Some of it was probably from Sara's clinging to me, and the rest of it was most likely something I'd picked up during my time passed out on the alley floor.

Discovering just how many tidbits of grossness were clinging to me wasn't pleasant, but the relief I felt after I was clean was immeasurable.

Throwing on some sweats, I poked around in the drawers in the various rooms in the house until I found a pad of paper and some extra pens. Next, I went back into my room and made notes of what I already knew about this case, and the ties we'd established the necromancer had. Usually I liked to do this sort of thing on my computer—it made it easier to cross-reference—but that wasn't an option here. Spreading the papers out on my bed along with the map with the notations of where all of the attacks had taken place, I tried to see how everything fit together.

Fabian was now dating Clyde. He had previously dated Gideon.

Gideon was after Clyde's people, punishing the new beau instead of Fabian, who was supposedly the unfaithful one.

Why?

Most people, when cheated on, tried to retaliate by making their significant others jealous. Thus, Gideon's response made me believe that he was acting irrationally, but for a far different reason than a need to get back at Fabian. Retaliatory affairs were the most common reaction of someone who discovered he or she was being cheated on.

Granted, magi might have different thought processes than most humans, and who knew what drove a necromancer to act as he or she did—but attacking Clyde instead of Fabian didn't seem quite right.

My PI Spidey sense was tingling.

"You as suspicious of this mess as I am?"

I glanced over my shoulder at Sara, who was in the door rubbing her hair dry with a towel, and gestured for her to join me.

She tossed the towel over her shoulder and moved over to the bed, placing her hands on her hips. We both studied the papers, frowning down at them. Sara grabbed my pen and made a couple of small notations of her own, then traced some of the roads between the areas where the attacks had taken place.

None of them were too close to Clyde's home. Another thing that didn't quite add up if this was a case of Jealous Lover's Revenge Syndrome. If he really intended to hurt Clyde, and he was angry enough to commit murder in the process, then why wasn't he attacking the guy directly? Why the bit and piecemeal destruction of Clyde's empire instead of an all-out assault? He was commanding enough zombies that he should have been able to do or take whatever it was he wanted.

Sara tapped the map where Thrane's hideout was, on the spot where we had been attacked. "None of this is right. That stink was awful, but the zombies were still in pretty good shape, considering. If Gavin was right and they were out in the woods or whatever, from how uncoordinated they are, wouldn't they have been torn up from stumbling around? Or maybe a bit damaged from animals or insects? I didn't see much of anything like that."

I rubbed my chin, and then leaned over the map as my finger followed the path Sara's had only a moment ago. "Now that you mention it, yeah. Do you think Gideon's keeping them in a refrigerated warehouse? Or somewhere else?"

"I'm not even sure if it matters anymore. Are we really still looking for this guy?"

"Cripes, I don't know," I said, turning away from the mess on the bed to walk over to the windows and stare out at the little slice of ocean visible between the mountains. "I was hoping Clyde would decide to let us do this on our own so we could stay with the White Hats for a while. Devon probably wouldn't mind letting us stay there at night, at least until this mess with the zombies is cleared up."

"Yeah, maybe. You know more about the White Hats than I do. Will they help us? Or hide us, do you think?"

I thought about it, frowning out at the dim sparkle of moonlight visible on the water in the distance. "Possibly. I'll have to call Devon and see. Though I'm wondering if it might not be a bad idea to check some of the local cemeteries to see if that's where the bodies are coming from. Maybe that's why they didn't look so banged up. He might be getting them fresh from somewhere close, then putting them back when he's done."

"Huh. Didn't think of that," she said, a brow quirking up. "One other thing to consider—we don't know if Clyde's going to assign us another bodyguard or not. We can't exactly take a vampire's servant to a White Hat hideout."

"I know, but I don't have any easy answers. If we're going to get out of this alive, we're going to have to have some kind of backup plan. Even though we should probably wait until tomorrow to figure out what we're going to do, I get the feeling we're running out of time. There's too much we don't know about this mess."

"Like what Fabian is up to. I think he's got his own agenda, and that he's not entirely aboveboard."

I nodded, lightly slapping my palm against the window. "Why is it that everyone's been straight with us and given us information about the necromancer except the guy who should know him better than anyone we've interviewed so far?" I turned around, sudden realization making my eyes widen. "You don't think he's working *with* Gideon to take down Clyde's empire, do you?"

Sara regarded me very somberly, her already pale skin going ashen. "Shia, if that's what's going on here, we better keep our mouths shut. You saw how attached Clyde was in there—he may not listen to us. Plus they're already killing vampires. It wouldn't be a far stretch for that mage to take us out as collateral damage if we get in the way. We're in the middle of something much bigger than a lover's spat."

Much like Clyde had been doing earlier, I started pacing, unable to help my imitation of his actions. Adrenaline was spiking along with my fear, the sensation of being trapped squeezing my heart with heavy jaws. I needed an outlet for my nervous energy. Running my hands through my hair, I tried to think of a way out.

"We've got to think this through. Be smart about it. If Fabian succeeds at destroying Clyde before we get out of here, we're toast. If we don't keep looking for the necromancer, both of the vampires will suspect something, and we'll still be in trouble. As much as I hate to say it, I'm not as concerned about screwing things up for Royce at this point, either. If he had any idea what kind of danger we're in, I bet he'd agree."

Sara nodded. "You suggesting a plan of action?"

"I think we need to get the hell out of here."

"I'd rather you didn't," a male voice said from behind us. Sara and I both whipped around to see Fabian in the door, his head down and hands pocketed.

He only took a single step into the room, but it was enough to send us skittering back, both of us getting as far from him as we could in the small space. He lifted his head just enough to give us both a wry smile, raising a hand to gesture at us to stop what we were doing.

"Don't worry, my little lovelies. No need for that. I'm not here to do you harm."

I closed my fingers around the window latch at the small of my back, wondering if I could jump from the second story without breaking my legs in the process. That's assuming I could get the window open and leap out before he could catch me. Cripes.

He moved deeper into the room, looking down at all of the notes Sara and I had made. His lips quirked, though whether he was pleased or not with our work wasn't clear. His fingers brushed over the papers, his eyes flicking back and forth as he took in the details.

I hoped to God he didn't notice Gavin's name among the mix. It wasn't much of a secret that we'd been talking to the White Hats and to Thrane, but if he figured out I'd spent time among the werewolves known for hunting and eating vampires, who knew what his reaction might be. If he thought we were making too many allies among the people who might want to see him dead, then he might think *we* were better off being disposed of—if he wasn't considering as much already, that is.

When he looked up, he focused on me, his expression at first unreadable. Very slowly, his lips curved upward, though whether he was thinking I was amusing or that I looked edible was up in the air.

"You're smarter than Clyde gave you credit for. It's no wonder Rhathos saw something of merit in you, Ms. Waynest."

I didn't respond, my fingers twitching reflexively as his dark brown eyes focused solely on me. He put me in mind of a young Robert De Niro, all swarthy skin and smiles, and with all the Godfather connections and killer instinct that implies.

"You two are so quiet all of a sudden. But you had so much to say a moment ago." His grin became a bit more feral, his fangs lengthening as we watched. "Things that are best kept to yourselves. Gideon and I would hate to have our little surprise for Clyde spoiled."

Knowing I was right about a case had never felt so terrifying before.

"W-we won't say anything to him, we swear," Sara said, her voice wavering. I didn't take my eyes off Fabian, since he'd never looked away from me. "Please, we were trying to figure out how to stay out of this. We don't want to get involved."

"Correct," he said, moving closer to me until he could tip my chin up with a finger.

His eyes never wavered from mine, and his touch was bitterly cold. I didn't dare move, blink, or even breathe with him this close to me. Never mind biting me—the guy could snap my neck in an instant if I said the wrong thing.

"When Gideon and I are done here, as long as you have kept what you know to yourselves until then, I'll see you safely away from this city. It will be our little secret." He gave me a wink, like all this was just between friends. "I'm good on my word. You can count on it."

"Please," I choked out, trying not to faint, "we won't say anything, we swear!"

"Very good. I will advise Clyde to continue to keep a detail on you. What he knows—I know. Keep that in mind."

With that, he chucked me under the chin and then silently shot me and then Sara with a finger gun on his way out the door.

My knees gave out, and I slowly slumped down the wall until I was seated on the floor, staring up at the ceiling. This guy was going to kill Clyde, or at the very least take over his coterie, and who knew what he would do to us when it was over. We were in the middle of what was about to become a war zone with nowhere to hide and no way to escape what was coming. Fabian's promise notwithstanding, we had no guarantee that we would live through whatever the vampire and necromancer had planned.

Sara shoved away from the wall and shut the door, locking it. She leaned her brow against it, one fist pressed to the wood up by her temple.

Then she said exactly what I was thinking.

"What an enormous asshole."

We both burst into shaky laughter.

Chapter 20

We waited until daybreak to make a run for it.

We took Trinity's car. Not intending to steal it forever, of course—just to get us where we needed to go. As soon as we were sure Fabian was gone, I dug out the number Devon had given me and called him, letting him know that Sara and I were in hot water and needed a place to stay. He gave us an address and directions, and I told him we'd meet him first thing in the morning.

None of the vampires could follow us, and their human servants were more interested in keeping people out than trying to keep anyone from leaving. Though I was sure Clyde and Fabian would both be pissed, I was hoping they would consider us too minor a threat to put much effort into tracking us down.

Sara and I didn't have anywhere else to go. If we tried to return to Gavin, no doubt he wouldn't be happy to see us and might even kill us for showing up uninvited on his doorstep a second time. If we tried to go back to Thrane, Gideon might hurt him or other members of his flock. Without credit cards or IDs, I wasn't sure that we could travel, and we were not going to take a stolen car across state lines. At most, we'd take it across town and maybe mail the keys and a note with the address where we'd parked it to Clyde once we found a place to stay.

Unless he ticked me off. Then the keys might end up in a gutter somewhere. I hadn't decided yet.

We drove around for a while, taking a fairly circuitous route in order to lose any tail Clyde might have set on us. Once the sun had already been up for a while, and Sara and I were both starving, we thought it was safe to head to our assigned meeting spot with Devon. We hit a drive-thru first, grabbing some coffee and breakfast sandwiches, then headed to the address we had been given in Glendale, right on the edge of Eagle Rock.

The area was full of hills and winding roads, but we found our way easily enough with the directions we had been given. Though I didn't like the idea of having to march up the steep incline into the hills, I was afraid the car might have some kind of security system that Clyde or the cops could use to track it down, so I didn't want to park too close. If I'd had a choice, I would have parked it across the Valley and had Devon pick us up instead, but I didn't want to impose on his hospitality more than we already were.

Sara was only a little bit winded, but my chest was

heaving by the time we stopped at our destination six mostly vertical blocks later, our bags in tow. The address turned out to be a pretty nice house. Not of the caliber of Clyde's mansion, of course, but it was definitely in the upper-middle class range. White stucco walls and a red tile roof gave it a clean, homey look, while the tiny lawn with miniature palms and thick, manicured grass made it clear that whoever owned it took pride in maintaining the place.

Devon answered the door on the third knock, his hair still wet from the shower and wearing nothing but a pair of board shorts. He gave us both a boyish smile, far from the predatory or fake grins I had been seeing so often since I got here.

"Shia, Sara—good to see you two again. Come on in."

We stepped inside, following him deeper into the house. It was immaculate, with little artwork or furniture, though that seemed to fit with the pale gray tile floors and very white walls. It made the place blindingly bright, almost sterile.

He led us into a kitchen, gesturing for us to take seats at the table across the room. All of the appliances looked new, and the scent of coffee was permeating the place like the perfume of the gods.

Devon poured us both coffee, setting cream and sugar down before picking up a mug for himself and leaning against the counter. He gestured with his mug. "You guys look like you've been through hell. Are you going to be okay, or do you want to get some sleep before you go into the details of what happened?"

I rubbed my eyes with one hand, saluting him with my mug in the other. "Hell is a polite term for it. That necromancer is probably going to be looking for us as soon as the sun goes down, assuming Clyde's people don't find us first."

"Are you sure it's okay for us to stay with you?" Sara asked.

"Of course. You two are always welcome here. Though I do want to get you out of town as soon as possible. One of the other White Hats was planning a vacation in Vegas in a couple of days. If you want to hide out here until then, you can probably hitch a ride with him if you pitch in some gas money, and then catch a flight out of there back to New York."

That sounded like the sanest thing I'd heard since I had arrived in Los Angeles. I gave him a tremulous smile. "Thanks, Devon. You really are a lifesaver."

"Don't mention it. Though I would like to know what you two know about that necromancer. I don't like the idea of having one of those roaming free in my town. If you two ladies came across any info about where he might be hiding, I can have someone start looking for him now."

"I really wouldn't do that," I said, my grip tightening on the mug until my fingers burned.

"Why not? It's just another kind of mage. We can do what we do with Weres and other rogue mages. Snipe it."

Sara choked on her coffee.

Concerned, he grabbed a towel off the counter and pressed it into her hands, then thumped her on the back. It took her a minute to get her breath back. She blotted at the spilled coffee and thanked him, her voice barely a whisper.

As for me, I had to swallow a few times around the sudden dryness in my mouth to speak. And I wasn't going to start by correcting his use of "mages" instead of "magi."

"Devon, he's against hurting normal people. He doesn't deserve that."

Frown lines appeared between his eyes, and for the first time since I'd met him, I had the feeling I was on the opposite side of the playing field. "Don't be naïve. He's a necromancer, Shia. He deals with the dead. It's unnatural."

"It's true," Sara said, her voice scratchy from inhaling the coffee, "but he's not out to hurt humans. Just vampires. He's here because he's working with Fabian d'Argento, the master vamp from San Francisco, to do something to Clyde. We're not sure what yet—but whatever it is, it's bad."

The hunter withdrew, his normally easygoing expression gone grave, his eyes distant as he sized us up. I wasn't entirely sure what he was thinking. He'd saved me from the clutches of Max Carlyle long ago. He'd helped Royce in the fight against Max and his cronies, ensuring New York didn't fall into the hands of a bigger, badder monster. Would he see that, this time, the situation was no different?

Clyde might not have been the ideal biggest bad on the block, but I hadn't the slightest doubt that things around this town would rapidly worsen if the city fell into the hands of Fabian or one of his cronies.

Sara coughed into her fist, then started speaking again, holding Devon's gaze. "I know it's hard to believe, but it's true. Isn't there any other way of stopping him? There's been enough death already."

"I don't know. I'll have to talk to the others and see what they have to say."

I took another sip of my coffee, my thoughts racing. If we couldn't talk the White Hats out of sniping the poor bastard, that would be another death on my head. One was more than enough. There had to be something I could do to stop it.

Though I hated the idea of putting myself back in harm's way, I wasn't sure how else to warn the mage that he needed to get out of town. That was assuming I could find him before the White Hats did, or before the vampires found me, and that he didn't try knocking me unconscious again. Or end up setting his zombies on me.

Why did I have to grow a conscience now? Things would have been so much easier if I had just stepped back and let all of the monsters in this insane town do their thing and destroy each other.

The problem with staying out of the mess was that I had no idea what Fabian might choose to do to me or to Sara once Clyde was out of the way. Royce had made no mention of him as an ally, and

I was pretty sure that he wasn't the other "friend" Royce had mentioned we might have been able to stay with if not for Max Carlyle's interference.

It felt awfully coincidental that all of this was happening while I was in town. I hated that feeling, like someone had known in advance that I would be here, had planned for it, and was pulling strings behind the scenes to make sure I would suffer because of it.

"Sara, you look like you're about to fall over. You want me to show you to a room?"

Devon's words snapped my attention to my friend. He was right, of course. There were deep circles under her bloodshot eyes, her skin was more pale than usual, and she kept rubbing at her forearms through the fabric of her long sleeves as if they either ached or itched. It seemed a bit warm for that type of clothing to me, but then, it had been a long time since I'd seen her in any shirts that didn't cover her arms all the way to the wrist.

As if I wasn't feeling bad enough already, I felt like a shit for taking so long to notice that she wasn't feeling well. Hopefully it was nothing more than a combination of jet lag and lack of sleep catching up with her.

With a nod, she rose, setting her coffee aside. She'd barely touched it.

He offered her his arm and walked her out. I stayed where I was, cradling my drink as I considered what to do next. I wasn't going to abandon Sara again, but I was afraid of staying here with the White

Hats now that Devon had revealed they weren't beyond using tactics like shooting unsuspecting Others from afar. It shouldn't have surprised me—White Hats weren't exactly known for their temperance or compassion where Others were concerned—but it still bothered me that this was the same guy who had been so willing to work with Chaz and Royce for my sake.

I didn't know what kind of defenses a necromancer might have, but a bullet to the head was usually enough to stop anyone in his or her tracks. The idea of murdering the guy because he had no respect for dead bodies seemed a bit harsh, in my opinion.

Then again, I was now—sort of—friends with a number of vampires, and had even slept with one. Not all Others were truly monsters. Or, rather, even if they were by nature a monster, it didn't mean their actions or character were always villainous.

No more than the necromancer, anyway. He certainly wasn't an innocent, and his actions weren't completely aboveboard. Even if Trinity had been a bit of a skank, and kind of bitchy, it didn't mean she deserved to die either.

This was all too much to think about after an all-nighter without coffee. I downed what little was left in my mug and looked up as Devon returned, his hands pocketed and his expression pretty sober considering his state of relative undress.

"She was almost out before her head hit the pillow. You guys must have been working hard."

Saluting him with my mug, I made a face. "That's us. Workaholics. It's been nothing but fun-fun-fun since we got here."

His lips twitched in a smirk. "I can imagine."

He moved closer, and I couldn't help but admire the fine play of muscles on his abdomen when he walked. No doubt, that was a gym-made washboard, but that didn't make it any less fun to watch in action.

Once he reached the table, he hooked the chair next to me with his foot and pulled it out, sliding into it in a manner that I might well have called flirtatious if I hadn't known any better.

Who was I kidding? Of course he was flirting. He'd expressed interest in me before he had left New York—why wouldn't he want a few minutes alone with me? I could only imagine how quickly that was going to change once he knew what my relationship with Royce had become. If you could call what I had with the vampire a relationship.

Even so, I felt a pang of acute longing when I considered the possibility of staying here in Los Angeles and attempting to make a go of things with Devon. He might have been a hunter, but he was also human—the one thing I'd desperately craved in a relationship, yet for whatever reason had never been able to find.

Giving in to the temptation of that admittedly delightful body would smack a bit too much of betraying whatever it was I now had with Royce. Which didn't make it hurt any less when I took the coward's way out.

"I'm sorry, but I'm really wiped, too. Where can I crash?" And hide from an inevitable conversation I didn't want to have?

Chapter 21

I didn't get much sleep. When I took a look out the window, the sun was still high in the sky. There wasn't much point in trying to get back to sleep; my stomach was growling, and I had too much on my mind to drift off again with any ease anyway.

I pulled some fresh clothes out of my duffel bag, frowning at the contents. Saving the master vampire of the city from a devious necromancer didn't leave much extra time for laundry. I'd ask Devon what I could do about that later.

Sara was already downstairs and talking to Devon, Tiny, and a couple of other White Hats I recognized from that bar we'd visited. She was looking a little better, but there were still circles under her eyes, and there was something I couldn't quite put my finger on that seemed a bit "off" about her. Maybe she was coming down sick.

Tiny got up, drawing my attention off of Sara as he pulled out a seat for me, giving me a friendly clap on the back that nearly sent me sprawling. With strength like that, the guy could have easily been mistaken for an Other. Probably something Were. I grinned and thumped him back on the arm before settling into the chair.

"We were just discussing what to do about this necromancer," Devon said, giving me a look that I interpreted as "and you're really not going to like the direction this talk is going, but try not to make a fuss about it, thanks."

One of the other White Hats poked at the bowl of chips in the middle of the table, stuffing some in his mouth before speaking around half-chewed crumbs. "I like Sara's idea. Maybe wait until that vamp from San Fran makes his move, then see what the necro does next. If they're both from up north, he might just leave after they get what they want. And I'm all for someone taking out that poser, Clyde."

"It's less work for everyone if we just let them take each other out," Devon said, giving me a pointed look. Though I didn't like the turn of the conversation, I kept my mouth shut.

Letting the vampires destroy each other might not have bothered me so much if I hadn't spent time getting to know Mouse, Clarisse, Ken, and some of the others who lived under Royce's watchful eye. They were monsters, yes, but they were people, too. Even if Clyde was an asshole, I wasn't sure that he deserved what was coming.

Aside from which, if my doing nothing resulted

in one or more of them dying, that just didn't sit right with me—but I wasn't sure what to do about it. The White Hats weren't about to try to stop Others from killing each other, particularly if it made their mop-up job of picking off the survivors easier. Hell, the White Hats might even be pleased if the Others killed each other off and saved them the work of interfering.

Having to deal with the guilt of letting Clyde continue to be used by Fabian and of having more (relatively) innocent vampires die at Gideon's hands wasn't high on my to-do list. I could always call Royce and tell him to tell Clyde what I had learned, or maybe hunt for a direct number in Trinity's phone, but I wasn't sure that Clyde would believe me or have any way of stopping the gears Fabian had set in motion. There was also no guarantee that alerting Clyde would prevent all-out war. It might only act as a catalyst for a battle between the vampires for control of Los Angeles.

Perhaps Arnold would know how to neutralize the necromancer without hurting him. It was the only solution I could think of that might head off what was starting to look like an inevitable massacre.

"Guys, I just thought of something. Before we make any hasty decisions here, let me give one of my friends a call. He might know how to stop the necromancer. If there's anything we can do to make him back off before things get rough, we might save some lives, huh?"

Some of the hunters shrugged, none of them

too enthused, but nobody disputed my request. Probably because I didn't specify that I wasn't just hoping to save the lives of human bystanders.

Sara gave me a look, mouthing "who?" at me. When I lifted my brows and wiggled my fingers, she snorted and sat back. She got who I meant, but didn't seem to think much of my idea. Maybe she'd already asked him?

Even though I had Trinity's cell phone with my things in the bedroom, I didn't want to risk the battery running out of charge since it was the only way Royce had to get in touch with me. I turned to Devon, who put a plate of food in front of me. "Do you have a phone I can use?"

"Sure. After you eat. You and Sara both need to stop waiting until you're completely worn out to take care of yourselves."

Shrugging, I tucked into the food he set in front of me. He'd put food in front of Sara, too, but she was only picking at it, not really eating it. That wasn't a good sign. Whatever was going on with her was worrisome, but I had a full list of issues at the moment, so I'd have to find out what was up with her as soon as I was sure the rest of the immediate messes I was dealing with were under control.

The other hunters talked about things that didn't concern me. Where people I didn't know were hanging out tonight, who was coming along on the scouting party checking in on some of Clyde's properties later, local politics that didn't interest me, and when to meet at The Brand. It took a bit for it to sink in that Devon intended to go with a group of these hunters a little closer to sundown, and take Sara and me with him.

Barely tasting the food I was shoveling into my mouth, I set down my fork and pushed the plate aside, turning to frown at the hunter. "Why are we leaving? Shouldn't we stick around here if we're going to hide?"

Tiny snagged a piece of sliced melon off the side of my plate, shaking it at me to emphasize his point before shoving it into his mouth. "We need him tonight, and we're not going to leave you two alone. You'll be safe at The Brand. We've got enough hardware there to stop an army of leeches."

Though I didn't like the idea, I had no alternative to offer. Neither did Sara. She pushed her plate away, most of the chicken on her plate shredded instead of eaten.

"Devon, you want to show me to that phone?"

He nodded, gesturing to the living room just outside of the kitchen. "There's a phone in there."

I thanked him and headed over, spotting the phone on an end table next to a couch. It was wireless, so I took it up to the guest room I'd slept in and pulled my Rolodex out of the duffel I'd been carting around.

Arnold didn't pick up. A little bit annoyed, I scrambled for Trinity's phone, poking around the options to find the phone number before I ran out of time to leave it in the message. The battery still had about half a charge, but I would have to be careful not to mess with the phone too much unless someone had a charger I could borrow that would work with the phone.

"Hey, it's Shia. Sara and I need some help. There are a bunch of problems right now, but the biggest one is that there's a necromancer working with another vampire to take down the vamp we were supposed to be staying with. Long story, but we're with some White Hats right now instead, and they're talking about killing the mage. Any advice about how we can neutralize the necro before the White Hats hurt him or themselves? Give me a call as soon as you can. The number is . . . um . . . one sec . . ."

It felt like it took forever for me to find it, but once I did I got the numbers out in a rush, then a second time, a little slower, in case he didn't get it the first time—but the message cut off right in the middle. Frig. I hoped he got the numbers.

I also really, really hoped he'd have some advice on how to deal with the necromancer. The thought of facing Gideon again unarmed, and with the charm around my neck not blocking all of the necromancer's powers to mess with my head, was not a happy one. Even if he had no intention of hurting a normal person, he might make an exception for me or Sara if Fabian told him to.

Tucking the cell phone in my pocket, I brought the cordless back to where I had found it and rejoined the White Hats in the kitchen. The guys were talking about sports, while Sara was talking to the only other woman in the room, some girl I didn't know. I couldn't make out what they were saying, and no one paid me much attention except for Devon when I slumped into a chair between him and Sara.

"Any luck?"

I shook my head, not really wanting to discuss Arnold in front of the others. Devon had met him before, but I wasn't sure how much he knew about the mage, or what he had thought of him at the time.

"Well," he said, brushing imaginary dust off his pants before rising, "why don't we get a move on, then? Come on. Let's hit the road."

The other White Hats got up, some of them adjusting weapons I hadn't seen while they were seated. It wasn't particularly surprising, just unsettling. Sara didn't seem to have any problems standing or walking, so some of my concern for her faded. Like I'd earlier figured, it was probably just a combination of jet lag, stress, and exhaustion from all the running around we'd been doing.

Tiny slung an arm over my shoulders, then ushered Sara to be on the other side of him. It wasn't anything possessive or creepy; he was genuinely friendly and was grinning down at us both like Christmas had come early. Judging by the flat stares and looks we were getting from the other White Hats, I was guessing that he was having a hard time making friends out here, and was glad to see us because we had never judged him or kept him out of the loop.

Not that I had anything against these White Hats,

but so far no one I had met in this town had been anything other than crazy, inhospitable, or flat-out hostile. Los Angeles was not going on my list of places to visit again anytime soon.

The sun was still a long way from setting, and I found myself wishing for a pair of sunglasses once we got outside. We piled into the three cars filling up the driveway, and a couple people even headed to the street to get into a fourth. Sara and I stuck with Devon, Tiny, and one of the other guys in a big SUV. The car was nice, clean, and a lot more expensive than what Devon had been driving back in New York.

I had to wonder what these guys did for money in this town. Did they have some kind of day job? How did they make enough money to afford these nice things, as well as support their hunting habits?

Whatever. Not my problem.

We took yet another freeway I'd never heard of. Staring out the window, I watched the world pass by.

We hit a traffic jam on the 134. Devon poked at his GPS, but even with the alternate route it spouted out, we were at a standstill. At one point, a cop passed us on a motorcycle, weaving between the cars. A black-and-white soon followed, driving on the median. Then another. And another.

There must have been some kind of major accident up ahead, because the traffic going the other way had stopped, too. There was a park off to our left that seemed pretty packed with people, most of them moving in our direction, towards the freeway. Probably coming to see what was going on.

I craned my neck a bit, trying to see around the driver's headrest.

"What the hell is that?"

Tiny's words drew my attention to where he was pointing. The people in the park.

Wait.

That wasn't a park. There were gravestones set into the grass, so neatly laid that at first glance, I hadn't noticed.

It was a cemetery.

"Devon, those are—"

He cut me off. "I know. That's Forest Lawn Memorial. Shit. We're in a lot of trouble."

The necromancer's powers weren't as hindered by daylight or witnesses as I'd been given reason to believe by Clyde and Fabian. That crowd—those weren't people. Not anymore.

And they were headed right for us.

Chapter 22

"Get out of the car! Go, go, go!"

We didn't need any more prompting from Devon. Everyone piled out and followed Tiny, who was leading the way around the maze of stopped cars and trucks to the nearest exit. Some of the other White Hats were joining us, too, getting out of their cars as soon as they saw what we were doing.

I glimpsed some zombies milling around the other side of the freeway, stopping traffic. There were more marching up an on-ramp on that side, moving in our direction. I had no doubt they were coming for me and Sara.

It was still a heck of a run, but we had to get off the freeway and away from the zombies doing their slow shuffle in our direction. When I glanced over my shoulder, even more of them were already over the fences surrounding the cemetery and what looked like a wide, man-made river past the road that ran between the park and the freeway. Despite all the obstacles in their way, most of the zombies were moving straight for us, even altering their path a little bit to adjust to our change in position.

How the hell did they know where we were? Why were they after—?

No. Stupid question. I knew why they were after us.

Rather than focus on the monsters coming toward us from the south, I put my attention on what lay ahead. People were rolling down their windows, sticking their heads out to see what was stopping traffic or watch us, though no one attempted to stop us. A passing cop on a motorcycle hollered at us to get back in our cars, but he kept going—probably on his way to face whatever was holding things up ahead.

The nearest off-ramp on our side was about a quarter of a mile away, and the traffic there was completely backed up, too. We dodged around the cars, working our way over to the side of the road, some of the White Hats pulling their guns or knives and holding them ready. It made me wish desperately for my own gear, but nobody had offered to outfit me with anything, and I hadn't thought to ask for any weapons before we left Devon's place.

I almost smacked into Tiny's broad back on the downslope of the off-ramp. I sensed something was wrong long before I saw it. Or smelled it.

The sick-sweet charnel reek of decaying bodies hit me like a smack in the face. The other White Hats were gagging, one of them on his knees at the side of the road, puking his guts out. Tiny's hand groped behind him, making contact with my shoulder, shoving me back.

I skidded on the dry, brown dirt and gravel, grabbing at a nearby side-view mirror to catch my balance. The cheap piece of crap came off in my hand when I put my weight on it, and I ignored the "Hey!" from the driver as I twisted around and ran back the way we had come.

The rest of the White Hats had stopped at the top of the ramp, their eyes wide and mouths open as they stared at what was behind us. So far I hadn't seen, but I was sure it would probably be a great deal like what Sara and I had witnessed outside of Jimmy Thrane's hideout.

One of the guys slapped a pistol into my hand when I hit the top. I spun around to see how close the zombies might be and to make sure the rest of the White Hats were out of harm's way.

Sara was lagging a little behind, but Devon had her around the waist and was dragging her up the incline. The other White Hats had their guns out and aimed at the zombies, but no one had fired any rounds yet. There was another gaggle of zombies at the bottom of the ramp, marching toward us in a loose formation. They weren't moving very fast, and some of the people in the cars were screaming or leaning on their horns, drowning out the sounds of radios and hush of commands being bantered between the hunters. One of the panicked drivers tried reversing, and the crunch of breaking glass and metal followed the squeal of tires on the asphalt.

Distant gunfire rang out from the direction the cops had been headed, echoing against the hillsides. A sharp crack, followed by a more full-throated boom, like a shotgun. More screams.

We had to get the hell out of there. The only way left to go was down the hillside along the off-ramp, opposite the cemetery, unless we wanted to risk running back the way we'd come. It was the only way we could go that wasn't being cut off by a swarm of walking dead. There was no way we could keep going forward. Whatever was up ahead was enough to keep a cop from stopping to question us when we left our cars—and from the look of all the lights flashing out of the corner of my eye and the thunder of a helicopter approaching, there were plenty more police on the way.

Cripes, was I wrong about Gideon and Fabian's plan? Were they trying to start the zombie apocalypse? This was a *much* bigger horde than we had encountered outside of Thrane's hideout.

A nearby cry from behind whipped my attention onto the White Hats at my back. There was a large group of animated corpses behind us, another group crossing the freeway, and a third coming from where all of the gunfire was originating, all moving to converge on our location. The screams from the cars around us were getting louder as the zombies approached, and more people were panicking and backing their cars into the ones behind them as they tried to escape the solid gridlock. Couldn't blame them for that, though escape at this point was a hopeless cause. There were too many monsters, and they were coming from multiple directions.

The White Hats had yet to open fire. I thought it might have been because of all of the innocent bystanders, but it might have been because of the police and witnesses, too.

Then I heard a roar. Not mechanical. The sound drowned out everything else, even the screams of terrified people around us.

Tiny gave me a not-so-gentle shove in Sara's direction, most of the White Hats and even the zombies turning in the direction the sound had come from. I couldn't be sure, but I thought the ground was shaking in rhythmic thumps.

I'm not sure if I screamed or not when I saw what had made that sound—what was causing the ground to shake. I was a bit too terrified at the time to tell.

Now, I've spent more than my fair share of time around werewolves. Their half-man, half-wolf form was nothing new to me. When shifted, they usually stood on their hind legs, upright like a man, with the head and tail of a wolf, complete with clawed hands and furred bodies. They're bigger than people in that form—unquestionably. Since I had dated one for a while, you would think I would have been fairly inured to what they were, what they looked like, and what they could do.

Then again, I'd never seen a shifted Goliath
before.

Rohrik Donovan was the largest shifted Were I
had previously run into, and he had easily been the
size of a particularly beefy Bengal tiger.

What stood before me was something completely
different.

Imagine a school bus. Now imagine a werewolf
that, from the tip of its snout to the end of its long,
swishy tail, was half the length of that bus.

You'd have a Goliath.

It galloped down the empty stretch of freeway
until it reached the nearest clump of zombies, tearing into them with all the aplomb of a chainsaw.
Rotted people parts flew every which way, gore spat-
tering its mottled gray coat, and the screams of
people in nearby cars were deafening. Most of them
stayed in their vehicles, but a couple tried making a
run for it. I couldn't tell if they got away or not.
There were too many zombies blocking the view on
the street for me to be sure.

The White Hats started shouting orders, and
some of them aimed their weapons at the Were. I
barely had time to scream, "No!" at them before a
few of them unloaded on the creature.

It yowled and looked our way, liquid golden eyes
swimming with hatred. Some of the teeth it bared
at us looked like they might be close to a foot long.

Real smart. That's right, go ahead and piss off
the gigantic, oversized, murderous werewolf.

The stupidity of the White Hats was going to be

their undoing, not mine. I tucked the gun into the waistband of my jeans and made a grab for Devon, who was still holding on to Sara, and for Tiny, tugging them after me. They all looked petrified, the White Hats' guns aimed at the gigantic werewolf stalking in our direction.

Its broad head swiveled toward us, and the teeth it had been baring at the hunters parted as it made some sound that was half growl, half whine. It made an annoyed gesture, that clawed hand sweeping in a negative motion, before it ducked its head and took a chunk out of a zombie that was still moving toward us.

Thank God it was only annoyed by the bullets instead of enraged. If it hadn't been so intent on tearing apart the walking dead, I'm sure it would have been White Hats spattered across the concrete instead. Hell, judging by the size of the thing, it probably could have thrown a car at us without breaking a sweat if it had been so inclined.

Gideon must have noticed something was wrong with the zombies. Maybe that they were being mowed down faster than they should have been, or possibly he sensed the way they were dying. I had no way of knowing how his tie to them worked other than through his ability to command them. Whatever clued him in, the bulk of the zombies shifted their focus from Sara and me to the Goliath that was tearing them apart.

I winced in sympathy when a few of them dug their rotted fingers into the Were's fur, some latching on with their teeth. We didn't have enough time to see what else the zombies or werewolf were about to do. Or if the bites made the Goliath turn into a zombie-werewolf. The thought alone was enough to make my blood run cold.

Devon, Sara, and Tiny didn't need much additional prompting to follow me. We rushed down the hillside, past some bushes and trees, and straight to the ivy-covered chain-link fence surrounding the blacktop of a parking lot behind an office building.

Tiny gave Sara a boost, while Devon and I scrambled to get over the top of the fence.

A womanly screech nearly shattered my eardrums and startled me so badly that I lost my grip on the top and landed so painfully on my back on the other side that all of the air was knocked out of my lungs. I stared up, gasping for air, as Tiny spun around to deck the zombie that had grabbed him. I could hardly believe the big guy had made such a high-pitched noise.

His fist went right through its rotted ribcage. I had to swallow back the urge to throw up, scrambling to my feet so I could help Sara over the fence while Tiny and Devon shoved at the creatures grabbing at them and reaching for us.

One of the zombies had Devon pinned against the fence, pulling him down before he could get onto the other side. His arm under its jaw kept the snapping teeth from latching onto him, but its long, dirty fingernails were clawing at his ribs, tearing up his shirt and leaving bloody streaks behind. Sara placed a piece of wood into my hand. A thick gardening stake or something. It didn't feel very sturdy, but I would make whatever use I got out of it count.

Hastening back to the top, I braced myself with one hand, hefting the piece of wood with the other. "Devon, down," I ordered, swinging up and over with as much strength as I could muster. He slid down, his thin wifebeater catching on the chainlink fence as he pushed the zombie toward me.

It was awkward, but it worked. The wood shattered but did an adequate job of staving the thing's skull in. We both got spattered with stinky gobs of some kind of pink and brownish fluid that had a mixed stench of chemicals and rot strong enough to make my eyes burn. Though my vision was blurred, I saw Devon shove the now limp body off of him and step in to help Tiny. He kicked at the corpse that was latched onto the other hunter's shoulders, gnawing at his upraised arm. I was amazed Tiny wasn't making a sound, other than a few pained grunts as he pushed at it with his good arm.

The thing didn't seem to notice Devon's attacks. Not even when tendons snapped as its knee buckled. I still had the gun, but I was afraid to use it for fear I might accidentally hurt Devon or Tiny in the process.

"Head shot! Go for the head," Sara called.

Devon backed up a step and kicked at the exposed jawbone poking through a hole in its cheek.

I didn't remember much about the specifics in my self-defense classes, but to my relatively un-trained eye, it looked like he had pretty good form for a thrust kick. The blow was powerful enough to stun the zombie, sending it crumpling to the side, yellowed teeth scattering across the ground like marbles. Its fingers clawed weakly at the patch of ivy it had fallen into, but it looked like it might be down for the count.

The two hunters scrambled over the fence, though Tiny had a hard time with his injured arm cradled against his chest. His dark skin was tinged a bit gray, and he was sweating profusely, but I hoped that was from the exertion and not because the zombie had infected him.

The four of us left the other White Hats behind, dashing across the parking lot. If we could get to the main drag, we might be able to flag a cab or catch a bus away from this crazy part of town.

Of course, Gideon had to be waiting for us at the entrance to the lot, hands on his jean-clad hips. His glowing eyes watched us over the lenses of rectangular, greenish sunglasses that should have looked ridiculous, but somehow fit perfectly on the guy. There had to be fifty zombies crowded around him, blocking the way out, waiting for us.

The way this trip had been going so far, why was I even surprised?

Chapter 23

"You two are really starting to get on my nerves," Gideon said, glaring at Sara and me over the tops of his sunglasses.

That startled a laugh out of me. "*We're* getting on *your* nerves? What the hell are you doing here? Starting the zombie apocalypse?"

Sara gave a slight start, and my gaze flicked over to her. Her brows had shot up, lending her an expression of mixed confusion and recognition.

It only then occurred to me that Gideon's "fade" spell might have been in effect in that alley outside Thrane's place. Sara must not have remembered what the necromancer looked like, though I certainly hadn't forgotten. Maybe that meant the charm on my necklace was working after all. It could cut through illusions and spells that were meant to affect a broad area, but wasn't powerful enough to resist a direct attack, like his command to make me sleep. Good to know the charm had its limits, though I wished Arnold had said something so I didn't have to learn through experience.

For his part, Gideon didn't appear very thrilled with us, either. "What? Of course not!" His lips pressed together, spots of color appearing high on his cheeks. Stalking forward, he stabbed a finger in my direction. "You need to stay the hell away from Clyde. What are *you* doing here with a bunch of hunters, hmm?" he demanded, waving a hand at Devon and Tiny, then in the direction of the other White Hats fighting in a clump just up the hill.

"She's a friend," Devon snarled, leveling a gun at the necromancer's head.

Gideon was not impressed. He rolled his eyes, waving a hand airily in Devon's direction. "Oh, please. Spare me the theatrics. Put the gun down."

"Get out of our way, and I'll put it down."

"Mmmm . . . no."

Gideon's gaze met Devon's, and his lips moved as if he were whispering something to the hunter.

Devon lowered the gun. His eyes glazed, his jaw going slack. Gideon was doing something similar to whatever he had done to Sara and me before when he had commanded us to sleep. A black enchant— the worst kind of way to mess with the mind. Stealing away a person's will.

There wasn't anything I could do about it. By the time I recognized what the necromancer was doing, he had finished toying with Devon's mind. Devon was clutching at his temples, the barrel of the gun pointed at the sky. Gideon grinned, pleased with himself, and was now looking at me.

Fuck.

"What did you do to him?" I asked, hating how my voice shook. I wondered if I could get off a shot before Gideon could pull the same trick on me.

"Oh, nothing much. Just kept him from getting any ideas about pulling that trigger when he's pointing that gun at me. And I won't hesitate to do the same to you." The necromancer's gaze flicked from Devon to me and back, his lips pursing. The hand he had been waving at Devon stilled, then clenched, one finger ticking back and forth between us. "You two . . . ?" One brow cocked in question.

"No," I said, imitating his earlier stance, hands on my hips. This guy was so obviously full of himself and what he was capable of that it made me briefly regret I hadn't turned Were. There was no way that I could see to hurt him back for what he had done. The best I could do was to hurl sarcasm at him. "What's it to you, anyway? We weren't coming after you *or* Fabian *or* Clyde." Not yet, anyway. Hoped he couldn't detect the little white lie. "We were going to meet some friends. How the hell did you know where we were?"

"Girlfriend, do not try me. You have no idea what kind of headache I have from raising enough zombies to make a bridge across the LA River and block the freeway, then simultaneously hold off police, a pissed off werewolf, *and* a bunch of vigilante hunters with *far* too high an opinion of their fighting abilities. Not to mention while holding a rational conversation with you. Cut the crap and give me the skinny. Why are you headed into town, and what the hell are you doing with a bunch of White Hats?"

A pained noise made me look over at Tiny. He had fallen to one knee, still clutching at his injured arm with his good one. Devon and Sara both rushed over to his side. The necromancer didn't try to stop them, but the zombies started inching forward. We had to get out of there.

"Please," I said, the words spilling out in a rush as I gestured frantically at Tiny who was now flat on his back, "we don't care what you and Fabian are up to. You want to kill Clyde? By all means, be my guest. Just let us go so we can take my friend to the hospital. I swear, we're just friends. I originally met them in New York. They helped me and Alec Royce out when another vampire tried to take over—"

"Max Carlyle?"

"Yes, him. He was attacking a bunch of the vampires in the city, and these guys helped us out. Royce sent Sara and me here to lie low with Clyde while he sorts out a mess I made back home. It's my fault we're here, not the White Hats'. Fabian said you guys were going to do something awful to Clyde, so we thought we'd be safer with the White Hats. That's all. Okay?"

Gideon considered this, one hand stroking his chin as he regarded me. The intense glow in his eyes faded a little. "Fabian informed me that you two had run off. He thought you were getting reinforcements to stop us. Stay out of our business, *capiche*?"

"Yeah, whatever—can we go now?"

He shook his head, stalking forward. Some of the zombies inched closer, though for the most part they hung back, still blocking the way out of the lot.

Gideon—unnecessarily, I might add—made sure he took a path that gave him a reason to give me a little shove on the shoulder, then bent to slide one hand in a very provocative way up Devon's back. "Out of the way, lover boy."

The hunter wasn't expecting the touch and fell on his side, scrambling away on hands and knees, before he remembered his gun and held it at the necromancer with both trembling hands. His finger tightened on the trigger, but not enough for the gun to go off. He cursed, the muscles and tendons in his arms and hands standing out in stark relief as he fought the mental suggestion preventing him from shooting.

All Sara did was lean back, but she didn't leave Tiny's side.

Tiny had closed his eyes, one huge hand engulfing Sara's. She glared over Tiny's prone form at Gideon, who wasn't paying any of us much mind, muttering to himself as he examined the bite marks.

The glow in the necromancer's eyes brightened before he shut them, resting both of his hands on Tiny's injured arm. He didn't say or do anything that I could see to cast his spell, but the bite marks were knitting themselves shut, and color was coming back to Tiny's normally dark skin. His breathing evened out; his eyelids were fluttering.

Of all the things I was expecting the necromancer might do, healing Tiny's injury was one of the last on the list.

Blowing out a breath as the last of the gray tinge left his patient's skin, Gideon withdrew, falling back a bit ungracefully on his ass. A couple of the zombies fell over, completely still.

Tiny groaned, one hand lifting to his forehead, though he remained on his back. "What the hell happened?"

"You had a close call," Gideon replied. He lifted his glasses and rubbed under his eyes, making no effort to hide the strain in his voice. "And now I'm exhausted. Perfect."

Devon still hadn't lowered his gun. One hand fumbled at Tiny's shoulder, then pulled him away from where Gideon was seated. The mage watched with dull interest for a moment, then turned his attention on Sara.

"You might want to do something about those runes, sweets."

She paled, withdrawing to cross her arms, fingertips curling around her forearms. "What? How . . . how did you know?"

"How did you think I found you? Makes it easy for anyone like me to tap in and take a taste. You're lucky I have some scruples, unlike whoever branded you."

My brows furrowed, and I took a step forward to

put my hand on Sara's shoulder. She looked like she was about to be sick; her breathing sped up to the point I was concerned she might hyperventilate. "Hey, someone want to hit me with a clue-bat over here? What the hell are you two talking about?"

Gideon smirked, reaching over Tiny to snag one of Sara's arms and pull it out straight. She didn't resist, though she made a little sound in her throat like a wounded puppy. One hand held her wrist while the other tugged on the cuff of her sleeve, pulling it up to reveal the inside of her forearm.

My eyes bugged. I had to sit down, my palms scraping on the concrete and the gun digging into my hip.

Why the hell hadn't she told me about the scars from marks that had been obviously, deliberately carved into her? They were an angry red against her otherwise pale skin, not the smooth, shiny gleam of normal scar tissue. Like there was blood pooled just under the surface, making them appear even more unnatural.

"Someone's been naughty. This is the darkest of the dark stuff, my dear. Believe me, I should know. Care to tell me how it happened?"

Sara didn't answer, tears pooling in her eyes. She yanked her arm out of his grip and cradled it to her chest, pulling her sleeve back down and ducking her head. I leaned over to pull her into a hug, though I was so tempted to throttle her to get answers out of her about how it had happened and why she had hidden something so important from me that I was shaking almost as badly as she was.

Gideon slowly rose to his feet, though he staggered before catching his balance. A couple more of the zombies fell where they stood—leading me to believe he was even more exhausted than he had let on.

His smile aimed at Sara was dark and sly, disarmingly charming. "I don't suppose you'd let me take a bit to freshen up, would you? Just a smidge?"

"Stay away from me!"

She practically hollered her demand, though it was muffled against my chest since she refused to look at the guy. My grip on her tightened, and I turned a death glare on him.

"I bet whoever did it made it hurt. Made you think you were dying. Right?"

"Stop it! Can't you see you're upsetting her?" I snapped at him.

"Did he or she make it feel like you were turning inside out? Like every scrap of energy was being burned out of your blood with every breath you took?" His voice lowered to a seductive whisper. "Like he or she was inside you, feeling it all, knowing everything about you—leaving no part of you untouched?"

Sara shoved back from me, her hands on my shoulders, twisting to look up at Gideon. His lips twitched, curving into a self-satisfied smirk as she screamed at him.

"Yes! Yes, you fucking asshole! He carved me up

and burned me out, and now I can't fucking stand it because I will never be able to forget what it was like having him in my head and everywhere else! It's like he never left, you insensitive prick!"

"There, that's good. Savor that anger. Don't you feel better already?"

She twisted away from me, putting her head in her hands and not answering him. He reached out to touch her shoulder—I thought maybe to comfort her, showing just how damned naïve I can be—but the scream that came from her and brief flash of light from the runes even through the fabric of her sleeves made it clear that wasn't it.

I'd never heard her make a sound like that before. It curdled my blood, shocking me so badly I nearly screamed myself.

Tiny and Devon both shot to their feet, I hoped to defend her, but Tiny couldn't keep his balance. Devon had to catch Tiny before he collapsed.

As he pulled away, Gideon looked much better— but Sara was now choking for every breath, the angry flush in her cheeks having faded until she was ghostly pale. Straightening his cuffs, Gideon turned that dazzling smile on me as I gaped up at him, grabbing at Sara so she wouldn't fall over.

"Sorry, lovey. Needed to get her revved up before I took a taste. She was looking a bit too peaked to be much use. Give her a couple days of bed rest, and she'll be good as new."

I pulled her limp form into my lap, still staring up at the necromancer, unable to believe this vicious turnaround. She felt so cold, like all the warmth and life had been drained out of her by that brief touch.

Gideon spread his arms and breathed deep, like he was totally invigorated. I don't know how he could stand to breathe in that stink—not with the zombies so close—but he soon turned his attention and that sunny smile back to me, like nothing at all had happened.

"Now, if you'll excuse me, things to do and all that. Speaking of . . ."

He turned and gestured at the zombies that had fallen. They started clambering back to their feet, and he headed toward them, giving us a little finger wave over his shoulder without looking back. By the time I thought to reach for my gun again, he was already surrounded by a protective wall of zombies, his voice fading fast.

"Remember, stay away from Clyde. If you ask nice, when I'm done dealing with him maybe I'll get rid of those pesky blood runes. Ta, ladies!"

Chapter 24

"Christ. We are fucked."

I looked over the top of Sara's head at Devon, who was still holding Tiny up by bracing his legs and offering a shoulder to lean on. He must have been stronger than he looked to support the big guy like that.

Then I saw the slight tremble at his knees. I was afraid to let go of Sara, but I was even more afraid that Tiny might fall down and squash Devon if I didn't help. Carefully setting her down, I got to my feet and rushed over to get under Tiny's other arm. He shifted his weight a little so Devon wasn't completely supporting him. Good lord, the guy was heavy!

"We're not fucked," I said between pants. "We're in a bad place, yeah, but we have one less vampire and one less necromancer after our butts. This is a good thing."

"Shia, we can't leave that thing running around loose on the streets. Look what he's done!"

I didn't bother to argue the point. "Where are we

going to go? We can't carry Sara *and* Tiny out of here." From the sounds of fighting and gunshots still coming from the freeway, we couldn't go back to the car, either. People were starting to gather in the doorway of the office building, too. "I don't see any cabs. . . ."

"Uh. This isn't like New York," Tiny said. "You have to call for cabs to come to you. Here, let me sit—"

The sudden shift in his weight nearly sent all three of us to our knees. Devon and I both had to do some fancy footwork to prevent a spectacular face-plant. Together we eased Tiny to the ground until the three of us were seated and breathing like we'd run a marathon.

"Thanks. Give me a few minutes to catch my breath, then we can get out of here."

Sara was stirring. I inched closer to her, checking her forehead and her pulse—not that there would be much I could do for her at this point, but it made me feel like I wasn't completely helpless. She was still a bit chilled, but not as bad as she had been when Gideon first stole . . . whatever it was he had taken from her. Ruminating on whether it was her life force, or part of her soul, or what, was going to be eating at me for a good long while.

What had happened to her? How could Gideon feed off her energy like that?

I wracked my brain, trying to think of when or how it might have happened. I didn't want to think Arnold could have been responsible for it, but it was clearly magework.

Then it hit me.

Sara had always been more elegant in her manner of dress than I was. When we were working, she had *always* worn long-sleeved blouses for as long as I'd known her. She wore T-shirts and jeans now and again, sure, but the long sleeves hadn't become a part of her after-work ensemble until after I became contracted to Royce.

After the battle with the sorcerer. David Borowsky had kidnapped Sara for the better portion of a day—a period of time she never talked about. Not even with me.

The kid dealt in the worst kind of blood magic, summoning demons and who knew what else. It was not a far stretch of the imagination to think that he might have been using his skills in the dark arts to do something to hurt Sara. And considering how strong she was, how much she hated being told what to do or how to do it by anyone, being under some magical being's control wouldn't have been any picnic for her.

I knew. I'd experienced what it was like being a puppet to Max and to Royce. It was one of the most frightening things that had ever happened to me. Even knowing Royce had no intention of hurting me and wouldn't do anything to abuse the power he held over me, those few days of having no conscious choice in when or how I answered to him had been a special kind of hell to live through.

It had been more terrifying than answering to Max—at least I had known what the crazy-ass douche-canoe wanted from me. To use and discard me, just a pawn in his games to take whatever Royce cared about from him.

Royce was still in many ways a mystery to me. A puzzle I wouldn't be able to solve until I returned to New York.

As for Sara, I couldn't imagine how much scarier it must have been to have something so incorporeal as your energy sucked away instead of something physical, like blood. Being bitten by vampires was already enough to give me the heebie-jeebies. Having my soul sucked out with no more than a touch was a thought too horrid to bear.

As much as I wanted to throttle her for keeping it a secret from me, I pitied her for it in the same breath. The shame she must have felt being used that way was incomparable to anything. I should know.

And if the necromancer could draw from her, too, that meant there must be other things she was vulnerable to that we hadn't counted on. I wondered if Arnold knew that. I wondered if that was why she hadn't thought it would do much good to talk to her boyfriend. He had to know—and, oh, did it burn me that Arnold had known about the runes before I did—but that also meant that he must not have any way of fixing the damage.

Which also made me wonder if he had ever used her for energy the way the necromancer and sorcerer had.

If that Borowsky kid hadn't already been dead, I

would have hunted him down and murdered him all over again with my bare hands.

I wanted to chase after Gideon, to beg and plead for him to do something for my friend to make this awful thing that had happened to her go away. If Gideon knew how to remove the runes, then that meant it was in our best interests to make sure that Clyde was deposed as the master of Los Angeles.

This was a drastic change in plans for me. My earlier ruminations about the morality of informing Clyde about Fabian's plans be damned. Clyde had nothing to offer me anymore, whereas the necromancer's survival and success was of vital importance.

Royce wouldn't like to hear it, but then, he wasn't here to deal with this mess. The complications were tremendous, and I hated that I had so little say in any of it, but Sara's health and well-being mattered to me far more than the life of a stranger who had forced us into dealing with his mess at the first opportunity.

Damn Clyde, and damn Fabian, and damn Royce, too, for sending us out here.

For the moment, all I could do was hold Sara's hand and wait. Tiny was too weak to walk, and there was no way Devon and I could drag him *and* Sara. I would have to be cool, calculating, and as devious as the vampires if we were going to make this work.

And it had to work. I *had* to fix this for Sara. It was my fault she had been hurt that way, my fault she was a living battery for magi to suck the life out of at any given moment. Without Arnold here to protect her, God only knew how safe she was. Considering how easy it had been for Gideon to use her, probably not at all. As far as I was concerned, her survival mattered more than any vampire's, no matter the cost. If we couldn't make it back to Arnold for a while, then I needed to do the best I could to take away as many of the dangerous threats to her health as possible.

I turned to Devon. "We've got to make sure Fabian and Gideon win. If they don't, Gideon can't fix what's wrong with her. Damn it, Devon, I hate this. I hate that there's no right answer, that every choice I've had to make since I got here has just made things worse for somebody—maybe even long before I got here. But there's got to be some way we can round up the White Hats who are left and get them to help in this fight. I need that necromancer to fix . . . whatever those are."

Devon and Tiny were both looking at me like I was crazy. Maybe I was.

"Girl, you are nuttier than a squirrel turd under an oak tree. You want to let that *thing* have control of LA? What do you think he's going to do once he's won?"

I shook my head, frowning severely at Tiny. "I don't know. I don't really care. What I do care about is fixing that," I said, stabbing a finger in the direction of the runes on the inside of Sara's arm.

Devon spoke gently, like he was trying to keep me from storming off or doing something equally stupid. "You're not thinking straight, Shia. Of course you're scared right now. We all are. But we can't let that monster win."

"You don't understand," I snarled.

His tone grew sharper. "Yes, we do. You're afraid of losing her. So are we. But we're more afraid of losing our city to something that could destroy us all if we give him a chance. I know you want him to fix what's happened to Sara, but you have no guarantee that he will, even if he wins."

I didn't want to consider that. Shaking my head again, I rose to my feet and started pacing, though I stayed close to Sara. It felt like the hairs on my arms and the back of my neck were crackling with static electricity, standing at attention. My vision was feeling a little funny, too. Something was wrong with me, more than just the overdose of adrenaline pumped into my system from the buildup of terror while facing down the zombies and the necromancer.

This was what Sara had been talking about when she said I never thought things through. The thing was, I *didn't* want to think them through. Not one bit. I wanted to go rampaging through the streets until I found Clyde and destroyed him.

That was my clue that not all was kosher in my head. Had the necromancer messed with my mind somehow? Or was it something worse?

Feeling sick, I stopped my pacing, hanging my head and taking deep, steadying breaths. When my gaze fell on my hands, those deep breaths caught in my throat. The veins under my skin were clearly visible.

Black. Not blue.

Fuck me sideways. Was *nothing* going to go right for me?

I closed my eyes and fought off the looming panic attack, forcing myself to take deep, steady, *slow* breaths. No hyperventilating. No rushing off to attack things with my bare hands. No succumbing to the corruption in my blood.

Once the worst of the desire to rush off and attack Clyde with nothing more than my teeth and nails subsided, I focused again on Devon and Tiny. That odd haze to my vision had cleared up somewhat, though the two hunters were both watching me warily now. Were there other visible signs of the change? Was I starting to turn Were? That thought cooled my ire faster than anything else.

"No matter who wins, we all lose. My only hope at this point is to find something I can give to that necromancer to make him fix what's wrong with Sara."

"He can't fix it," Sara muttered, one hand lifting to her brow. My attention shot to her, and I quickly knelt by her side again.

"How do you know?"

Her eyes fluttered open. She tried to sit up, but couldn't quite manage on her own, so I gave her a hand. Once she was sitting up, she addressed the three of us, her voice soft and features twisted in a grimace of discomfort.

"Arnold checked every source he has at his disposal. There's no cure for this, Shia. I'm going to end up living with these things for the rest of my life."

She might as well have told me her parents had died all over again. My heart ached for her in a way I couldn't put words to. All I could do was wrap my arms around her and hold her close.

There was no way I could ever be sorry enough for what had been done to her. Knowing it was my fault was like having a dagger buried in my gut, twisting and turning and digging its way all the way up to my heart. David never would have taken her if she hadn't been connected to me. Helping me fight his plans to make the Others of New York his slaves. Who would have thought some puny human women would have the power to stop a mage who had control over the will of New York's most powerful Others? The sorcerer had obviously felt threatened by me at the time—threatened enough to drag Sara into my mess and hurt her when he couldn't get to me directly.

And the joke was on him. I was alive. He was dead. All that mattered now was finishing cleaning up the mess he'd left behind.

A small part of me wanted to hope that Gideon hadn't been lying—that he had some way of making this right again.

The rest of me knew it would be stupid to take anything he said at face value, and that if Arnold said there was no way, I should leave it alone.

Still, I wanted to give him a chance. Just once. Just to see. Maybe this would be the one epic fuck-up in my life that I could fix.

Sara pulled back from me, running a shaking hand through her hair. We all looked like hell, covered in gore, tired, shell-shocked. Tiny somehow managed to stagger to his feet first, his hands braced on his knees as he bent over to catch his breath. Devon soon followed, then me. I helped Sara get to her feet, though she did take my unspoken offer to lean on me for support once she was up.

"Look," I said to the White Hats, as we all limped toward the exit together, "you told me yourselves that you want to see Clyde dead. There will be no better opportunity to see that happen than to help Fabian and Gideon get rid of him. But"—I added hastily, cutting them off as they opened their mouths to protest—"if we let them win, then they'll be weak and vulnerable, and that will put us in a better position to get rid of them, too. Maybe we can get Gideon to tell us what he had in mind for Sara first. He might know something that our mage friends in New York don't about how to get rid of those scars."

No one seemed very happy with the idea.

That was okay. I wasn't either.

"I guess that might work," Devon grudgingly agreed.

Hallelujah. It was the least I could ask for, and the best possible outcome.

Now, if only things turned out the way I hoped they would, then everything would be golden, and I would have an honest shot at atonement.

Chapter 25

"Tiny, why don't you take Sara somewhere safe—" I started to say, but Sara cut me off.

"No. I'm coming with you guys." That didn't sound like a good idea. She looked like a stiff wind would knock her on her ass. She lifted her fist, giving me a fierce glare in return for my dubious look. "You can't keep me out of this fight. If the necromancer has been following us through me, then it doesn't matter where I go. He'll find me again, and I'll end up leading him right into one of the White Hats' hideouts."

Devon rubbed his temples. "This is too complicated. So we need to help the necromancer kill Clyde, but then we have to wait just long enough for one of you two to ask him for help removing those runes—and then we have to try to kill him? How are we supposed to know the right time to get involved? It's not like he's going to be an easy kill, even after he's worn down from the fight with

Clyde. Not if the mess up there is anything to go by." He gestured at the freeway, encompassing the sounds of gunfire and screams, punctuated by the occasional roar from the shifted werewolf, only a few hundred feet away.

That gave me an idea. I could have kissed him if it wouldn't have sent the wrong message about my intentions.

"Follow me!"

Devon helped support Sara. Tiny wasn't too quick on his feet, but he was able to follow without much trouble.

I led them around the fence and up the freeway off-ramp, thrusting the gun into Devon's outstretched hand. Better not to face the Were while armed. Didn't want an unspoken threat to piss off our one shot at turning the tables on the necromancer and both vampires right off the bat. Werewolves were so touchy about those visual cues.

The Goliath was still rampaging across the freeway, gallumphing its way from one clump of zombies to the next. Most of the people who had stayed in their cars were watching with their hands and faces pressed to their windows, only withdrawing when a zombie came too close.

Earlier, I hadn't noticed, but the Goliath was making a sincere effort not to damage any of the vehicles around it. It moved its great body gracefully considering all of the many places its skin was torn and bleeding, chunks taken out in human-sized bites. Every now and again it bumped into one of the stopped cars, but it never knocked any over or even scratched the paint. It had developed a system for killing the zombies still coming after it, getting up on its hind legs to grab a torso with one paw, and using a foreclaw from the other to pop the head off.

What was left of each zombie flopped bonelessly to the ground once the Goliath let it go. It was a pretty efficient, if disgusting, system.

There weren't too many left. I scrambled on top of one of the nearby cars, some expensive luxury sedan with a long, low-slung front end, ignoring the owner's indignant shouts as I got up on the roof. Sara, Tiny, and Devon crouched behind it, all three of them hissing variants of "Get down! Are you crazy?"

Why, yes, I was feeling a bit on edge at the moment.

A quick glance farther along the freeway gave me a glimpse of flashing red and blue police lights, and a better view of the helicopters hovering overhead. One had "LAPD" on it and seemed to be more focused on the jam ahead, but it looked like the rest were from news stations. A handful of them were closer to this end of the jam, probably videoing the Goliath melting zombie faces.

"Hey! Hey, you . . . werewolf!" I waved my arms over my head, shouting at the Were. It growled as one of the walking dead grabbed at its hind leg, shaking the cadaver off and then pinning it with that foot, before looking at me. "I need to talk to you!"

The Were lifted its lip, turning its attention back

to the remaining zombies. I stomped my foot, making the roof of the car make a hollow sound that didn't do anything to get the Were's attention, other than making it flick its ears back. The guy inside yelled again, but I ignored him.

"C'mon, you asshole! I haven't got all day!"

This time it looked at me over its shoulder, hackles raised and pearlescent fangs gleaming as it turned narrowed, golden eyes on me. Finally. A hand was grabbing at my ankle—Devon or Tiny, I was sure—tugging at my pants leg for attention. I couldn't listen to them right then. I had hundreds of pounds of pissed off werewolf leaning meaningfully in my direction.

"Listen to me, and listen good," I said, adopting as dangerous a tone as I could muster. It must have worked, because the Were was paying attention, even if it was still bristling at me, meeting my challenging stare. There was something to be said for the lessons Chaz had imparted about what kind of dominant behavior a Were deferred to. My asshole ex hadn't been good for much, but the lessons I'd learned, I'd taken to heart. "You want to stop what's controlling all of these things? Find your alpha and tell him to bring the rest of his pack to Clyde Seabreeze's place. Help me, and I'll help you. Santa Monica. Midnight. Tonight. Got it?"

It flicked its ears in my direction, then went back to tearing apart the few remaining walking dead. I hoped that meant yes. If not, I had no idea how we were going to stop the necromancer.

That was assuming Gideon could destroy Clyde's retinue and heal Sara before then.

Maybe it made me a cold, heartless bitch—too much like the vampires I hated, calculating and cruel like Max, Fabian, and Clyde—but I wasn't going to leave any loose ends. If Gideon could remove Sara's curse, I'd find some way to distract the Goliath werewolves once they showed up until he was done. Possibly by setting them after Fabian. If Gideon couldn't deactivate the runes, heaven help him, because I would do everything in my power and use every resource at my disposal to see that he was hunted to the ends of the earth for hurting her like he had.

In many ways, it might have made me as monstrous as the thing I had feared turning into, but there wasn't even the slightest twinge of my conscience when I saw the way Sara's skin was stretched tight over the bones of her hands and face as she looked up from her crouched position behind the car. The dark circles under her eyes had worsened, and if I hadn't known better, I might have thought she'd been bitten by a vampire given how weak and parchment pale she'd become.

Hopping down from on top of the car, I shrugged off Tiny and Devon's hands, flexing and then clenching my fingers until my knuckles gave a satisfying crack.

"Let's get back to the car."

It would take a little while for the gridlock to clear up, but we still had a couple of hours before sundown. If we couldn't use the freeway, hopefully there would be another way to get across town in time to reach Clyde's place before Fabian and Gideon attacked. Perhaps Gideon would be too distracted by the fight and the number of zombies he had to control to notice we were coming.

"Shia, this is crazy. What the heck are you trying to do?"

I paused so Sara could catch up, hooking an arm through hers and slowing my pace to help her the rest of the way back to the car. "Trust me. I've got a plan."

Devon's hand was heavy on my shoulder as he fell into step on my other side. "We deserve to know. Especially if you expect the rest of the White Hats to help."

"Fine. First, we're going to help Fabian and Gideon take down Clyde."

All three of the others shot me horrified looks.

"Then we're going to let Gideon fix those marks on Sara. If he can't fix it before the Goliaths arrive, we'll set them after Fabian. If he does fix it, once he's done, we'll let the werewolves mop up what's left of the vampires and get rid of Gideon."

"Shia." Sara's voice was hushed, strained. "Shia, no. You can't—"

"Can't what? Can't fix this?"

"Can't treat them like pawns. This isn't your fight, and it's not like you can fix what's been done to me."

Hissing a breath between my teeth, I shrugged

his hand off my shoulder and stomped forward, half-dragging Sara with me. The sound of mixed fear and pain she made was enough to jolt me out of my anger.

I stopped, setting my hands on her upper arms, both to keep her on her feet and from pulling away. It gave me a good view of the engorged, blackened veins pulsing under my skin, further drawing me out of my rage and reminding me that I needed to stay calm. Something was trying to break its way free of this flimsy cage of flesh. If I couldn't stay focused, couldn't keep my emotions under control, who knew what kind of monster I might turn into.

"Listen," I said, noting that my voice was unnaturally deep—still wasn't totally in control yet, had to focus. "Listen. I'm not going to let you suffer the consequences for my mistakes. We're going to make that damned necromancer try to fix this. You hear me? I'm not leaving this goddamned town until I know for sure if he can make this right. And I'm not going to abandon Devon and Tiny and Analie's family to deal with him by themselves when it's over. Give me a chance. This can work. We just have to time it right."

"But what if it doesn't?"

I turned a flat stare on Devon. He didn't give an inch.

"What's plan B? What if Clyde wins? What if the werewolves decide to attack before midnight, or don't show at all?"

Fear as much as rage threatened to overwhelm

my better sense. I wanted to do something physically violent to make the questions stop—which meant there was far more wrong with me than I had originally thought.

Closing my eyes and counting to ten didn't do much to help, but I gave it a shot anyway. The others were looking at me expectantly when I opened my eyes again, as were a few of the nearby people who had remained in their cars.

The sense of something dark and hungry compelling me to lash out was new, but not entirely unfamiliar. It bore an uncanny resemblance to the desire for vampire blood that had coursed through me when I was bound by blood to Royce and Max. The unnatural hunger to absorb some part of them and keep myself in their power at one point had had me literally begging Royce to keep me bound to him. Anything to stop the pain.

Whatever this was, it bore the same flavor of compulsion. I wasn't going to give in to the need to lash out or act irrationally. No matter what. I wasn't a monster. Not in that sense, anyway. I was stronger than this. Had to be stronger than it. Whatever it was.

The words came slowly, thick, like there was cotton stuffing in my mouth.

"Maybe you're right," I said.

Devon arched a brow, and I pulled away from Sara to face him. He wore an expression of wary concern. Whatever signs of change I was exhibiting, he hadn't quite caught on to them yet. Good.

"Maybe Clyde will win. If he does, you still want him taken out, right? So the werewolves can take care of that. Same thing with Fabian. No matter what, the vampires need to be destroyed. Gideon is dangerous, but without Fabian driving him to go after Clyde, or if both vampires are dead, he has no reason to stay here. This isn't his city or his fight. If he chooses to stay, there's no way the Goliath pack will tolerate it. Even if you can't set them after him, isn't there a local mage coven? You can set the local magi after him, too."

Tiny spoke up, his deep voice threaded with apprehension. "We'll never be able to get there before the fighting starts. Not without a car. Not in this mess."

Good. They were starting to see things my way. "That's fine. We don't have to be there when the fight starts. We just have to get there before it's over. If I can find Gideon after, I can get him to see to Sara, and we can take it from there."

"Are you sure he'll fix it?"

"No." I bit my lower lip, glancing at Sara as a tingle of foreboding squeezed around my heart with cold fingers. "We can't trust him—but he's the closest thing we have to a shot at disabling whatever that sorcerer did to her."

Privately, I vowed to myself that I would make the time to study the different branches of magework and learn enough to protect us both against something like this ever happening again once this mess was behind us.

"I don't think this is going to work, Shia. If Arnold couldn't fix it, what makes you think that Gideon can?"

I gave Sara's arm a reassuring squeeze, though I was nowhere near as confident as I forced myself to sound. "Arnold doesn't deal in the dark arts. This guy does. What he knows is closer to what David was doing than the magic Arnold uses. Gideon's the best chance we've got."

And damn whatever fates were responsible for making that the sorry truth.

Chapter 26

It was long past nightfall before we were able to make it across town to Santa Monica.

Tiny had taken the wheel. Not that there was anywhere for us to go for a while—not with the mess in front of us.

Gideon had planned his diversionary tactics well. There were just enough zombies still stumbling around to keep the cops and local news stations frantic with activity, drawing everything from the National Guard to the CDC. Not only did the mess keep us locked in place for hours, unable to chase after him, but it also meant that any rapid response teams that might have come after him at Clyde's place would be delayed and unable to stop whatever plans Fabian and Gideon had in mind for the master of Los Angeles.

We had to get the hell out of this trap, but there wasn't anywhere to go. Cars were stopped bumper-to-bumper in both directions.

The anthill of activity centered on the worst of the jam was disrupted when a few people figured out they were about to be detained by the government for "testing;" they then drove over curbs and bumped other cars out of their way to escape.

It wasn't a bad idea. We took off with some of the initial rush, maneuvering around the abandoned cars, before any barricades could be set up to keep us from hightailing it. We'd lost a couple of precious hours, but it had given us the time to work together to come up with a stronger plan than just "show up and melt faces." Once we got off the freeway and away from the cemetery, there was little traffic on the surface streets.

Devon had been on his cell phone nonstop. Making arrangements with other White Hats to bring weapons and meet us not far from Clyde's place. We were going to need to try for stealth sneaking into the gated community, which meant we needed a back way in. A half dozen or more cars and trucks carrying vigilante hunters bristling with weapons wasn't going to fly with the security guards.

Neither were the zombies, I was sure, but Gideon had the advantages of an insider who might clear a path for him and a lack of moral compunctions preventing him from messing with the minds of people who might try to stop him on the way in.

Plus, none of us were magi, so we didn't have that power. Damn it.

We would have to hope that we arrived either

shortly before or after Gideon and Fabian attacked. My assumption, based upon what little experience I had in Other-to-Other wars, was that Gideon would be responsible for handling the remainder of Clyde's bodyguards, while Fabian would be the one to attack Clyde. Most likely, Gideon would stop somewhere to pick up a few extra zombies on the way and attack shortly after sunset.

There was a slim chance we were wrong. He might be waiting for sunrise, when Clyde would be at his most vulnerable, but I had to hope that Fabian was too cocky and impatient to wait that long. They wouldn't want to give up the advantage of the mess Gideon had created on the freeway.

If I was wrong, we were all screwed.

Either way, both vampires had to die tonight. The thought of Fabian being killed didn't give me so much as a twinge. On the other hand, as much as I didn't like Clyde, I was sorry he was caught in the middle of this. He was a prick, but that wasn't enough to merit his death.

Still, I wasn't sorry enough to stop it.

Even if I had a last minute attack of conscience—ha!—it was far too late to stop the gears that had been set in motion. Everything was about to come to a head.

Some of the other White Hats were held up on the freeway, and a few others were caught up in other activities Devon didn't choose to explain. By the time we arrived at the rendezvous point on a service road that ran around the perimeter of the community, the sun had set about half an hour ago, and there were maybe thirty White Hats in a variety of tactical gear waiting for us, hovering in the shadows just outside the cones of illumination from nearby street lamps.

It surprised me to see so many hunters out here. The New York chapter boasted maybe half this number. Probably even fewer now that Jack was out of the picture.

Some of them gave deferential nods to Devon as he walked down the line, exchanging a word here and there.

The guy from the White Hat bar we'd visited on our first night out on the town—Jesus—was passing out weapons to some of the other hunters. Tonight he was wearing a vest, combat boots, and cargo pants—no shirt, no jacket—and carrying a long, heavy duffel. He put what had to be an illegal assault rifle into my hands. It was so unexpected and heavy that I almost dropped the stupid thing before I got a good grip on it.

He didn't bother to see if I was okay. He kept moving at a good clip, pulling a sawed-off shotgun out of the bag and thrusting it at Tiny, and following up by tossing Sara an Uzi. Thank God she didn't drop the damned thing, or accidentally flick the safety off in the process. She looked at the weapon in her hands like she'd never seen a gun before, though we'd both spent time at the range together.

After the initial surprise wore off, we both gave

the guy death glares, but he didn't appear to notice, continuing down the line to toss weapons at the few White Hats who didn't have their own. No one else seemed ruffled by his actions.

Someone had disabled the alarm and security camera by a recessed gate in the thick stucco wall surrounding the property, and the door was being held open for the White Hats to slip through. Most of them were wearing dark colors: grays, browns, greens, and slashes of black, blending into the deep shadows of the towering bushes and trees that had been grown close to the wall for an extra layer of privacy from prying eyes.

As the White Hats filed inside, I examined the rifle that the walking arms dealer had put in my hands.

Damn. The guy meant business. It was an AK-47, matte black, and a magazine was already attached. I wasn't used to anything bigger than a handgun, and it took me a moment to figure out how to check if a bullet was chambered.

Once I figured out the bolt action and barrel extension, I could see that, yes indeed, this gun was ready to go. If I weren't already in so much trouble, I would have been having a minor panic attack at holding a gun that wasn't registered to me and that I wasn't technically trained to use. Dim recollections of the information the sentient hunter's belt had given me about the use of various guns would be enough for me to get by, but if the gun jammed or anything else went wrong, I was screwed.

I couldn't be sure if the magazine was full, but hopefully whatever was in there would be many times more bullets than I would need to use tonight.

When I looked up, Sara was still examining her gun. She was running the thumb of her free hand over the safety, frowning down at the weapon. The knot between her eyebrows didn't ease away when she tilted her head up to look at me. She must not have been pleased at this turn of events either.

Hefting my rifle up so the barrel was to the sky, resting against my shoulder, I sidled closer to her and nodded at her gun. "Bet that thing will cut right through a zombie."

"Maybe," she said, lifting it one-handed to give it a more critical eye. "I hear they have a tendency to jam, though. Hope the White Hats aren't planning on putting me in the front lines. I'm not sure I'm going to be much of a shot with this thing."

"I'm sure we're going to be the last line of defense. If Devon or anyone else thinks we're front lines material, we're all screwed."

That prompted a hollow laugh out of Sara. We shared weak grins and followed the trickle of remaining hunters through the door and into the private domain of the obscenely rich and most likely famous.

The homes in the community had bigger lots than most of the others I'd seen so far in my time in California, even counting Sara's sister's place in Malibu.

Many were large, imposing structures, but none of them matched Clyde's for casual intimidation. A few had lights burning, cars in the drives, and the sounds of the occasional radio or TV drifting through windows, but I didn't see any people moving around except for White Hats skulking through the bushes like the bad guys in a cheesy action flick.

The enormity of what we were doing didn't sink in until I saw the moving vans. A half dozen of the big haulers, the kind you used to move an entire household, were lined up on the street in front of a house around the corner from Clyde's mansion.

Maybe it was the way the wind was blowing, but the stink of them didn't hit me until we skirted around the side of a house down the hill from Clyde's. Gideon must have been hauling zombies from all over the county in those things, maybe raising them by the dozens from other cemeteries and using Forest Lawn in Hollywood Hills as a distraction or cover of some sort. One of the trucks was the telltale U-Haul with the Golden Gate Bridge decal on the side the lady we'd interviewed at the Laundromat had told us about.

There was nothing in the trucks now; the cabs and cargo doors stood open, the loading ramps still down. Small gobbets of unidentified people-bits, a few bugs, and that unmistakable stench were all that remained.

It was a wonder none of the neighbors had noticed or complained. This was not the kind of neighborhood where you could haul in zombies by the truckload and have them go unnoticed. Someone, somewhere, had to have noticed the smell. Even a couple blocks away, even though I was covered in long-dried dead people juice, the concentrated stink of decomposing bodies left to rot in a hot truck all day (or maybe days) was making my eyes water.

Some of the other White Hats were muttering about it, one of them retching in the bushes nearby. On a hunch, I tugged Sara's arm to get her to stop, and I edged closer to one of the windows of the house we were using for cover. Peering inside, I spotted what I was looking for. When Sara tapped my shoulder, I answered her puzzled look by pointing to the prone body on the kitchen floor, only the designer jeans-clad legs and part of the torso visible from our angle.

Gideon must have done something to put the people in the neighborhood—or the ones closest to Clyde's home, anyway—to sleep while he did his dirty work. Since he had so casually sent Sara and me into unconsciousness outside of Thrane's hideout, it didn't surprise me. Though I was glad none of the White Hats had shown up early enough to be caught in the spell, I wasn't too concerned about the neighbors. He hadn't added them into his army of undead. They'd be fine, if a bit groggy, once the spell wore off.

The question was, where was Gideon now? And Fabian, for that matter.

"*Madre de Dios.* . . . That monster will pay." Jesus's voice startled me, though he spoke in a low growl. He must have crept behind Sara and me when we were looking in the window.

"They're sleeping," Sara explained, "not dead. They'll be fine."

"You know what did this?"

We both nodded. "A mage. A bad one who doesn't follow the rules."

Frown lines appeared between his eyes, but he didn't say anything. We followed him as he moved from shadow to shadow, bringing us ever closer to Clyde's property.

It was so quiet—no dogs were barking, no early evening birds rustling in the trees, no bugs chirping, no nothing—that I couldn't help but worry. There was no sign of security, no vampires wandering around watching for intruders, and no sign of movement in the windows of Clyde's house. The other shoe was overdue to drop.

We kept going, though, moving with more stealth than I would have thought a bunch of dudes carrying tons of weapons and acting like Navy SEAL rejects would have been capable of managing. Nobody made any effort to stop us or investigate, which didn't make me feel any better, no matter how good these guys were at this. Vampires had senses far superior to those of humans, so even if Gideon didn't have some magical radar that would tell him Sara was here, someone from Clyde's household should have detected us by now.

This had to be a trap of some kind, but I didn't know where Devon was, and it was too late to tell him we needed to back out and rethink this plan.

Then the first gunshot rang out, and it was too late to do more than regret ever coming to this god-forsaken town.

Chapter 27

Gunfire sounded from all sides. Jesus plowed ahead, so Sara and I continued to follow him. The zombies came from around the trees and bushes in Clyde's front yard, having hidden until we got close enough for them to do the dead man's version of a rush on the nearest White Hats. More approached from behind us, too, somehow having snuck around to cut us off from our escape route.

Cursing under my breath, I flicked the safety off the rifle, hefting it to my shoulder, and took aim at one of the zombies moving our way. It was farther back than the ones Sara and Jesus were concentrating on, with little between us other than a couple of low, ornamental bushes.

The thing was withered and shrunken, yellowed teeth bared in rictus as it shuffled in our direction, grasping hands held out before it. Blowing out a breath, I focused down the sights, aiming carefully for one of the raisin-like eyeballs.

At first, I didn't think I had hit the thing. It took another step forward. And another. Then toppled forward, the back of its head laid open like some grisly flower. Man, this gun packed a punch. I'd have to see about getting one from Jack for my very own anti-zombie kit when I got home.

Wait. Jack wasn't leading the White Hats anymore. Maybe Royce could hook me up. Either way, I loved this rifle.

Taking careful aim, I popped off another few rounds. More zombies fell under my bullets, and now that the initial surprise was wearing off, the White Hats were doing a good job laying a suppressive fire, rapidly regaining the ground they had lost. A couple of times, I heard curses and shouts of pain, but I didn't see anyone getting dragged down by cold, dead hands.

It was probably just a couple of minutes, but it felt like a lot longer before the last one fell, jaws still moving as it tried to latch onto one of the nearest hunters before the rest of the body caught on that its brain had just been turned to mush by the .22 bullet that rattled around in its skull like a crazed bumblebee in search of escape from its smoking hive.

Still, no vampires. And no Gideon.

Despite the adrenaline rush from the battle, I was getting more and more worried that this was a setup. We had to get the hell out of here, and we had to do it soon. Something bad was waiting for us in that house. I just knew it. Devon wasn't anywhere in sight for me to tell, and Jesus had separated from us during the battle. There were other White Hats nearby, but I didn't know any of them by name, and I wasn't sure they would listen to me if I tried to tell them this must be some kind of trap.

It was too late, anyway. Half a dozen White Hats were already sprinting for the front door. One of them kicked it in even as a couple others were stage whispering at them to wait. After all the gunfire, I wasn't sure waiting mattered or that the few with half a dozen brain cells between them were heard by the idiots rushing in. Any element of surprise we might have had was long lost, and whatever was waiting for us inside was going to force us to fight on its terms.

A garbled scream came from inside. More White Hats moved in. Devon and Jesus were among them, and I thought I saw Tiny, too. Sara and I clutched at each other until we grabbed hands, dashing forward to see what had gone wrong.

All the lights were burning inside the house, but there were so many hunters crowded in the foyer that I wasn't sure what had happened or what was going on. There was blood on the floor and walls, but only a little of it was recent. Some had already started drying to a tacky coat, evidence of a different battle that must have taken place before we arrived.

Movement somewhere farther along in the ranks had me standing on tiptoe to see. Soon there was shouting, but no one was firing—probably didn't dare in such close quarters. This was not the best thought-out firefight I had ever attended. Jack had kept better rein over the New York White Hats than whoever was in charge of this branch. I was starting to hope it wasn't Devon, because that meant he was far less competent than I had thought. Though it answered my questions about why he had temporarily defected to New York a few months ago.

Then someone was thrust up until his spine and back of his head cracked against the ceiling, and the shouting reached a decibel that made it impossible for me to tell what the hell was going on.

People were being shoved this way and that. Sara's fingers slipped out of mine, and then it was far too chaotic to keep track of anything.

We were all shoving against one another, panicked, animals in a trap. A spatter of warm, wet liquid against my cheek was all the warning I had as to what was going on, and why everyone was so desperate to get out of there.

One of the vampires had found us. And he was tearing through the people like paper dolls, a frenzy of deadly motion like nothing I had ever encountered before.

No Other I had ever seen had so blatantly disregarded human life before. Not this way.

Yes, Max Carlyle had killed an entire club full of people once. That was calculated, cold; he had been making a point. He had even killed one of Royce's donors right in front of me. Again, it hadn't been because he had lost his senses. He had known exactly what he was doing. Feeding because he needed it and establishing his dominance over an already beaten people.

A pack of werewolves had once torn apart a vampire and a sorcerer, too. Feasted on them like lions taking down a pair of gazelles. It was coordinated, predatory, and brutal—but again, they had known who they were attacking and why. That had been an act of revenge; payback for enslaving them.

This was different. There weren't words for this kind of slaughter.

This was a vampire gone mad.

Warm blood fell like summer rain, sprinkling over the screaming, running hunters. I fought my way through the crowd until I reached the nearest stairwell, needing higher ground for what I had planned.

Once I was up a few steps, I turned around and hefted the rifle to my shoulder.

The vampire's face was covered in a thick, red coat, even his hair color unrecognizable under the mess. His face was twisted with demonic hunger, eyes matching the liquid splashed all over his skin and clothing and fangs fully extended, but he didn't bite anyone. He was using his hands, moving like a whirling dervish as he cut a swath of carnage across the room, following the thick of the crowd as they fought one another to flee from the monster in their midst. Not an elder. His movements were visible, if inhumanly fast.

One breath. Hunter in front of him. Two breaths. The hunter was ducking, screaming as talons raked down his back. Three. The vampire was looking at me.

Four. The bullet entered the pinpoint of crimson gleaming in his right eye and exited the back of his skull, leaving a spatter of brains and blackish blood on the wall behind him.

From somewhere deeper in the house, a howl of anguish split the night. The windows and even some of the framed pictures hanging on the walls rattled at the sound of it. The White Hats stopped in their tracks, wild eyes searching for the source, hunting for what was now undoubtedly hunting them.

Or, rather, hunting *us*.

Things were truly fucked if I was the one with the level head around here.

The chilling sound petered out, leaving nothing but the pounding pulses and heaving breaths of the people around me. As I shouldered the rifle again, it struck me that I *could* hear their pulses. The hammering of their hearts against their ribcages, calling out to me, stirring a strange hunger for something I was not about to put a name to.

Yeah. One crisis at a time.

Clamping down on the mixed desire to start licking the blood painting the walls and to toss my cookies, I moved down the stairs, breathing through my nose. Not that it helped much. It only made the sick feeling roiling my stomach worse with the mixed stink of the blood, piss, and rotting flesh sticking in my throat and nostrils.

Sara, stepping around the puddles of blood on

the marble floor, was making her way back to my side. Pale and shaking, she handed me a hunting knife. I wasn't about to ask where she'd gotten it from, but I tucked it into my jeans at the small of my back. Here's hoping things wouldn't get so up close and personal that I would need it.

I approached the vampire corpse slumped on the floor, toeing it onto its back. One of the security guards. I vaguely recognized his features under the blood, twisted as they were with the rabid hate and hunger that had driven him. It seemed unlikely that he would have acted like that without severe provocation, but I had no idea what could have set him over the edge.

"The hell was that about?"

Devon had come up close behind me, spattered with blood, his shirt plastered to him with sweat. He smelled delicious. Like food, delicious. I could really sink my teeth into—

Christ, there was something really wrong with me.

Closing my eyes and gritting my teeth, I took a moment to compose myself before answering. "Something must have driven him to it."

"No shit. Any idea what?"

I shook my head, not daring to open my mouth. Running my tongue over my teeth was a bad idea. The taste of blood filled my mouth as one of my canines sliced through my tongue. Fuck, fuck, *fuck*. What was happening to me? And why *now*, damn it?

Swallowing the few drops, willing the taste away, I followed Devon as he turned away and led us deeper into the house. The desire to do something violent to him was getting worse. Having his back to me was such a bad idea, but it was impossible for me to tell him that right that moment without sounding like a crazy person. Even if that's exactly what I was.

The only thing keeping me from falling on him in a frenzy was knowing that there were a necromancer, two elder vampires, a mess of zombies, and maybe a couple dozen more vampires of indeterminate ages after our asses.

Had to keep it together. Had. To.

Devon had stopped. His mouth was moving. The sound wasn't quite registering. I shook my head. "Sorry?"

He was looking at me like I was a few beers short of a six pack. "Didn't you hear me? I said we need to figure out where Clyde is holed up. Do you know where he might be?"

"Oh, sorry. I—no, I—"

"Yes. I think I know where they are."

Everyone, including the other White Hats who hadn't fled deeper into the house, turned to Sara. She ran her arm across her forehead, her sleeve smearing the blood on her brow instead of wiping it off.

"Downstairs. Remember, Shia? The first night we came here, there was a big party, and everyone was on the first floor except for Clyde and Fabian. They were down in some private place—maybe Clyde's daytime hiding spot. Why don't we look there first?"

"Yeah. Oh, yeah. That's as good a place to start as any."

This place was a maze. Downstairs really was the best place to start as far as my addled senses could tell. Though running into the vampires no longer seemed like such a great plan. Even in the haze of hunger and with the need for violence crawling under my skin like thousands of invisible ants, I knew attacking Clyde or Fabian fell under the category of "epically bad idea." Without the belt to augment my strength and speed, even the rifle wasn't going to do me much good. Not in close quarters like this.

I was starting to see the wisdom of picking off Others from afar with a scope like someone had suggested at Devon's house as a solution for our necromancer problem.

"Who has the grenades? I want you two in the lead in case we need to—yes, Jesus, Phil, you guys scout ahead. If you see the necromancer or the vampires, bombs away. Got it?"

The pair followed Sara as she led the way to the stairwell, the rest of us following a few steps behind. Devon looked to me and then Sara when we reached the door, but we were never given the security code. Jesus shouldered his way to the front and examined the pad. He punched a few buttons and the lock gave an audible "click" as it disengaged, the door swinging open.

He glanced at me over his shoulder, grinning in response to my look of surprise.

"That's a vampire for you. Smart enough to lock away the goods, but too behind on technology to know anything about password exploits. Glad his security admin didn't know enough to reset the default code."

Devon gestured impatiently. "Enough showing off. Go check it out."

Jesus and the other guy, Phil, gave him a sarcastic salute and disappeared into the dark of the stairwell.

Devon put an arm out when someone tried to follow the two down the stairs, lifting a finger to his lips for us all to be quiet and wait.

It didn't take long for the two to come barreling back up the stairs, shouting, and the rest of us to scatter.

Right into the waiting arms of several vampires who had crept up behind us. Their eyes gleamed like bloody jewels and fangs glistened with saliva as they jerked the nearest hunters into their arms. Gideon stood behind them with a sly smirk and his arms folded.

"Well, look who decided to join us."

Chapter 28

Jesus pushed Sara and me to one side with a sweep of his arms, putting himself between us and the open door leading to the basement level. It was just in time, because an explosion blew a wave of stench and deadly shrapnel of wood and metal chips through the opening. Some of the other hunters were cut down, screaming in pain and fear, clutching at their wounds.

Gideon flinched, but otherwise didn't move. Some of the vampires paused, their expressions turning blank; others tightened their grips to the point at which the hunters they were holding cried out in pain.

"That was uncalled for. Now, who's in charge here?"

Nobody said a thing.

Frowning, Gideon unfolded his arms, placing one hand on his hip, the other making a sharp gesture at the vampires. They moved as one, snapping the necks of the hunters they were holding.

My mouth dropped open, and some of the others in the room started screaming, scrambling back. The vampires dropped the lifeless bodies of the hunters they had just killed and swept forward, grabbing a new round of hunters—Jesus and Devon among them. A couple vamps leaned forward, their fangs stopping just short of sinking into the throats of the people they'd grabbed, but a hissed command from Gideon kept them from closing the distance.

"Let's try that again, shall we? Who is in charge?"

Jesus was frantic, struggling against the unnaturally strong arms of his captor. "*¡Chingue a su madre! ¡Voy a matarte, hijo de la chingada!*"

The necromancer was nothing more than amused. "You kiss your mother with that mouth?"

"*¡Hijo de puta!*"

"Right, that's quite enough of that."

With a snap of Gideon's fingers, Jesus was out cold. Devon surged against the vampire holding him, grunting with effort. "Stop! I'm in charge. Just stop!"

"Ah, progress!" Gideon beamed. "You, pretty boy, are going to tell the rest of your hunters to vacate the premises. You, a-a-a-and . . . ah, yes. You two." He pointed at me and Sara. I barely registered the movement before two of the vampires dropped the hunters they were holding in favor of grabbing onto us instead.

Perfect. My day just couldn't get any better.

Sara squirmed, panting, but the vampire holding her gave her a shake until she stopped. She looked like she might faint at any moment. Anger drove me to fight against the cold fingers wrapped around my upper arms as well, a low growl vibrating in my chest.

Gideon moved forward to poke me in the shoulder with a manicured finger. "You just don't know when to leave something alone, do you? Well, you ladies are in luck. You three are going to stay here with me and answer some questions. Doesn't that sound fun?"

"No! Let them go. I'll stay," Devon shouted.

The necromancer shook his head, waving his hand airily at the remaining hunters. "Go on. The rest of you get out of here. And to make sure . . ."

With another curt gesture from Gideon, in unison, the vampires who weren't holding Sara, Devon, or me took a menacing step forward.

Cowards that they were, the remaining hunters didn't need a second invitation. They ran off, most of them rushing out as fast as they could. Only a few had the decency to assist the ones who were too hurt to accept Gideon's offer under their own power, helping the injured get to their feet or dragging them when they couldn't walk. Half a dozen vampires followed them out, probably ensuring that they got the hell out of Dodge instead of regrouping and coming back to save us.

I bit my lip so hard it bled, trying not to get us all in a world of trouble by saying something that would dig us a deeper hole. I wondered where Fabian and Clyde were, and if they knew what Gideon was doing down here with the younger vampires who were so obviously under his power. I wondered, too, if he had some version of the *Dominari* Focus that the sorcerer, David Borowsky, had used to control the Others of New York, or if being a necromancer was what gave Gideon his power over them.

The vampire holding me tightened his grip, his empty eyes shifting in the sockets, focusing on my lip as I tilted my head to look up at him. He nearly vibrated with hunger, lips peeling back from his fangs as he leaned in over me.

"Hey! Hey, hey, hey! Teasing them isn't going to get them to let you go," Gideon scolded, flicking the vampire in the temple. The vampire went rigid, no longer acting like he was on the verge of biting me. Instead he was frozen in place, fingers digging into my upper arms so hard it hurt.

The pain was good. It would make it easier to focus, not give in to the urge to scream or become a ravening animal.

Gideon waited until the last of the hunters were gone, then ran a hand down his face. "By Crowley's gods-forsaken ghost, I can't believe you guys threw a grenade at my minions. Do you know how long it took me to raise that many zombies? Fuck!"

He was more annoyed than genuinely upset, I thought, though the bodies of the hunters littering the ground around us might have indicated otherwise. Hard to tell. The guy was nearly as unhinged as I was.

Without another word, he stalked off in the direction of the stairwell I had earlier used as high ground. The vampires dragged us along like errant children, taking us up the stairs and ignoring our squirming.

The room he led us to was wide and open and gave an excellent view of the front yard and the straggling White Hats still limping their way across the grass. No fucking wonder the zombies had been able to flank us out there.

I supposed we were lucky the vampires hadn't thought to snipe us from here.

Speaking of, Clyde was on the floor, flat on his back, his eyes closed and blood trickling from the corner of his mouth. His bare chest didn't rise and fall, but I didn't think he was actually dead. Stunned, maybe, or out cold, but not the permanent kind of dead.

Fabian was thoughtfully picking between one of his fangs with his thumbnail, leaning against a desk by the windows, his gaze distant. He gave Devon a once-over—a rather lascivious once-over at that—and then turned a disinterested glance in Sara's and then my direction. He then turned a pleased, cat-that-got-the-canary smile on Gideon.

"Very good. Yes, this is very good indeed."

I didn't like the sound of that.

"What's with . . . ?" He jerked his chin in Devon's direction.

Gideon arched his brows. Fabian's sly smile grew, and Devon visibly paled. A sick fear for Devon coiled in my stomach like a serpent, waiting for a moment of weakness to strike.

"The stud's a bit of insurance. Maybe a bonus, depending on whether we finish up here before the rest of the hunters regroup."

Fabian nodded, then folded one sleeve up past his elbow. He lifted that hand, clenching and un-clenching his fist a few times. He then raised his newly bared wrist to his mouth where he quickly cut a gash. Fangs gleamed with the splash of crimson before they were licked clean.

He pushed off the desk and knelt beside Clyde's prone form, pressing his cut wrist to the other vampire's lips. Clyde didn't move at first, but then I detected a feather of movement at his throat. Swallowing, maybe involuntarily. Fabian stroked his hair in a loving, possessive gesture that did a fantastic job of creeping me the hell out.

It was eerily reminiscent of the time Max bound Royce's house guard Mouse to him by forcing her to drink some of his blood. A shiver of foreboding crawled down my spine, but there was nothing I could do to stop any of this. With Clyde under his power, who knew what Fabian might do to this city, or how he might abuse his power over the weaker vampire.

Gideon yawned and stretched, then leaned an

indolent elbow against the shoulder of the vampire holding Devon. The hunter shifted his weight, trying to pull away, but his captor had such a tight hold of his arms that Devon could barely move.

"One down," Fabian said, pulling away. He rose in a smooth, predatory motion, stalking across the carpeted floor in bare feet. He stopped in front of Devon, smiling down at him with just a hint of fang. "One to go. . . ."

"No!" Devon and I both cried out at the same time.

"Stay away from him!" Sara shouted.

Fabian didn't bother looking at us, running a fingertip down Devon's cheek. This was like a surreal reenactment of Max's takeover in New York, only . . . the vampires were more interested in the dudes than the women.

I don't think I have ever seen Devon look that frightened in my life. Fear for him as much as my own remembered terror drove me to renew my struggling against the vampire's hold, knowing, but not caring, that it was futile.

And then Gideon was stumbling forward, blood bubbling from his lips.

I couldn't see at first what was going on, but Fabian was whirling, aghast, anguish twisting his handsome features into a caricature. Then Tiny stepped into view, the machete he had used to stab Gideon in the back spraying thick red droplets in an arc as he tugged it free and slashed at Fabian in one deft motion.

The elder sidestepped, stumbling back, clearly too startled and shaken by this turn of events to immediately retaliate. Tiny didn't give him the opportunity to regain his footing. He had a Desert Eagle in the other hand.

Though I'd been listening to gunfire all night, the mini hand cannon was deafeningly loud in the enclosed space. The shot must have missed, because Fabian was lunging at Tiny, his eyes burning with the hellish red of agitation as he sought to grab the hunter.

The fingers on my arms briefly tightened—then loosened, the vampire holding me shaking his head and pulling back slightly. "Wha . . . ?"

The ones holding Sara and Devon were also coming to. Devon's didn't quite let him go, still holding him with one hand, the other lifting to his temple. Sara's did release her, taking a step back to clutch his head with both hands.

She fell to her knees, creeping forward to check on Gideon. God, he was her only hope of ever being free of those runes. If he was dead, I'd never forgive Tiny for that, even if Tiny's actions were the only thing that could have saved Devon from becoming Fabian's eternal, unwilling boy toy.

Devon jerked out of the arms of the vampire holding him, pulling a small knife out of his boot. It would be about as effective as a toothpick against a vampire as old and powerful as Fabian, but with two experienced hunters after Fabian's ass, I wasn't sure if it mattered. Devon could probably find a way to make a weapon out of anything in the room if he needed to.

The vampire holding me finally let go, all three of the younger vampires skittering out, running for the exit with inhuman speed, clearly knowing better than to stay anywhere near the necromancer in case he might recover and enslave them again. Without Clyde awake and capable of protecting them, I couldn't blame them for wanting to get out of there as fast as they could.

As Devon and Tiny went on the offensive against Fabian, dangerous as it was, I tuned them out, all of my focus on Gideon and helping Sara with the wound.

Those incredible green eyes were open wide, and he was gasping for air, every breath wet and flecking his lips with beads of scarlet. Sara looked up to me, stricken.

"I don't know how to deal with this. His lung must be punctured."

Medical treatment for wounds like that wasn't in my repertoire either. If he stayed on his back, it seemed more likely he would either bleed out or drown in his own blood. I yanked him up into a sitting position, his hands weakly clawing at my shoulders and breath hot on my neck as he rested his cheek against my collarbone. Shock, maybe. I didn't think he was entirely conscious of what he was doing.

Sara tugged at his shirt, pushing it up to bare his back. The snarling and cursing and gunshots didn't get my attention, but the shattering glass as something was thrown through a window did. Craning my neck to see, I gaped at Fabian, who was forcing Devon to kneel at his feet with the fingers knotted in his hair and holding Tiny by the throat out the window. The fall might not kill him, but I wasn't about to risk it.

"Don't! Don't you do it!"

Fabian glanced in my direction, fangs bared, eyes burning crimson. As soon as he saw that I had pulled the knife I'd been keeping at my back and that I was holding it by the back of Gideon's neck, panic quickly replaced the anger in his expression. "Stop! Let him go!"

"You first. Don't drop him—bring Tiny inside and put him down. Do it now!"

Slowly, carefully, Fabian drew Tiny back into the room. The big man was gasping for breath, his hands clawing at the fingers closed vise-like around his throat. Tiny easily had a hundred and fifty pounds on Fabian, but the vampire held him like he weighed no more than a house cat.

Once Tiny's feet were no longer dangling out the window, Fabian thrust Tiny away with a harsh snap of his wrist that sent the hunter sprawling on the carpet. However, Fabian didn't let go of Devon, instead taking the opportunity to haul him to his feet by the hair and then hold the hunter against him, nails biting into his neck and abdomen where he rested his hands.

"Let's make a deal. Give me Gideon, and I'll give you the hunter. Yes?"

"Don't do it, Shia! Kill the fu—"

Devon's words were cut off as Fabian's nails dug deep furrows in his throat. I narrowed my eyes and dug the point of my blade into Gideon's skin, drawing a drop or two of blood and making the guy hiss audibly and jerk in my arms.

"Don't fuck with me, Fabian. You let him go. Do it, and do it *now,* or so help me I will gut Gideon right here and now."

Not really. But Fabian didn't know that.

The ancient vampire's lips peeled back until I swear I saw his molars—and then slowly slid into a thin-lipped smile, the red tint to his eyes growing brighter. "Alec Royce was wise to take you under his wing. I can appreciate such ruthlessness."

"Now!"

He shoved Devon away, nails swiping over his throat and leaving crimson streaks behind. "Done. Now you step away from Gideon, or you'll see what it truly means to be merciless."

Chapter 29

Sara and I carefully backed away from the necromancer, though I kept my knife on him as long as I could. Fabian stalked forward as soon as we gave him some room.

As the vampire knelt beside the necromancer, I checked on Devon. Sara knelt beside Tiny. I was pretty sure Tiny was just out cold; Devon, on the other hand, was bleeding profusely from the wounds on his throat, and awake, but not moving save for weakly clawing at his neck and gasping for air.

I cut a strip off my shirt with the knife, using the least filthy swatch I could find. I pressed the wadded material against the cuts to staunch the flow. His voice, when he managed to choke out a word or two, rasped and squeaked like that of a kid going through puberty.

"The hell . . . did you . . . did you do that for?"

"To save your life," I hissed at him, hoping Fabian was too busy to pay us any attention. "Here, hold that compress—yeah, right there. Come on, we're getting out of here."

I hooked his free arm behind my neck and helped him to his feet, staggering slightly to one side with the weight of him. He wasn't deadweight, but not far from it, either. Judging by the groans and wincing, Fabian had done a number on him. Getting out of here wasn't going to be easy, but we needed to get moving before the vampire finished seeing to Gideon and decided to retaliate.

I turned us toward Sara, opening my mouth to tell her and Tiny to hurry up, but the words caught in my throat when I saw her tear-streaked face. My gaze slid from her to the downed hunter, and it felt like the blood in my veins froze solid.

Tiny wasn't unconscious like I'd first thought. His neck was at an unnatural angle. There was no rise and fall to his chest.

Fabian had killed him.

"No . . . Tiny, no!" Devon's voice was faint, hoarse—and broken.

The two had been good friends for as long as I'd known them. Tiny was a good man. I'd never really understood what drove him to hunt Others, what led him to live the life of a vigilante, and now I'd never have the opportunity to ask.

Did he have family? A girlfriend or a wife? Someone out there who would never know how he had died, someone waiting for him to come home?

Devon pulled away from me, dropping to his knees beside Tiny's prone form, bowing his head.

Sara set a hand on Devon's shaking shoulder. He didn't make a sound, but I had no doubt he was crying.

My hand fell to the hilt of the knife I'd tucked into its place at the small of my back. Drawing it once more, I hefted the blade and stomped over to Fabian, who was ignoring me in favor of cradling Gideon to his chest, crooning encouragements to the necromancer as he pressed a bleeding wrist to his mouth. It would heal his wound, yes, but that didn't mean it was worth the price. The two might have been lovers, but I had to wonder if Gideon had any idea what kind of personal hell he was in for, being bound to the vampire.

I pressed the tip of the knife against the underside of Fabian's jaw. He tilted his head to the side, looking at me out of the side of his eye, one fang visible as he sneered. "What do you want now?"

"You killed him."

Jerking back from the blade a bit, he tilted his head a little more to see what the others were doing. Then back to me, his expression neutral. "Perhaps. He attacked Gideon. I saw no reason to be careful with how I handled him."

With a snarl, I put enough pressure on the blade to give him a shallow slice, only enough to let him know I meant business. "As soon as that necromancer wakes up, he's fixing what you did. You understand me? He fixes it, or I will kill you and whatever miserable remains of your bloodline I can get my hands on."

A blur was the only thing that registered before I felt the bite of my own blade against my throat, his hand wrapped around mine, my other arm pinned, and Fabian pressed behind me, close as only lovers should be. His fangs brushed over my cheek and then earlobe as he whispered in my ear, his voice a seductive hiss.

"Oh, will you now? You think you have what it takes to kill me, little girl? Do you know how many have tried over the centuries?"

"Not nearly enough if you're still here," I spat.

He laughed softly, mocking, reminiscent of someone I had heard before but couldn't quite place. "You just wait. Gideon told me what he promised you and your little friend. He can't reverse death—that power is beyond him—but he can do something about her curse. Isn't that what you came here for?"

I stopped squirming against his hold, some of my anger fading. The promise of help for Sara was the only thing that could have cut through my murderous rage at that moment, sending the bestial need to hunt and kill back to the depths it had clawed from.

"Watch."

I did as Fabian directed, turning my attention down to Gideon. The necromancer was stirring, grimacing and rubbing the back of his head where it had thumped against the carpeted floor when the vampire let him go.

Gideon sat up with a groan, then staggered up to his feet. His shirt was still bunched up near his shoulders. The only sign of the wound was an angry

red line that showed Tiny had expertly sliced deep
into his back, right between his ribs. That he was still
alive meant Tiny had missed his heart, but it couldn't
have been by much. He was coming out of shock re-
markably fast.

Gideon tilted his neck to one side, then the
other, rolling his shoulders until a sharp crack
sounded. When he finally opened his eyes, they
turned to Fabian before anything else, hot with
desire and an adulation that hadn't been there
before. I wondered if that was how I had looked at
Royce and Max when they gave me their blood the
first time.

Dimly, I heard the sound of tires crunching on
gravel drifting in through the windows. Police?
Backup? The first few Goliath warriors, here to
even the odds? I could only hope. The quiet hiss
of tires on cement and brief flash of headlights
through the curtains and broken window heralded
a newcomer, but whether he or she would think to
come upstairs to find us was anybody's guess.

Fabian didn't seem terribly concerned. He continued to hold the blade to my throat, keeping me
from pulling away, but he lifted his other hand to
brush the back of it against Gideon's cheek. The
necromancer leaned into the touch, giving a visible
shudder of ecstasy. It was hard to tell whether to be
horrified, disgusted, or saddened by what the bond
had done to him. Seeing someone that powerful
made into a fawning puppet was like seeing a wild
lion de-fanged and de-clawed. It might have made

it safer to be around him, to some degree, but in its
way it was still heartbreaking to witness.

"You promised to do something for these ladies.
Do you remember?"

Gideon's gaze briefly flicked to mine, the glittering green color flaring brighter. There was a tug
in the back of my mind, like he was doing something to mess around with me again, but it didn't
last long. With a nod, he turned his attention back
to Fabian, awaiting direction like an eager, demonic
puppy.

"Good. Go take care of it."

The necromancer moved with purpose, showing
little sign that he'd suffered from shock and severe
blood loss only a few minutes ago. He reached
Sara's side in moments, pressing a hand lightly on
her back. She didn't look up, still holding Devon as
he shook in silent grief over Tiny's body.

Though she refused to be budged, it didn't
appear to bother or slow Gideon down. He flicked
his wrist, dislodging a small, slender blade. I stiff-
ened, but Fabian hushed me and held me tighter,
keeping me from rushing over to stop him.

Gideon put the blade between his teeth, using
long, slender fingers to roll up the sleeve of her free
arm, holding her forearm out in front of him. She
watched him from behind a curtain of blond tendrils, clinging to Devon a bit tighter.

Gideon said a few words, the sounds foreign and
strange to my ears. Guttural, almost. Something
Slavic, maybe. It didn't sound like any language I was

familiar with. Having heard Arnold cast spells before, this felt . . . different. Darker. More ominous.

Sara jerked her arm, but his grip was too tight. She couldn't pull away.

The fae glow in his eyes grew brighter—and the runes on her arm began to glow, too.

Devon tilted his head up, red-rimmed eyes staring dully at what was going on. Then widening. His fingers tightened around Sara's, but there was nothing he could have done. Interrupting the spell could have disastrous consequences, not the least of which being a backlash of whatever energies Gideon was summoning right now. From the look and sound of it, they weren't beneficial, either.

The bluish-white light slowly faded, the color draining away until the symbols were left in stark relief, black against her white skin. Sara made a sound of pain, soft in her throat, that grew into an agonized scream as Gideon whipped the blade out of his mouth and slashed the tip down her wrist— a line directly over the runes, cutting each of them in half.

She never stopped screaming as he held her, keeping her still, the words flowing like the black and yellow pus that seeped from the wound. Devon must have known the consequences of letting the spell be interrupted, because he helped hold her still, even though his eyes were wide and it was clear he was just as afraid for Sara as I was.

She writhed and twisted, kicking at Gideon, but

he didn't stop until every last rune had been cut in half.

The fluid corruption flowing from the wounds became clear, the stink of death and rot that I had thought must have been zombie leftovers abruptly clearing out, leaving something that seemed almost sweet in its place. Gideon slowly ran the flat of the blade over her arm, and the stuff began to sizzle and pop, but left her previously scarred skin unblemished.

He had done it. The runes were gone!

I could have kissed the crazy bastard. Now Sara wouldn't be in danger from every passing mage. It felt like a hundred pounds of worry were lifted from my shoulders in that moment, knowing that she was no longer going to suffer for my mistakes.

I had finally made something right.

Sara slumped against Devon once Gideon let her go, her eyes wild with pain and terror, but she had clearly been too weakened to do anything to fight him off. The necromancer tucked his dagger away, flicking some of that clear goop from his fingertips, before turning an expectant look back to Fabian. A dog looking to its master for a treat after performing a neat trick.

The vampire finally loosened his grip on me, and I immediately ran to Sara's side, wrapping my arms around her and Devon both.

I would never forgive Fabian for Tiny's death, but knowing that he had a hand in making sure

Gideon kept his word and healed Sara went a long way toward keeping me from feeling a need to exact revenge on him.

Which reminded me—I wasn't sure what time it was, but if Gideon, Fabian, and Clyde remained here, they'd no doubt be killed by rampaging Goliath werewolves. The pack was supposed to show up at midnight. We had arrived not too long after sunset, and the battle had not taken terribly long. They still had a couple of hours to get a head start and find a safe way out of town.

I looked up from Sara's bowed head, my fingers running through her hair, trying to console her as best I could. Gideon had returned to Fabian's side, folded into his arms like a child seeking reassurance from his parent. Fabian watched us over Gideon's shoulder, a sly smile I didn't like hinting that he still had something up his sleeve. But whatever he hadn't put on the table yet wasn't going to stop me from doing the right thing.

"You should get out of here while you can. There are werewolves coming to kill him," I said, tilting my chin in Gideon's direction.

"We weren't planning on staying much longer."

Gideon glanced up at Fabian, then nodded as if he had been given some instruction. He turned back in our direction, flicking his fingers in a "come on" gesture at Clyde. The prone vampire finally opened his eyes, blinking a couple of times before rising slowly to his feet. He moved like he was buzzed—not quite sure on his feet, hands out to catch himself in case he bumped into something or fell—coming to an unsteady, swaying halt at Fabian's side.

"Come on."

The command was directed at Devon, Sara, and me. She wasn't in any kind of shape to be on her feet, still shaking from aftershocks of pain or fear or who knew what, probably caused by Gideon's spell. Between the two of us, we were able to get her up, though Devon wasn't too happy and was having difficulty keeping pressure on his wound with the hand not being used to steady Sara.

"I can't just leave him here. Not like this."

Fabian was unmoved by Devon's unspoken plea. "We'll make arrangements. If it is as you say, and werewolves are going to be coming along any-time now, we need to be gone before they arrive. Let's go."

We didn't argue, following the three Others out. The acrid stink of smoke was still drifting from somewhere deeper in the house, mixed with the smell of zombies. There might have been a fire on a lower floor; I wasn't sure, but I was beginning to wonder why Fabian had already planned to leave, even before we mentioned the Goliaths. Now that he had control over the vampire in charge of this city, why wouldn't he take over his seat of power?

The trio of Others stepped aside for us once we reached the front doors, letting us go out first.

I figured they were just being polite. Though

once I saw what was waiting for us out there, my heart clawed its way from my chest to lodge high in my throat, choking off thought, reason, and air in one fell swoop. That moment of shock and panic was all Fabian, Clyde, and Gideon needed to swoop in from behind to grab us, keeping the three of us from running off or escaping back into the house.

We were so fucked.

Chapter 30

Max Carlyle grinned, spreading his arms as he approached the steps. "Hello, kids. Daddy's home."

In a surge of panic, I tugged at the arms holding me captive.

Half a dozen other vampires were leaning against the outside of the cars, all radiating power and danger the way that Fabian and Clyde did. Not as old and powerful as Max, but close enough to it so as to make no difference to the three of us, even if we hadn't been confined.

Max looked just as dapper and handsome as I remembered. The suave, fashionable businessman look did a great job of slapping a passable veneer of polite professionalism over the crazy underneath. Was I the only one who could see the madness roiling in those cold, gray eyes?

"Sire," Fabian said from behind me, his voice the warmest and most sincere I had ever heard from him. "I do hope you'll accept my first tribute as master of Los Angeles."

Oh, God, *no.*

That smile could have charmed the angels from the heavens. It wasn't my imagination. He looked right at me as he nodded. "Yes. Tribute accepted. Very nicely done."

"Excellent. Thank you, sire. Gideon, if you would?"

Gideon, who was holding Sara, slid a hand up to her temple, commanding her to sleep. Her struggles ceased, her body slumping in his arms. One of Max's henchmen strode forward, scooping her up in his arms and carrying her toward the car.

The necromancer took care of Devon next, probably because he was struggling against Clyde's hold like a man possessed.

As for me, I didn't move. I didn't dare. All I could do was stare at my death warrant, signed, sealed, and delivered, all in that razor smile curving Max's lips. He held up a hand for Gideon to wait a moment, just before the necromancer reached me.

"Shiarra Anne-Marie Waynest. How I have looked forward to this moment."

How the hell did he know my middle name? He must have done his homework after our last encounter in New York. How he could have known I was here, though—

No. Fabian had addressed him as "sire." That meant Max had made him into a vampire. I would bet my last shares in H&W Investigations, whatever remained of the business, that Fabian had alerted

Max to our presence long before now. Max had just been biding his time, waiting for the perfect moment to make his entrance. He was that kind of guy, the bastard.

"Put her under, and make it last long enough for the trip home. I've got unfinished business with that one."

"Yes, sire. And the other two?"

Chill fingertips brushed my temple, a whispered breath tickling my ear.

I was out before Max gave his answer.

Acknowledgments

This book has been a long time coming, but it wouldn't be here if not for the help of a few friends.

First, a big shout-out to my agent, Ellen; my editor, John; my publicist, Vida; and the rest of the team at Kensington. They make me look good.

Next, a word of thanks to my beta readers. Kristin, for always lending an ear when I need it most. Tori, your words of wisdom shall resonate through the ages. Kate, you know I've got some special Devon-related business I'm working on just for you. Eve, for being your inimitable self—Thrane and Co. thank you, as do I, and you'll always hold the title to most devoted and disgruntled fan in all the land.

To the others who had a hand in this one, you know who you are—thank you.

Lastly, a word of thanks to the readers, bloggers, and book reviewers who have helped this series stay alive. Your support and encouragement has done more than you know to keep these books coming. It's been a rough road for Shia, but I'm deeply grateful to those of you who have followed her on her journey, and I hope you'll stay with her to its end.